Dear Reader,

In the dark of winter on mid-we _____ _____ ____on made its way through the airwav_ _____ ___ _he magic of cowboy heroism and romance from the very heart of its origin: Texas. Night after night when our cows were milked and the supper dishes put away, ballads of lonesome riders, lost love, misplaced trust, bullets spent, and lives gone wrong were crooned to the sad and lonely chords of strummed guitars. Sometimes a zesty mouth organ, or twanging jew's harp, or mourning violin chimed in to underscore the mood.

The repetition of those melodies and words were impressed in my mind more than I realized, although they disappeared beneath experiences that occurred in following years. It was only after my travels brought me to sagebrush land that this story, Sagesong, found its way into my computer. And with scent of the sage and the jolt of an inexperienced rider, snippets of those melodies popped out from the dusty caves of memory. Each episode begged for the song of the range, a jealous heart, a yearning, a heartache, or a tragedy. Each event demanded words from those western songs to set the scene and I didn't resist.

If you wish to know the song lyrics or the writer of the lines used as chapter titles, go on an Internet search to refresh your memory or introduce you to the history of the old, wild, and romantic west. Listen to the original hit recordings of many of those melodies performed on YouTube, a wonderful Internet feature.

I excel in creating situations where the chemistry of love surprises people. More than diverse backgrounds clash in unexpected places when those who thought they were aged beyond passion that only trips the young. They may recoil from the electrical charge at their first touch, indeed, even deny the binding attraction of their first penetrating look. Just as with first love Sarah and Matt were destined for each other. Greed of young charges heightened the drama and threw them together in situations they could not escape. I hope you enjoy the suspense as much as I enjoyed its creation.

Naomi Sherer

Sagesong

Naomi Sherer

iUniverse, Inc.
New York   Bloomington

iUniverse books may be ordered through booksellers or by contacting:

iUniverse
1663 Liberty Drive
Bloomington, IN 47403
www.iuniverse.com
1-800-Authors (1-800-288-4677)

Because of the dynamic nature of the Internet, any Web addresses or links contained in this book may have changed since publication and may no longer be valid. The views expressed in this work are solely those of the author and do not necessarily reflect the views of the publisher, and the publisher hereby disclaims any responsibility for them.

ISBN: 978-1-4401-1950-7 (sc)
ISBN: 978-1-4401-1948-4 (ebook)

Printed in the United States of America

iUniverse rev. date: 01/29/2009

My First Love

CAST OF CHARACTERS

Sarah Nelson – A widow drawn into dangerous intrigue when she vacations at a working ranch where dudes participate in trail rides through sagebrush grassland. She is totally ignorant of horses, but is captivated by the western movie atmosphere and the lean handsome cowboys recalled from childhood memories.

Matt Bannister – Wealthy landowner established "*The Singing Ranch*" for boys refused by adoption agencies. He gets along with his life just fine until the widow becomes irresistible, invades his privacy, and saves his life.

Lou Petrosky – Sarah's best friend who insists horses are irresistible.

Buck Bannister – Matt's son whose jail sentence changed the lives of unwanted boys.

Steve – Manager of Bar X, which produces the revenue for all ranch operations.

Eric – A runaway from abusive adoptive parents.

Rusty - Kidnaps Eric for delivery to pornographers..

Table of Contents

Chapter One

An Old Cowhand

"Horses? What do I know about horses? Lou. Did you think because I showed you the drawings of horses that I would want to spend two weeks with them?" Sarah exploded. She wasn't about to go to some dude ranch. What was Lou thinking of anyway? Sure, Lou was into horseback riding, Sarah knew that but Lou never invited her along before now. She always went with her sister-in-law.

"What's up with Caroline?"

"My brother had a heart attack and Caroline won't leave him," Lou explained.

The wild west of the movies Sarah watched as a child was romantic and tugged at something deep within her being. Her determination to refuse gave way and she agreed to meet Lou for the two week vacation at the Bar X.

"Why am I doing this?" Sarah Wilson asked herself, "I'll surely end up the fool." She worried over her decision. She got a free ticket when Lou's brother's wife canceled because her husband suffered a stroke. Neither horses nor cowboys were part of Sarah's childhood, but she fantasized over the ranch life she saw in Western movies when she was a kid. She loved old country songs heard on the radio. Lyrics told stories of love, heartaches and humor. Hearing them night after night she memorized the music and words. From movies and those songs she thought of a ranch as a romantic place to live.

"You can forget those cowboy fantasies, Sarah, the Bar X is working ranch. Nothing like the movies." Lou teased her. Sarah dropped her face in her hands. Now she was going into the thick of it on a real ranch. "What a crazy thing to do," she thought. She opened the dude ranch brochure she retrieved from the side pocket of her carry-on bag. She was doubly silly to take up sketching. She enrolled in a drawing class at the Community College because it was interesting and challenging. The instructor suggested she start with horses when he learned she would be absent for several sessions because of her vacation at a dude ranch. She chose to copy a head, and as instructed, used big bold strokes. Each attempt resembled a moose more than a horse. She tried sketching legs and hooves. When that proved as much a failure she turned to a clean page and wondered how much practice it would take to bring even a hint of success. Sarah harbored misgivings about horses. Horses were never of interest to her and she seldom found herself in their vicinity. She found them smelly, awkward and cumbersome, with eyes and feet big and unattractive. She went out of her way to avoid getting too close.

Her friend, Lou and her brother's wife booked two weeks at the working cattle ranch. Lou called her with sad news last week. "Sarah, my brother had a heart attack and Caroline won't leave him. Why don't you come with me? The reservation is paid for. You can go in her place." At first she felt badgered into going but, in all fairness to her friend Lou, Sarah wasn't really going against her will. Since the death of her husband, she refused to do anything she didn't want to do. She often took her time to think things through but the decisions were always her own. She thought again of Lou's brother and hoped he would fully recover from his heart attack.

Sarah's husband had not. In her five years of widowhood Sarah gained an unprecedented independence, enjoyed the freedom it offered. However, recently she come to dislike the loneliness it entailed. Pressing her nose to the oval airline window, Sarah tried to blot out unpleasant thoughts as her plane moved on toward the city airport where Lou would meet her. She strained to get the fullest possible view of the sprawling farms below. In a wild scattering of unusual textures of plantings in rectangles, trapezoids, and circles, the fresh spring green color identified thriving wheat. Occasional brown patches indicated fields only recently prepared for planting.

The farms represented more to Sarah than geometric shapes marked on the soil surface. Their very existence revealed a human endeavor more complicated than manipulating the earth's surface. During her work in the publishing division of an agri-business corporation, she ate, slept, and breathed, farm economics. Sarah's paycheck, until she took early retirement, depended on the success of farmers whose names and faces she never knew. In fifteen years, technology encouraged more sophisticated responses to adversity, resulting in dramatic changes in the business of farming, particularly in the size and design of machinery.

Raising crops of any kind was a mysterious challenge, one that always intrigued her. She endorsed the hope and optimism of those who worked the land, and admired their courage and perseverance against unpredictable, capricious aspects of nature. It was no wonder that early peoples centuries past attributed the success of plentiful food to magic. Or in times of famine did they accept the failure of nature as a fault of their own. That wasn't so far fetched considering how quickly humans today accept blame unnecessarily when things go wrong. Saying a prayer to prevent an oncoming storm from laying their grain prostrate which prevented harvest could be expected when relying on

4

mysterious vagaries of nature. Their attitude wasn't one of giving up - acquiescence - but part of what they were; what it took to face reality when confronted with acts of nature they would prefer to control in the raising of raw products.

The thoughts always left her is a state of amazement. She turned to the window. Her gaze followed the green and brown patchwork passing below with a twinge of restlessness. She agreed to fill the last minute cancellation and was apprehensive about spending two weeks on a dude ranch. It was an unexpected vacation, at least unplanned in her usual long range conscientious manner.

Sarah spoke to Lou the night before and heard her exuberance for the venture. Lou had enthusiasm and curiosity. Two overpowering features led Sarah to fill in for Lou's sister in law. The most pressing was friendship. Lou was gregarious and met all strangers as though they were long time friends.

"You do love country songs but forget the movie concept of western heroes." Lou said. "You must be curious to see what a real ranch is like."

"I don't like horses and never tried to ride. Bicycles and cars I can handle. Do you think they will let me ride a dirt bike around the cattle?" Sarah worked diligently to improve the things she was good at and patiently practiced any new activity she attempted, but she carefully chose things which would not shake her confidence.

"I might have made a mistake in this dude ranch thing, Lou." Her confidence was shaky as Jello, "but I'll be on the plane tomorrow." She was determined to handle it, one way or another. Even though it implied a promise to ride. Sarah suspected her chances of staying off a horse were slim at a working ranch, inexperienced rider or not.

Lou was certain with every ounce of her tightly girdled body that Sarah would fall in love with horses once she tried riding. "You're gonna love it. I just know you will." Sarah imagined

Lou's downward jerks of her fuzzy prominent chin she used to emphasize every word she so adamantly uttered.

As Sarah watched the passing scenes below, the wispy clouds allowed only occasional glimpses of the Rocky mountains. The elusive clouds obscured her vision and let her mind dwell on the coming adventure.

She returned to her sketch pad to practice her hobby. She took sketching classes at the community college during the winter, a promising pastime for her retirement hours. In the next two weeks she hoped her drawing would improve with the use of live models. If she benefited no other way the vacation would be worth every day.

That old strawberry roan, a faithful pinto, the piebald paint, and a dozen other lyrical descriptions in song strummed through her memory as she sketched the time away. Lyrics of songs about cowboys and cattle roundups ran like endless herds in her fancy. Gene Autry's television theme song came to mind: *I'm riding the range once more, totin' my old forty-four.* The movies were fantasy, but the vision was real in movies recalled.

She practiced drawing the parts of horse anatomy her art instructor pointed to in a sketching manual. The calendar photos of horses were inspiring and she tried to copy many disconnected parts in the poses she studied. Her efforts to make a whole animal were way out of perspective and she soon gave up, tucking her pad and pencil into her carry-on bag with the hope that she would be more successful with real life models. She settled back and closed her eyes.

And shortly thereafter, her ears felt the declining pressure of descent into the airport.

Lou's voice echoed across the milling passengers at the arrival gate.

"Yoo hoo, over here," Lou hollered as she barreled her way to Sarah's side through the crowd. Everyone but Sarah seemed completely assured of their goal. She waited for Lou's guidance, not having had any part in the planning of either the trip or the vacation. Traffic flowed generally in the direction of the arrows pointing to the baggage claim. Sarah dodged bodies to reach Lou and avoid being swept in the wrong direction.

Lou clasped her in a smothering bear hug. She leaned back without totally releasing Sarah to give her a thorough appraisal.

"Looking good, my dear." She nodded an approval and dropped her hands, satisfied with Sarah's healthy glow.

"Your plane was late and I worried you changed your mind," she said as she took command of the carry-on bag in Sarah's hand.

"Lou, you know very well I wouldn't refuse to take a vacation I already paid for." Sarah felt a rush of excitement at Lou's effervescence.

They laughed as they walked arm in arm toward the baggage claim, aware of many ways to pinch pennies to make their pensions cover the travels they chose.

"I'm glad you consented to come in Caroline's place," Lou said, "She felt bad she had to cancel, but after John's heart attack, she just wouldn't leave him."

"Is your brother going to be all right?" Sarah asked.

"Yes, thank goodness. He's got to take it easy but the doctor says he's got a good chance to fully recover. My sister-in-law's a dear and he couldn't do it without her."

Lou's impatience with the unpleasant thoughts were reflected in her voice, "Now let's get going. I'm raring to ride for two weeks."

A ripple of alarm flowed through Sarah at the thought, a thought which she couldn't hold in the struggle against the pressing bodies intent on retrieving luggage from the moving belt with as much persistence as her own.

After collecting Sarah's suitcase, they were on their way to the Bar X, a working cattle ranch with the false promise that it was for dudes. Comfortably settled in the soft spacious bucket seat of Lou's car, Sarah recited from the ranch brochure.

"Guests share cabins separate from the main lodge and dining room," she read, "ride gentle well-trained American Saddle Horses and enjoy fresh mountain air in the foothills of the Bitterroot Mountain Range, participating in routine ranch work." Sarah waved her hand while she attached her own opinion, "They might be willing to let greenhorns do chores but here is one dude who is going to sit back and watch."

The view opened up to a wide expanse of azure blue sky as they drove out of the airport and left buildings behind. Rangeland roamed up and down the hillsides, cattle scattered to graze. Calves ran with tails raised high and Sarah smiled as they butted heads, imitating their elders. Just like any kids learning what life is all about, mimicking adults to better get the instinct honed properly.

"Dudes may not be given the option. Cowhands will show us the chores and help us learn. I think you'll get into the swing of things once we get there," Lou maintained with her usual confidence.

"I'll try my best, you know that," Sarah conceded, "but it all sounds formidable and very difficult if you ask me. More like work than a vacation."

"Have you kept up that video exercise routine?" Lou asked. Miles of hilly terrain swept past. In her defensive driving posture, Lou's hands gripped the suggested safety positions of eleven and two o'clock designations when relating the steering wheel to a clock face.

"Of course. Why?" Sarah was serious about taking care of her body since the day she'd turned fifty. She tried going to health clubs and aerobic classes but they took so much more of her valuable time than she was willing to give. She worked a forty hour week, as did her husband, and together they attended wholesome activities for their daughter in the evenings. Or simply stayed home and enjoyed simple hobbies or discussions.

Workout videos with movie stars became popular and she tried several. The idea was successful. She could follow a thirty minute tape before she went to bed. At first it was difficult to force herself to follow the exercises, as weary as she was from the day's stress. She promised herself to give it up if she was too completely worn out at the end of the first week.

She discovered, surprisingly, she was enervated and slept better. And best of all, her protruding tummy flattened and her sex life improved. Sarah couldn't get Lou interested in exercising to a video. Lou did not work outside her home and preferred to hike everyday while her children were in school. Those days were a long time ago.

Sarah frowned at Lou, "Why did you bring that up?"

"You might find some muscles you didn't know you had," Lou insisted.

"Lou, I already guessed that. That's why I'm nervous. My stomach gets upset every time I think of it." She held her hands on her stomach and bent forward.

"Oh pooh, just relax and go with the flow. There's a bottle of antacid tablets in the glove compartment. Have one. I take them all the time just on general principles. Hand me one, will you?"

Sarah flipped open the tiny storage compartment that held the car manual and looked for the bottle of antacid.

"There is no bottle here."

"Are you sure?"

Sarah searched through the assorted papers and manuals once again to be certain. "Maybe they're in your suitcase," she suggested.

"No. I always keep a supply there. I must have used them all. I can't get along without them," Lou complained. "I have to stop and get some." She stretched her neck to peer ahead at the highway. They searched the horizon for a sign of a town where that could be accomplished. It didn't look hopeful for some miles. A green directional sign came into view and named a town at the next exit. Surely there would be something. Lou slowed in preparation of turning on the marked exit.

In the distance a silvery oblong tank hovered on spindly steel supports, looking like a giant spider hovering protectively over captured prey. The small town water tank added a technological exclamation mark to the cluster of buildings. Would one of those buildings include the store they needed? Sarah doubted, but even gas stations often carried such basics. Lou turned off anyway to search for a store where she could purchase the over-the-counter relief from her stomach acid condition.

The car rumbled across unguarded railroad tracks and turned down a narrow street, lined with old fashioned store fronts. Sarah read the signs and recited a running tally.

"Sally's Dry Goods has children's summer clothing, women's leisure wear and colorful shorts and shirts for men. Hank's Hardware has electrical and battery tools and insists there are advantages of doing it yourself. Shoes For You has, oooohh, the neatest cowboy boots. Valley Bank is austere and tasteful. The Coffee Cup boldly boasts 'Breakfast anytime.' This town has everything but a drug store, Lou."

"Keep looking down the side streets. There's got be a place for these folks to get remedies. I'll bet I'm not the only one to get acid indigestion."

Lou proceeded slowly along the parked vehicles. Dark colored trucks with white vanity stripes, and colorful cars pointed into the sidewalk at a 45 degree angle. All cars were just as dusty as the pickups and most had stuffed toys stacked in the rear windows.

"Hey, I think they've got something down that way," Sarah announced, pointing down a side street. She saw four large windows with a mixture of toys, a conglomeration of colorful gadgets, and lawn furniture.

"The sign says Variety and Drug Store."

"That's it," Lou exclaimed happily at the discovery. She turned and found an empty space among the diagonally parked pickup trucks and cars.

Sarah stepped out of the car and stretched slowly. She looked over the small town atmosphere with curious satisfaction before following Lou inside.

Lou strode purposefully toward the large overhead sign in the rear of the store proclaiming the pharmacy she sought. She would find what she needed and be back on the highway in no time.

Sarah perused the shelves in the combination variety and drug store, welcoming the chance to stretch her legs. She was always amazed at the variation of merchandise jammed in the limited shelf space in variety stores. Customers appeared to search with definite products in mind, not merely browsing out of curiosity as she was.

Bottles and boxes, in cluttered displays fascinated her and she gave them her complete attention. She converged on the shelves, intent on exploring the colorful items, totally absorbed in her idle browsing with no desire to buy. She lingered by the stacked shelves in the narrow aisle. Other folks appeared to be serious customers absorbed in their own explorations.

Sarah found a small puzzle and studied the label closely, moving on to other items. She looked at the boxes of round playing cards never having seen anything like them before. Straining intently she carefully bent her head to read around the label, touching the precarious stack with great care.

Unstable piles of boxes quivered. She groaned and clutched at the trembling stack with both hands and successfully steadied it. But that movement nudged the adjoining stack and that, too, threatened to collapse.

She held her breath. The stack settled as it was instantly supported by a large brown hand. She gingerly patted her stack in place and quickly withdrew her hands, casting a collaborative smile sideways, as her impish gaze followed the wrist and chambray shirted arm to an amused face.

Sharp male features were overshadowed by a dusty Stetson.

"Thanks," she breathed in an incredulous whisper, relieved at the diversion of disaster. The catch in her midsection intensified when she caught a glimpse of his masculine mouth. She felt an intimacy uncalled for and unfulfilled when he went on about his business. She was at once repelled and intrigued. Her brows wrinkled in annoyance.

"My pleasure," the man replied over muscular expanse of his shoulders and moved along, making way for others in the aisle.

Her elbow was jostled and she turned, expecting Lou to be at her side to get her attention. Lou was nowhere in sight.

A boy, not a child but neither a full fledged teenager, deftly stepped between her and the stacks of merchandise, stopping briefly to examine small objects which he picked up, turned over, replaced, then handled again. His hair was a golden red, fashionably cut but poorly combed. His face was baby like and his fair skin sprinkled with freckles. His poor manners diverted her first impression of his unpretentious appeal.

Sarah went around him to look at the CD display, a circular free standing rack that she turned to read all the titles. Her side vision caught the movements of the boy, that were oddly suspicious, and she watched him browse among the crowded shelves. He moved between the aisles, alternately in view and obscured from sight.

He was agitated and Sarah thought she saw him slip one of the objects he handled into his pocket. He picked up several other small items which he slowly and deliberately replaced before returning his hand to his pocket.

Sarah did not see anything in his hand. She scowled and wondered if this was an accomplished shoplifter in action. Her gaze sought the boy more openly while she considered what to do if she actually witnessed him stealing.

She put up her hand to draw Lou's attention but without the care nor the intervention of another steady hand, the stack of boxes she touched began to teeter. Lou was not within reach.

Items tumbled off the crowded shelf behind her and scattered on the floor. Sarah's gaze shot sidelong on the pieces but her concern was for the drama she wanted to bring to Lou's attention.

A lanky man appeared behind the boy and put a firm hand on his shoulder, admonishing him, Sarah thought, although she did not hear the words. Suddenly the boy twisted from under the big man's hand and dashed down the aisle toward Sarah, unconcerned about obstacles. His rushing feet kicked the scattered merchandise even further and she bent to retrieve it, groaning at her carelessness of moments before.

The man's long strides covered the space proficiently in pursuit, his broad shoulders and slim hips maneuvering smoothly around the haphazard displays. His eyes were shaded under the turned brim of a cowboy hat, warped by the weather and sweat stained from the sun, so well fitted to his head Sarah considered it an extension of his body.

The man moved with grace and determination. In passing Sarah, he dipped his head in a cursory nod and confessed a dispirited, "S'cuse."

He caught the boy by the arm and pushed him through the door. He moved forward with powerful strides without a backward look. His brown boots barely escaped through the heavy glass door before it swung closed. His agile form moved fluidly away. The departing figure looked like Roy Rogers, a real cowboy movie star.

Sarah stared after him, recognizing him as the man who came to her rescue, craning her head to see past the store displays, trying to discover where he took the boy. He must be the store detective, she thought, not aware of how unlikely a security guard would lurk in a shoestring operation of a small town store. The hat, the jeans, the boots, suddenly registered in her mind as the definition of more than a lawman. He was a cowboy, a real cowboy. She was astonished, and looked around to see if others were available for closer scrutiny. This small town was in ranch country and there would be other cowboys around for sure. A sense of excitement swept through her. Would she find others fitting the role of handsome heroic cowboys she idolized in the western movies she saw as a child?

Chapter Two

Don't let the stars get in your eyes

Sarah did not take her eyes from the door. Her hand was on the revolving rack of DVDs. Her searching expression only stopped Lou for an instant.

"Are you going to buy something or stare at the cowboy? Buy that one in your hand if you're going to," Lou suggested, not convinced Sarah's mind was on any compact disc in particular.

"Oh, sure," Sarah remarked, her attention brought back to the one she held. The disc had some obscure title but she recognized several individual songs that were not in her present collections.

"Get on with it so we can get back on the road," Lou insisted, brusquely abrasive that Sarah could overlook and accept as an endearing characteristic.

Sarah immediately chose to buy the compact disc of old time cowboy songs. The song titles she vaguely remembered, songs no longer sung by contemporary country singers.

"I want to hear familiar tunes and words. Every singer writes their own lyrics these days," she complained to Lou as they left the store.

"Didn't they always? The things happening out there in the world where they are don't strike a familiar chord in me."

"Me either," Sarah admitted, "although there are still lost lovers, cheating hearts, and spurs that jingle, jangle, jingle. The reasons for the lyrics are the same, I suppose, just the picture looks different these days."

Sarah buckled into Lou's car and brought her portable CD player out of her overnight bag. It was loaded with new batteries for just such an occasion. She was anxious to hear her new album. Lou drove on the smoothly paved canyon road, slowing to accommodate the sharp uphill turns that brought them to the high desert plateau.

Solitary junipers stood as sentinels among sage and bitterbrush. Unusually abundant cheatgrass covered the areas among the shrubs with a verdant green, a vivid reminder of the exceptional rainfall in the past months, combined with the snowmelt gathered behind a breached earthen dam that had washed away a small town not long past.

Sarah increased the volume of her CD player and Gene Autry's television theme song filled the cool, dry air in the car. Sarah looked toward Lou for approval. She admired Lou's reddish blond, carefully coiffed, hairdo. Her chic red pant-suit was a lively accent in the car's dark gray interior. Lou jerked her chin to the music, enjoying the guitar beat. Sarah hummed the strains, lost in nostalgia.

Autry's crooning faded away in elaborate orchestration. The piece that followed began with the strumming of a single guitar. Softer and more romantic music than more recently made with electronic instruments, the piece charmed Sarah. A single fiddle joined in with a melancholy that touched her strangely.

Lou wasn't touched at all. "That's awful," was all she said.

Sarah listened more attentively to the familiar tune. It was a rendition like nothing she heard before. The simple lyrics were crooned with such sorrow her breast filled with a wistful yearning. She leaned closer to catch every note over Lou's objection.

"That's the worse thing I ever heard. What song is that, anyway?" Lou asked.

"It's an old country classic. At one time every singer who wanted to win a reputation recorded that one. A haunting melody but I never heard this voice before," Sarah defended. The deep rich voice prickled her skin with inexplicable power and touched a deep core within her.

Lou was expressive and impatient. She backhanded the air toward Sarah and turned away, screwing her face distastefully. It was up to her to get them to the ranch and she indulged Sarah patiently, wondering what held her attention in that mournful tune.

"Oh, Lou, doesn't that put you in a tender sympathetic mood? I want to go right out and meet him tonight in the moonlight. I feel compelled to console him," Sarah said, following the guitar chords with a strumming hand.

"Well you won't get the chance. Nobody sings like that anymore," Lou snorted. "I'll bet nobody even sings that song anymore."

"Maybe. But I like it and I'll bet there are others who'll like it, too." Sarah reluctantly removed it from the player, snapped it into its hard plastic container and returned them both to her overnight case.

Lou cocked her head thoughtfully. "Wouldn't it be fun if we got turned on by a couple of cowpokes?" She giggled in a clucking sort of way.

"Oh, Lou, that's not likely." Sarah glared amusingly at her attractive friend. Lou's skin was clear, although softly lined with smile crinkles by her eyes and mouth. Pale short hairs caught the sunlight when she smiled. She was as vibrant and healthy as Sarah.

"Look how that song affected you. Doesn't a real flesh and blood cowboy sound better?" Lou wondered if Sarah could unleash real passion if given the right target.

"Are you looking for an affair?" Sarah asked, with a puzzled frown, "You told me you weren't interested in marrying again."

" Well I wouldn't exactly rule it out, but the fellow would have to be very special - you know - the chemistry would have to really click."

Lou flicked a sideways glance at Sarah. "I'm not talking marriage, here."

"You can't be serious." But the thought aroused a bizarre curiosity in Sarah.

"You haven't got your mind closed have you?" Lou challenged, her glance warily scanning Sarah before returning to the road.

Sarah shrugged her shoulders. "Do you really believe chemistry could 'click' at our age?" She pondered over that very feeling in the years since her husband died.

"I get to feeling pretty frisky sometimes," Lou said. "I don't know much about clicking chemistry. A real man with a live touch might feel good."

Sarah grinned at the implication Lou put on the word frisky. Her own sexual longings surfaced all too often lately. There were very few single men her age to encourage the speculation of a frisky relationship.

"I wouldn't 'mess" around," Sarah said. Tying herself down in a permanent relationship since the death of her husband was beyond her comprehension in all those five years.

Lou hit the brakes and Sarah braced herself against the door as the car spun round a sharp curve in the road. The road straightened out between open fields of meadow grass. She saw trees protectively bunched toward the horizon.

"Is that our dude ranch?" Sarah asked. They topped a rise and looked across undulating hills where buildings were visible among distant trees. She opened her window to get a clearer view and her nostrils were assailed with the pungent smell of sage,

Artemesia tritentada was its Latin name, she recalled. It was the most pleasant odor she remembered from the country beyond the city limits, although not one that penetrated the blocks of groomed and irrigated lawns where she lived. She concentrated on the unfolding scene.

Far away hills gently rounded and the widely scattered shrubs looked like freckles on healthy cheeks. Trees half hidden between the hills emphasized the rolling terrain. A row of poles connected by the gentle sweep of electric wires raced along the road, alternately peeking over the hills and disappearing into the next valley. Jagged rocks and basalt outcroppings tore the horizon.

Lou nodded as she deftly turned her car onto a narrower graveled road, "That's the Bar X." And straightening her hefty shoulders, Lou took a deep breath and added, "Get set, all you handsome cowpokes. Here we come."

Sarah winced and laughed nervously, "Are you going to launch an all out attack? I think I prefer a quiet invasion."

"Whatever works, my dear, whatever works."

Beyond a cattle guard with an overhead Bar X sign, they had nearly a mile to go before driving past large sprawling barns and hay canopies. Several residential buildings nestled among towering trees.

"I guess they really do run cattle here," Lou said as the wheels rattled over the cattle guard. The open device seemed an unlikely barrier to cattle but it was most effective.

The smooth iron tubes, spaced several inches apart, allow passage of wheeled vehicles. When cattle attempt to cross such a barrier, the cloven hoof, too short to step on more than one tube, slips in between, and the animal rests, to take the next step, on its hocks, a part of the anatomy that cannot possibly bear any weight. After avoiding that first painful experience, a second step is never attempted.

"I wonder if we get to go on a cattle drive," Lou asked, ever hopeful of getting into every activity known to horseback riding and ranch life.

"I hope not," Sarah exploded, her face screwed in a disbelieving frown, " On a working ranch let the ranch hands do the working, not me. How could you expect such a thing?"

"Hey, where would you expect to find the cowboys?" Lou hadn't forgotten her announcement about getting turned on by cowboys.

She searched the maze of driveways that branched off among the trees. "Can you tell where we check in?"

Sarah looked down one driveway where several pickup trucks and a beat-up jeep were parked under the trees. A two toned gray van stood in front of the long low building.

"Over there, on that big log cabin, I see an office sign." Lou parked in front of an impressive log cabin, undoubtedly the lodge.

Sarah looked up at the wide veranda running the full length of the building, supported by a three foot high fieldstone foundation. Ornate wooden columns supported the tiled roof that swept down to shade the open porch on which colorful furniture was randomly spaced.

A gangling boy rose from a chair and came to attention in front of a tall cowboy stepping out of the office door. The sculpted masculine profile of the man in a broad brimmed hat was clean shaven and bent briefly to the apprehensive boy, whose well combed hair bounced buoyantly with each jerky movement.

Sarah's mouth fell open when she recognized the lanky cowboy and the young shoplifter from the variety store.

The cowboy spoke to the boy, motioning him away. The boy nodded his golden red head, sent a wary glance toward Sarah, and cautiously hurried off the far end of the veranda.

Sarah's eyes followed the boy's retreat, oddly curious at finding him at this ranch. He had been combed and cleaned, not the untidy picture she saw in the store. The dismissal seemed hasty and unnecessary. Wouldn't guests be welcomed by all workers? But then was the boy a worker? Or for that matter was the older man? A burgeoning warmth that ran like a river swept her length at the sight of him. Sarah breathed deeply to regain control of her emotions.

Her gaze swung to the cowboy whom she studied now with critical interest. The lean figure walked with a deceptively easy stride toward the stone steps. She remembered him manhandling the boy in the variety store. Distrust crept into Sarah's mind and that puzzled her.

Lou noticed Sarah's apprehension but she attributed the reticence to her dislike for working with horses.

"C'mon, once you meet your horse you'll love it." Lou thought everyone would love horses the way she did. "You just have to give it a chance to get acquainted."

Sarah wasn't ready to get acquainted with a horse. She wasn't ready to get any closer acquainted with this real life cowboy either. She met him briefly already and was enamored in spite of her distrust. Instead of chancing another jolt in her stomach, she stared at the wide stone steps.

High-topped hand-tooled travel-weary boots paused at the top. Sarah's eyes clung to the leather tooled morning glory pattern for a moment when they invaded the top step where she so studiously glared. When she could no longer quell her curiosity, her gaze traveled up long denim-clad legs converging below a wide belt and a pale blue chambray shirt.

Her eyes swung sideways to take in the breadth of his shoulders, then upward across a red bandanna and sun browned features. The stone rugged jaws tilted in question. She had not noticed in the store how handsomely they blended in the curly sideburns beneath the distinctively fondled hat. With eyes in lids permanently squinted from facing day-long sun, poised like an eagle atop its aerie, the imposing cowboy examined the new arrivals from his stance on the ranch house steps. A friendly smile toyed with the corners of his thin lipped mouth. His eyes were darkly penetrating.

He found himself strangely curious about the woman he rescued from disaster at the crowded shelf. Her corroborating smile flashed so quickly it surprised him then and he was pleased at her spontaneity. He saw a light heartedness in the moment their eyes held. He perceived she wasn't as worried about the tumbling items as her groan implied. A sense of humor lurked in her impish expression. She might have laughed about it if they had failed to keep the boxes from scattering.

She looked far too serious and apprehensive now as she stared at him from the car. Had she reacted harshly to his capture of the boy? Her impression of his actions did not cross his mind at the time. His eyes looked for signs of disapproval.

Sarah didn't stop staring. Was he the ranch manager? The owner? He came down to greet them. The large brimmed hat, pushed back, revealed a lighter band of forehead above the dark piercing eyes. Why did she get the feeling he was not looking at her but looking through her? Over Lou's excitement she put such thoughts aside.

Lou resolutely grabbed the steering wheel with both hands, thoroughly admiring what she saw.

"Now will you look at that? Does that look like a man who knows cattle? Or what?"

Sarah couldn't answer that. Her imagination was building a habitat around this individual that was foreign in itself and she was afraid to enter. His likeness appeared in the western movies of her childhood, yet here he was in the flesh, taking the measured stride of a stalking predator down the wide stone steps. That image disconnected with his authoritative manner toward the boy on the veranda. What were they doing in the store? Was it his son sent off to do chores? Or was the boy sent away to avoid introduction to the newly-arrived ranch guests?

The questions had no answer, although a manager was not likely to allow loitering on the porch. If the kid was a derelict, was the cowboy concerned that Sarah saw him stealing? If the kid was his son, was he removing an embarrassment? Or might there be essential chores on a real ranch? The tall handsome man looked like a cowboy in her estimation filling the role of a cowpuncher, but what did Sarah know about cattle? A lot less than she knew about horses.

She was uncomfortable with his stance, his entire appearance. In fact, she was uncomfortable with the whole vital image of the man. She could not remember ever before feeling a runaway heart trying to burst out of her chest as it did at that moment. His dark eyes bored into her from his bronzed features, as if he could see right through her. She felt under siege and she didn't like it. She fretted over ways to explain herself to the alarming image. She squeezed her eyelids tightly closed and shook her head to wipe away her trepidation. This was a dude ranch. No one was expected to be anything but a dude, an unaccomplished rider. An early questionnaire asked for experience level and she underlined beginner. The fact that she was less than that - totally inexperienced - was not something she should be accused of, even though she had never been on a horse.

It was preposterous that she should feel accused by a penetrating look of his sun-squinted eyes. She had a close glimpse of his deep brown eyes when he stabilized the toppling boxes in the store at a brief moment of shared appreciation of an accident averted. He was simply a stranger who reached out and prevented a minor catastrophe, a stranger never to be encountered again after briefly crossing her path, although she did not dwell on the fact at the time.

And now that path must be recrossed. He was here. Suddenly because of the store thievery she witnessed, question of the coincidence assailed her. She stiffened gravely. Sarah never backed down from anyone before and she had no intention to start now. This was her vacation and she gathered her composure to face it like the guest she was. She straightened her shoulders and stepped out of the car.

Slowly the long-legged cowboy came down the wide stone steps, his thumbs hooked in the side pockets of faded jeans, loosely fitting his narrow hips.

Sarah warily met his gaze. She mustered a stance against her fear. A fear she could not readily explain. Suddenly the reason occurred to her. She was starstruck, intrepid with anticipation but wavering with childish disbelief. She feared her knees would not support her when she stood. This long-legged man was the startling image of a movie cowboy - a regular Gary Cooper - straight out of High Noon. His confidence radiated awareness of his new guests and their identity. He knew who they were and was expecting them. The cowboy's heavy jaw was ruggedly handsome and his wide-set eyes were hidden in sun squinting wrinkles. In his late fifties, he possessed an odd remoteness reflected in the exaggerated sway of his broad shoulders as he sauntered down the steps. The air of vanity in his bearing was so overpowering that Sarah viewed him with caution.

"Howdy, ladies. Welcome to the Bar X. We're expecting a Lou Petrosky and Sarah Wilson." His slow uncultured voice made the statement a question and the deep gravely sound sizzled along her spine. Without the slightest move of his head, his eyes conveyed the query to each woman.

"I'm Matt Bannister," he said, extending his hand to Lou who was the first to step forward to identify herself. When he moved on, Lou promptly placed her hands on her hips and strolled off to the side of the building, looking to see where the red-haired kid was sent off to. She nodded to herself with satisfaction at the overall impression of the ranch house.

"You can sign the register when Melanie returns. I'll show you to your room," Matt said with quiet authority as he walked around the car to meet Sarah at the open trunk. His blue cotton shirt molded his chest with the slightest movement of every muscle. Beside her, his height was not as great as she first thought, but every inch was filled with controlled power and assurance.

"Then you're Sarah." That question was a definite statement in his confident and deep unhurried tone. His eyebrows nevertheless remained raised in question when he held out a large welcoming hand that compelled her to share a warm handshake.

"I apologize for the boy in the store," he said, holding her hand firmly, as if insisting the apology be accepted with no further explanation of the boy's action, nor his own. There was no indication of why he felt this need to apologize. Indeed, he was uncomfortable with the realization and dropped the thought in his attention to the darkly tanned woman and her luggage.

Sarah smiled tightly, uncomfortably aware of her unsettled feelings. She wanted to follow her first impression and not trust him but all of her senses rallied to adore him.

Holy Toledo! She was weak-kneed with the first firm acquaintance of a fantasy cowhand.

Matt Bannister looked every bit like a movie-set cowboy. His faded blue shirt stretched firmly over his muscled shoulders when he reached for the luggage. His very breath put a strain on the pearl inlaid snap closures. A clean red bandanna enclosed his neck and the ends hung down where a black tangle of hair appeared unrestrained within the unbuttoned collar.

Sarah nervously hauled her large suitcase out of the trunk and thrust it into Matt's outstretched hands.

He took it from her as if it was a feather.

Sarah hefted Lou's enormous leather suitcase out of the trunk. Matt reached to take it with the same nonchalance.

He grunted in surprise to discover the bag was much heavier than he expected from the way she handled it. A bushy eyebrow raised ever so slightly as his approving gaze bounced from the bag, then up and down Sarah's figure, coming to a penetrating halt on her hazel eyes.

Sarah's felt her heart give a little leap as she acknowledged the silent compliment as her due. She reached nervously for Lou's cosmetic bag, feeling uncomfortable at his unmasked appraisal of her strength. And she became more uncomfortable at the unbridled response of her body. She dropped her gaze in the hope it didn't show.

"I've got an overnight case in the front," Sarah mumbled, avoiding his eyes. Before he could set a bag down to free his hand and close the trunk lid, Sarah reached and slammed it, an angry reaction to the primitive response of her body.

Matt was annoyed with the haughty way Sarah closed the lid. He couldn't understand what brought her dander up in such rejection. She didn't stand helplessly awaiting his assistance, which was surprisingly different from other female guests. He admired her strength and self possession but was confounded when she didn't respond to his implied compliment with humility or grace.

He felt a twinge of regret that she was not the humorous guest he anticipated. She seemed to have soured since the encounter in the store. He frowned ever so slightly to think the boy's intrusion may have caused that change in her. He didn't like that implication one bit.

No matter.

It was his intention to be no more than politely courteous to the guests, even the occasional promiscuous female who openly invited liaisons with every man on the ranch. When he felt an unquenchable need for female companionship, he knew where to find relief in the city. Sometimes he doubted the worthiness of the rare trips he made there over the years. Lately he longed for more than sexual satisfaction in his life. He was surprised at the way his curiosity stirred and continuously returned to this woman after he left the store with the boy. Something about her made him want to linger at the time, never expecting to see her again. He did not know she was to be his guest.

Now he shrugged it off. The first ignited spark he felt from Sarah didn't catch fire. At least not alighting her tinder as it had his. He felt an odd smoldering in the kindling of his soul but he thought better of pushing her, regardless of how flammable he felt. Her surliness made him decide to back off before any serious sparks could fly.

The trim little woman was going to require cautious handling to prevent friction with other guests if she continued to bristle like this. That shouldn't be his worry. The managers handled guest relations. He was a temporary fill-in for Steve and Melanie.

Still, the silver haired woman ignited his interest. She sparked a challenge to his manhood to which he would normally give a swift and virulent response. He gritted his teeth refusing to give her the satisfaction. Resolutely he turned from her to direct Lou, with a nod of his head, to follow the left path. Sarah got her overnight case and followed with the two small bags. Doing her best to disregard the easy swinging gate of his lean hips below the broad muscled shoulders, she concentrated on the colorful tulips that lined the cobbled walk. The grounds between the lodge and the guest cabins were informal, the paths meandering among old trees with overhanging branches. The lovely parklike setting put her at ease and at once she was glad to be here.

That thought caused her eyes to swing to the cowboy. She could not deny his presence. His ambiance lingered to tantalize her senses. Trailing in his wake marked with the smell of leather and something she did not recognize, she was reminded of a spicy relish. It was unique. The worn heels of his scuffed boots clicked on the field stone walk. Her unsettled attention skittered from his impressive image to an encroaching racket.

Hissing geese propelled themselves around the flowers toward her in a flurry of wings. She stiffened at their angry approach. They looked vicious and righteously incensed.

"Damn," Matt swore as he glanced back toward Sarah, pretending shame at his outburst, "Sorry, Ma'am," they're supposed to be confined in back." He strolled on, unconcerned.

Opened wings flapped an attack on Sarah, their fury fueled by frightening cackles. Like shields, the bags Sarah carried were flung forward to protect her legs from the onrush of the hissing geese. She was too uncertain to move.

Lou heard the ruckus and flew into action. She shouldered through the door, past Matt, flapping her bright red jacket at the cackling gaggle.

"Shoo! Shoo! Get back with you!" Lou shouted at the attacking geese. The red flurry stopped them before they reached the steps. They milled and circled in confusion.

The geese uneasily folded their wings, momentarily subdued by the flailing red jacket. The strange spectacle left them hissing with outstretched necks, chattering among themselves like a committee deciding the next course of action.

The geese reconsidered their attack against Lou and simply held her at bay with their cackling chatter. Their tongues arched in open beaks as their beady eyes struggled against a decision to retreat. Sarah shook her head, bewildered at Lou's bold action. With her eyes riveted on the scene she straightened and uncertainly backed into the open doorway to get far away from the action.

The door was open but the doorway was not empty.

It was filled with the solid length of her movie cowboy.

Sarah stiffened against his hard muscled body and caught her breath. She absolutely refused to return to the noisy geese and pressed persistently against him insisting on access to the building.

She expected protection inside the door.

She found a more significant refuge against a manly form.

Sarah stood her ground. This stranger would surely make way for her. She waited for his retreat but it did not happen. Her shoulders warmed from the touch of his chest, her hips fit a hollow below his and she could not breathe. The back of her head fit the concave between his shoulder and biceps. Somehow this position was terribly familiar. And it felt wonderful.

Her body prickled with memories.

She refused to move.

Matt stood insolently firm.

She came breathlessly alive.

She did not flinch from him.

Matt's eyes widened and his eyebrows raised an inch. He should move aside and let her by. She tried to force him to move with her persistent pressing, a move he decided to resist. She was afraid of the geese and that amused him. He was in no hurry to move. He alerted every muscle and stood his ground. He was not accustomed to giving in. Furthermore he liked what he felt – Sarah's body tucked against his full length.

He recognized her wish to avoid the geese. He would protect her from real danger, but the geese were harmless.

No matter.

Her genuine fear brought out his desire to protect. One more second of her pressing body and he would wrap her in his arms. His head told him that was a bad idea. He should never get this close to a guest. That was trouble he would always avoid.

She sought escape from danger.

He was determined to resist entanglement.

He clenched his fists to prevent his arms from surrounding her. Just a conditioned male reaction, he thought, to which he refused to respond like a Pavlovian dog. This was not the way he had in mind to meet the challenge she presented at the car.

At least he demonstrated how immovable he could be. That made him chuckle, nervously, not sure how much of a victory that was.

"That's something else," he thought, barely a murmur meant only about his response to Sarah. Her body quickened with a question and he realized he spoke his offhand appraisal of his response to her aloud.

He recovered quickly indicating he was only watching Lou hold the raucous birds at bay. Lou was something of an anomaly as she shook the resolve of the attacking geese. What a contrast there was between these women, he thought. Their mutual agreement about Lou broke the stalemate but not the body contact. He bent his head to her.

"The geese won't hurt you, Ma'am. Just dirty your shoes if you don't watch where you step." He held back a chuckle and his lips twitched in a tease.

Sarah's hair moved with the puff of his breath at every word. Another body lost for years was pressed in memory against her. How she missed that contact. How she savored the warmth of the body that rekindled the memory.

But it was only a memory. The long warm body at her back was a momentary substitute and a pleasant one at that. She held the memory but returned to reality when she decided to breath again. She turned, removing all but her shoulder from his touch and caught his condemning smile.

He was enjoying her fright and laughed. That raised her ire. She didn't like being the butt of a joke and her cheeks grew ruddy.

He stepped back and reached down, "Let me take your bags."

Color heated Sarah's neck and chin. She was embarrassed at her ignorance of geese but was not convinced they were harmless. She surrendered the bags to Matt with a shoving movement to push him a safer distance away.

Nevertheless, her discomfort lingered. She was unnerved by her reaction to his body contact. She followed him with an awareness that she had pressed against him unnecessarily and enjoyed the prolonged contact far too much.

She hoped he saw it only as a reaction to the attacking geese. There was no erasing her own sensation. And her mortification. She didn't meet his penetrating eyes when he glanced up as he set the bags inside the door of the room she would share with Lou for the next two weeks.

"Come into the lodge for coffee," the lanky cowboy offered.

He backed away to let Lou enter, touched his hat and turned to find Sarah staring at him. The message he returned with his eyes was as physical as if he had touched her with that calloused brown hand she admired in the store a short time past. A more intimate touch caressed her across the empty space than what she felt when his entire body pressed against her back.

She squeezed her eyes closed and turned away ignoring his polite gesture with a   sideways shrug of her chin. Surely he couldn't have read her mind, could he?

Chapter Three

I'm back in the saddle again

Sarah did not expect to be aroused in such an intimate way by any man. She had been embraced by men who hoped to stir her emotions but never had anyone touched her depths as this one had.

It was a fluke. A coincidence of body positions. That was all. The memory of it continued to disrupt her equilibrium just as much as the real performance had. The coincidence could not be taken lightly. She searched valiantly for a diversion that would wipe it from her memory. She tried to concentrate on what Lou was doing.

"I chased the geese away, Sarah. You just have to show them who's boss, that's all," Lou announced triumphantly, throwing her jacket to mark her choice of beds.

"I came here to ride horses, not herd cackling geese," Sarah insisted, irritated at the pleasure Lou showed in apprising their surroundings. She still smarted from Matt's chiding laughter, although her body tingled from a far more overriding emotion.

She wasn't too pleased with herself that she couldn't shrug off the arousing effect, conversely reveling in the warming it produced. Lou's wavy reflection smiled at her from the mirror.

"Isn't this quaint?" Lou deliberately examined the decorations and furniture, nodding her approval with her roving eyes.

Sarah watched Lou take in the furnishings but didn't bother to take more than a cursory look for herself. She tossed her linen jacket on the pillow and expelled a long sigh. Throwing herself across the bunk Lou left for her, she replied with great force, "No, it's not quaint. It's like a movie. It's unreal."

The doorway was flanked by spindled chairs and bunk beds. Cream colored wallpaper attempted to brighten the rustic room. Renditions of bucking horses hung in rustic frames around the periphery above the window and bunks. Below the window a low night stand was occupied by an electric lamp fashioned from horse shoes. The bunks were neatly covered with coffee-brown cotton bedspreads. The tufted chenille felt like ripples through her blouse.

Sarah rolled over on her back and declared, "It was a big mistake for me to come here."

A free standing wardrobe huddled between one corner of the room and the wide window through which a gentle breeze puffed out the gossamer panel that obscured the mottled shade from trees nearby. An ancient dresser with a mirror entwined by carved vines backed sedately out of the draft as if receding for protection into the other corner.

Sarah could not begin to describe to Lou where or how her feelings originated. An apprehension lingered after Matt's departure when his dark eyes impaled her with a directness she didn't want to face. She felt an intimacy then that could not possibly exist, not with a man so recently met. Yet it hung between them like a tangible thing. She regretted the imprudent manner with which she held herself against him for that short moment in the doorway. She was aware that she invited the intimacy if indeed it really was intimate, not simply an unavoidable happening. She considered herself a fool for having done so.

"I feel awful already." She thought that was reason enough for what she considered the big mistake.

Lou glared at Sarah. "What is this? A tantrum? This room is beautiful. Sure, it looks like a movie setting. So much the better."

"I don't know what I expected, Lou, but it certainly was not a movie."

Lou continued to thrust out short commanding sentences. "Well, it's not a movie. It's a vacation. We paid for it. But if you have to pretend, then make believe you belong here. Like neighboring rancher. Or the town hussy. Or a cowboy's" sweetheart. But get into the act. Enjoy!"

Lou's arm swept the room. She put her hands on her hips as if to emphasize her authority. "I'll unpack later. I'm going for a cup of coffee. It's over in the lodge. Mr Bannister is going to introduce us around."

Sarah didn't want to move. Lou was not about to give up. "C'mon. Let's go," she urged.

"You go ahead. I want to wash my face and put on a fresh blouse," Sarah said, sitting up with a resigned sigh. Maybe she should get into the fantasy. But it would take some pretending if she was to play the part of a cowgirl. She wasn't going to let Lou's insinuation of childishness spoil her day. She wasn't going to spoil Lou's day either. She would do her best to enjoy herself. Sarah smiled at her good friend, who admonished her from the doorway.

"All right, I'm off to find the coffee. I'll ask if we can meet the horses right away."

Lou pointed a slim finger at Sarah with the advice: "The quicker you get acquainted with the horses the quicker you'll see how nice it is to ride."

Lou set her mouth in a straight line, determined to have Sarah enjoy the ranch whether she liked it or not.

"Don't think you can hide in this room," Lou shook her pointed finger as a warning as she left and closed the door.

If Lou had her way she'd make Sarah enjoy her stay. The least Sarah could do was try to enjoy it herself.

For Lou's sake at least.

Sarah put the noisy geese out of her thoughts but not the quiet cowboy whose anatomy she so intimately encountered. It was the memory the encounter invoked, not the man himself that left her shaken.

Well, wasn't it?

Unusual longings she could not describe, inexplicably surfaced recently. Maybe those yearnings were only buried under the newfound independence after her husband's death. It was annoying that the cowboy rekindled memories at such an awkward time and place.

It was not the cowboy that brought about her unsettling response, she insisted, as she unpacked and put her clothes away. In no way could she deny the memories that swept her and she had no wish to deny them. What she should deny was the longing that his body revived to her consciousness. This was not the time nor was it the place to unleash dormant emotions. Lou triggered some foolish expectation when she spoke of romantic cowpokes before they arrived. Sarah tried to wipe that foolishness away.

She found the bathroom and washed her face with tepid water, finding it a useless endeavor with which to wash the cowboy's image from her mind. She tried to take refuge in the memories of those intimate moments with her husband but she had long ago stopped pining for what was lost and vague memories were no substitute for the live emotions that swept her. Taking her time toweling dry did nothing to wipe away the newfound feelings.

The knitted cotton pullover she chose to wear felt cool and soft against her shoulders. The alternating blue and white strips coordinated with her dark blue split skirt. She slipped into her running shoes, snapped on her fanny pack and turned to leave the room. Before opening the door she tucked her sketch pad under her arm.

Sarah's spirits were considerably better now that she had washed the dust off her face, and was no longer sticky from the plane ride she had endured earlier. Closing the heavy plank door, wondering where its solid form had been when she backed into the man instead, Sarah was again jolted at the memory of the cowboy's insolence as he refused to give way to her fright. She put the thought out of her mind as she watched carefully where she put each foot when she stepped out on the goose tracked steps. The geese were nowhere to be seen.

Small birds flew off at her appearance and twittered curiously in safe perches above her as if discussing the intrusion. Other outdoor noises raised her curiosity. She decided she might as well get acquainted with the ranch and this struck her as a good time to explore. She was on her own. Lou would be so busy meeting other guests she wouldn't notice Sarah's absence if she didn't come for coffee right away.

Mr Bannister – Matt, she remembered his name - invited them to coffee. That meant he would be there. She couldn't face him just now. She would go in some other direction. This real ranch called for an investigation. If she was going to sketch horses, she might as well look for some.

Turning away from the walk to the lodge, Sarah walked along the flower-ridden path. A broad shouldered cowboy, hardly fitting the role of gardener, pounded a stake among the flowers. He sneaked a glance at her as she walked by. Her sketch pad caught his attention, bringing him to his feet. He touched his hat brim in a stiff salute.

"Excuse me, ma'am," he called. "Are you the one with the art gallery?"

The idea of being associated with artists amused Sarah as it had in the plane with the curious flight attendant. People who noticed her sketching often questioned her, hoping to meet a real artist. In the same way she was curious about fancy dressed cowboys, wondering if she would meet real western singers. She looked at this tall cowboy, curious at his question.

"No. I'm not even an artist," she admitted, regarding her sketch pad rather forlornly, recalling that she seldom admitted that before.

"I took up sketching and thought I should practice drawing ranch animals." If a guest owned a gallery, Sarah would meet her soon enough. A connection like that would be interesting but not critical. Sarah was not planning to sell work any time soon. It amused her that she even thought her work could reach that state of acceptance.

"I'm Sarah Wilson, retired from reprographics. Are you one of the working cowboys we're going to watch?" Sarah extended her hand, looking up into the young man's face shadowed by the wide brim of his Stetson.

He stifled an amused smile at the thought of being watched at work. It was an important part of his job, to get the guests involved with ranch activities and watch over them while they took part in the work of the ranch. He was as tall and broad shouldered as Matt, his cotton shirt work worn but pressed. His face was clean shaven, deeply tanned, and wrinkle free. His gaze was guarded, his attitude friendly, but aloof.

"Yes, my job includes a little bit of everything. I'm Buck," he answered, taking her hand in both of his. "I'm interested in drawing. Perhaps we could compare ideas."

"I'd like that," Sarah agreed, "But you'll find I'm just a beginner." She had trouble pulling her hand away.

Buck held it as if expecting a more specific commitment, holding her gaze as well, waiting for her to name a time and place. His eyes flipped past her shoulder and his gaze immediately hardened. His hands dropped.

"Sorry to keep you," he exclaimed, nervously, "See you around." He backed off several steps and walked away.

That was curious, Sarah thought, looking behind her for the cause of Buck's abrupt departure. He reacted as though censured. Sarah saw no one around the buildings or the surrounding grounds. Buck's reprimand must have come from his conscience. Perhaps he was concerned he had taken too many liberties by stopping her and then expecting her to compare art work. She had nothing to show him and probably never would.

She hurried to find the animals. So far all she had seen were two cowboys, both tall and slim, and either could fit a hero role in her idea of a western movie. She shrugged away the notion of a movie set, complete with authentic cowboys. If the workers on this ranch were catering to paying guests, the authenticity was compromised to a role, not reality.

Movie or not, the ranch setting was real. Saddled horses were lined along a rail on one side of the barn. Cattle grazed on the hills beyond the barn in the sun drenched yellow-green grass, creating another authentic scene of western movies.

She softly hummed: Oh, give me a home, where the buffalo roam...

The nicker of a horse from inside the building drew her attention and she stiffened, wondering if she dared to investigate.

The barn seemed deserted although the heavy stomping of a large animal echoed against the empty walls. Waiting for her eyes to adjust to the shadows, she searched the depths of the interior for the noise.

Off to the other side of the building against an open door, Sarah could see the silhouette of the horse. Its head came up on an arched neck, ears pointed forward. Empty stalls stretched off to the right. She saw no gate through which to walk so she considered going over the top to get nearer to that beckoning horse. She put her sketch pad on a window sill, climbed on the feed box and raised up to look over on the other side.

An aisle ran the length of the barn so she jumped down into it. The barn floor was dusty and dry. The air smelled of fresh clean straw mixed with a faint animal odors that wafted lightly through the dimness of the building. Different from dog and cat smells, the odor was totally foreign to her and she wrinkled her nose to sniff more carefully before deciding where to place the scent in her unspoken list of likes or dislikes. It didn't occur to her that the odor receded behind her intent to reach the origin, the horse that raised its head to beckon her.

Only the front of the stall remained between her and the horse that had lured her into the large windowless barn. She inspected the horse with an artist's eye. The head was raised attentively, ears pointed forward in expectation. Its sleek neck was gracefully arched presenting an exquisite picture of natural power and beauty. A thrilling excitement replaced the tremor of misgiving Sarah felt when first entering the shadowed aisle.

The horse looked hopeful, inviting her approach. How ironic to be welcomed by a horse, the one individual she didn't want to meet. Her tension subsided and she walked slowly toward it.

Suddenly, Sarah had the feeling she was watched by more than the horse. Her spine tingled. She looked up and down the aisle but saw no one.

The horse nickered for her attention. She shuddered in delight at the welcome she thought it was. A blanket lay across its back. Was it being saddled? Should she be here? A worried feeling swept over her at the thought.

Perhaps she shouldn't have come uninvited. For a moment she wanted to flee but it was too late to avoid discovery. She was fraught with misgiving at the sound of approaching footsteps. A furtive backward glance verified what her radar suspected.

She had not avoided Matt.

She had gone straight to him like a homing pigeon.

Sarah stiffened and a strange heat swept her. What an affect this man unleashed in her hormones! *Get yourself under control, she admonished.* Playing a movie role in this western setting was going to be real tough, unless she cast herself as a besotted female.

She couldn't face him with her emotions running rampant. She moved toward the beckoning animal confined in the stall. She reached across the feed box to pet the glistening neck. The horse turned its head and nuzzled her hand. Long stiff hairs prickled her palm. The softness of the muzzle surprised her.

Sarah was never before this close to a horse. She was not afraid of horses, but she never wanted to get close to one before. This animal was compelling her to advance in spite of her tenuous tremor of fear. She was brave enough with this one. The beautiful dark red animal was securely tied.

She decided to go in beside the mare. Lou would be proud of her courage.

Sarah climbed up on the feed box, prepared to slide down into the stall. Her action was severely stayed by a hard iron band.

"Just what do you think you're doing?" Matt's forbidding voice was firm and rough in Sarah's ear as he dragged her away from the stall.

"Tryin' to get yourself killed?" This red mare was particularly wary of strangers. Horses don't relate actions to consequences. He envisioned a former guest who had been pinned between a horse and stall, sustaining serious injuries. The horse had turned suddenly and the guest was crushed. Liability insurance rates soared. Most accidents involving large animals could be avoided by using common sense.

Sarah struggled in his embrace, ineffectually trying to stand on her own. Matt released his encircling arms to let her catch her footing but he didn't want to leave her trembling. His hands slid from her shoulders to her waist to help her find her balance. He knew from the earlier encounter she wasn't hard packed into a torturous undergarment. It was a recollection he was ready to verify as fact once more.

Now his hands enjoyed the contact and he confirmed his discovery as he moved her to safety. For a second he reveled in the sensation. *God, it felt good to touch her!* "Don't ever get into a stall like that," he admonished, remembering his purpose in grabbing her in the first place. He must not get involved with a guest. He pushed her brusquely across the aisle and picked up the saddle he had thrown aside when he came to her rescue.

Sarah couldn't imagine what she had done that was life threatening. Her adrenaline pumped as she stared at Matt. The heat from the imprint of his hands left her as stunned as his violent action. She pressed back against a partition so hard it could have absorbed her. She put her hand to her mouth and kept her questions to herself.

Matt placed the saddle on the back of the glossy red horse and smoothed the corners of the underlying blanket until he was satisfied with its position. He dragged his hand across the glistening hide behind the saddle. The dawdling soothed the horse and gave Matt time to ponder the exchange between the horse and the woman.

If the mare intended to repel the woman, it would have been instantaneous. Sarah would have been bitten or at least lunged at with bared teeth. He could not have prevented it. But the horse actually welcomed her attention. He thought the nickering he heard was the horse's impatient response to his intent to ride because he had already placed the blanket on the mare's back. When Sarah appeared and the horse's attention was obviously on her instead of him, he was too amazed to move quickly. He arrived too late to rescue her if she had needed such an act.

He didn't know what to make of Sarah. Her approach was a spontaneous reaction to what he saw as an unprecedented welcome from his horse. She had read that right. He was surprised at her intuitive reaction and downright amazed at the way she scaled the stalls that barred her way. He was completely dumbfounded by the easy way his horse accepted Sarah's hand.

He expected the horse to bite her. That was the move he rushed to avoid when he pulled her away from the stall. Ruby was a well trained horse but rarely reached out to strangers. The horse was always ready to bite anything near.

Matt shook his head as he reviewed the incident. He wanted to make his guests happy and he wanted to keep them from injury. Where this little sprite of a woman was concerned he wanted to add more personal actions to that priority list. With her near, something kept getting in the way of his business like manner. He had to get his priorities straight. He reviewed the kindergarten lesson he had perfected to use on naive guests.

"This horse weighs a thousand pounds which is enough to crush you. It's well trained but we never know how it will react to strangers or unexpected actions." He watched her reaction from the corner of his eye while he tightened the cinch.

"I didn't know," she said, letting out a relieved breath, "It seemed so friendly." Her hand was drawn toward the horse beyond her intention.

When Sarah came into the barn to answer the beckoning nicker, she began to think Lou was right about liking horses. She agreed that a horse wouldn't be as easy to push away as a rollicking puppy. She took a confident step and reached her hand toward the horse.

"You're real anxious to ride." Matt chanced a glimpse at her. His pulse quickened at the way she stood up to him. The guest record listed her as a non-rider, yet in her first hour at the ranch she came to the barn. He could tell she had no experience with horses, yet she was drawn to this one. Furthermore, the horse accepted her, much to his astonishment.

"Whatever gave you the idea I was anxious to ride?" Sarah demanded, her feet firmly apart and her hands on her hips.

He shot a puzzled frown at her over the horse's back. He tried his best to keep his mind on the business of saddling his horse. He had planned to saddle his first, then two more docile animals for Sarah and Lou.

On sudden impulse he decided to let her ride Ruby. He feigned indifference. "I'll have this horse ready in a few minutes."

Her eyes widened in protest, "I am not anxious to ride."

Matt flipped the stirrup down and cocked his head to study the length. With aggravating patience, he hitched it up several notches. His glance flicked to Sarah and back to the stirrup to mentally verify the measurement.

"C'mon. Let me get these stirrups adjusted."

"I told you - I don't want to ride," Sarah repeated between gritted teeth.

Matt's eyes narrowed and the sun squint wrinkles grew hard. "Lou asked me to saddle up for both of you. She said you'd be reluctant."

Sarah drew in herself up and took a deep breath. She could successfully defy Lou but how could she defy Matt? Lou equated her actions to a spoiled child. Now that attitude was emanating from this cowboy - this authentic cowboy that gave her weak knees at the very sight of him.

She hesitated.

Matt untied the mare and led it around to where Sarah stood.

"So I scared you," he goaded, with a jerk of his head toward the horse, as if he forgot he just threw her from the stall.

Sarah clenched her fists to control her embarrassment. She wanted to slap his arrogant face.

"I'm not scared. I just can't ride."

"What do you mean, you can't ride?" He looked at her in silent disbelief for a long disconcerting moment.

He snorted.

"That's a new one. Most folks who come here call themselves riders and they don't know a thing about riding. Some don't even want to try to learn the right way to handle a horse. All you have to do is sit in the saddle and hang on. You can be that much of a rider. The horse does most of the work anyway."

To have come to a ranch where she was expected to ride horses she thought she didn't like, seemed more ludicrous now than ever. "I have a feeling it's not that simple." She didn't want to look foolish. Making a good impression on this supercilious cowboy would be impossible if it had to be done on horseback. It didn't occur to her that his opinion shouldn't matter.

The lovely red horse loomed beside her. The blocky hoofed feet moved daintily at Matt's bidding. Large darkly luminous eyes held a curiosity Sarah found intriguing. If there was an odor it was not offensive. Sarah was completely awed by its appearance.

The imposing saddle horse stood over fifteen hands high at the withers which were somewhat higher than the hips, dispensing with the uncomfortable feeling of being pitched forward or riding downhill as with the English jumpers. Mixed trotting and thoroughbred blood changed the conformation of the Kentucky saddle horse in physical appearance from gaited horses, although modification and refining that occurred in the mixed breeding did little to change the gaits.

The American Saddle Horse was a true breed and most of the thousands of registered pedigreed stock contained thoroughbred blood. Ruby was a magnificent piece of horseflesh and Matt was justly proud.

"I'll ride with you and you'll be just fine," he insisted, as he reached toward her with an outspread hand.

"C'mon. Get in the saddle so I can fix the stirrups."

His voice was firm but his patience was growing thin. Sarah could feel his rising agitation. She had no reason to test the limits of his anger. She noticed that none of his impatience showed when he turned to the horse.

He stroked the horse's neck and his voice held a softness when he uttered assurances into its eyes. He turned the mare's left side toward Sarah. Holding the reins against the mane with his left hand, he turned the stirrup toward Sarah with a glance to her foot. Her leg was too short to mount easily. He would have to upturn a bucket for her to stand on if she was going to succeed on her own.

"Can you reach the stirrup?" he asked. He couldn't judge her weight but he didn't want to lift her. Subconsciously he opened a possibility to touch her again. He let her attempt to reach the stirrup on her own.

Not believing for a minute that her heart was racing to flee from this potent male, Sarah gripped the saddle horn with one hand and the cantle with the other. Uneasily, she hopped while raising her left foot to the stirrup, a height beyond her reach.

The horse sidestepped and she lost her balance. Matt's right arm came round her waist and held her steady. Her body was wonderfully solid and impossibly soft at the same time.

"Grab the horn and swing aboard," he ordered, delaying until he cupped her hip in his large hand and gave a demonstrative lift. He felt her body shift and swooped her up.

She hoisted her own weight. He guided her into the saddle. In that one swift instant, she mounted. The horse jerked its head up in response to her sudden weight, swiveling its ears forward, reflecting its surprise, accepting without displeasure.

Sarah dazedly regarded the bounce of the flowing black mane as it settled neatly on one side of the blood red neck.

For a moment it seemed impossible.

The saddle was under her.

She was on the back of the tall horse. The barn floor was a long way down. She was amazed, her eyes round with triumph, her face bright with wonder.

Matt's hand lingered until her trim form settled securely in the saddle. He had a glimpse of her strength when she handed him the luggage but he never guessed she was so agile. By the look on her face, she surprised herself with that leap. The extent of her accomplishment radiated from her hazel eyes.

Matt forgot what he was supposed to be doing. He stood mesmerized. Sarah was beautiful.

She was startled at the expression on his upturned face and the admiration in his eyes which he nervously averted. Her eyes clung to Matt's hat. The crown was battered. The band was dark from hours of sweat. The wide brim showed signs of being handled but so far he hadn't tipped his hat once to her. He didn't fit the gallant cowboy role in the movies she remembered.

That fact didn't slow her heartbeat the least little bit.

Matt placed the tied reins over the saddle horn and his pleasant expression reflected her triumph, understanding her amazement perfectly.

"Zorro wouldn't have done better," he grinned. The lines of his rugged jaw were transformed into a seductive inference.

Her heart raced.

Of course it was because she was actually sitting on the back of a horse. She tested her running shoes in the stirrups by straightening her knees and slightly raising her body. Only one foot rested properly in the stirrup.

"Shouldn't I wear boots?" she asked, seriously considering her new status of horse back rider.

"Those'll do the first time out. Just keep your heels down."

Ruby was his horse. He was getting ready to lead the first ride of the new group of guests when Sarah entered the barn. Ruby was reserved for him and he couldn't explain his impulsive decision to assign it to this inexperienced guest.

The horse had made the decision. Ruby had chosen her. He crossed over in front of the horse and adjusted the right stirrup.

Sarah took the reins gingerly at first, then more firmly when the horse stood still under Matt's hand. She studied his way with horses. A delighted expression stole over her face as she regarded his features. Her stomach flipped at the softened line of his uncompromising mouth. She remembered how close it was to her temple when she leaned against him in the doorway.

Would she ever forget that moment?

With a racing pulse Sarah responded to Matt's adjustments of the stirrups. An odd confidence replaced the reluctance she felt just moments before.

Maybe she could learn to ride. Her thoughts were muddled, her eyes lingered on the broad shouldered cowboy with an unbidden yearning in her stomach.

She ruefully admitted to herself that she couldn't learn to ride unless she learned to keep her attention on the horse.

Chapter Four

There's a long long trail a'winding

Sarah sat with the confidence of an experienced rider.

"There. That's all the adjustment needed. Just grab the horn and slide off."

Matt stood aside to give Sarah space to do as she was told.

"You'll find her tied here whenever you're ready." He took the reins and looped them over the top rail of the stall.

Sarah felt his manner cool, she felt dismissed. He turned toward her and, looking up without moving his head, his eyes swung from her to the direction of the lounge, with an emotion she failed to define. She paused before leaning forward and bringing her right leg over the saddle.

"I see you met Buck." He mentioned it casually, waiting for Sarah to dismount, his manner showing far more interest in the answer than his tone implied.

"Yes," Sarah admitted, wondering at the significance of the younger cowboy. She recalled the silent rebuke in Buck's expression. It must have come from Matt, she thought. Her hand on the saddle, she waited for some revelation. He merely met her gaze, shuttered all expression, and ran his hand along the red mare's neck.

"You better go check in with Melanie, she's the boss lady in charge."

If Sarah felt dismissed before in her life, she felt it intensely now, ordered to be on her way immediately. Matt had made a judgment concerning Buck and she was perplexed. She hurried toward the ranch house, her elation over her horseback experience dampened by an undercurrent she could not explain.

Lou caught Sarah immediately by the elbow when she entered the lounge, bombarding her with a question but giving her no time to answer.

"Where have you been? I had Matt go saddle our horses. If you hurry you'll just have time for a cup of coffee before we go on our first ride. Come and meet Steve. He's in charge of the activities for the guests."

Sarah greeted the young man who reached to pour her coffee.

"I'd better skip the coffee," Sarah said, with a desire to blurt out that she already had her first ride. She couldn't actually call that exercise in mounting a real ride, but it was exciting for her all the same. Her enthusiasm had lost its edge at Matt's dismissal but the pride she had at the successful mount on the welcoming horse did not diminish. She missed the announcement of the introductory ride, foolishly thinking Lou's influence was so great that Matt had saddled the horses for them simply at her bidding.

"Whatever," Lou shrugged. " We'll only ride a few miles. They want to see how we handle the horses."

"That's right," Steve admitted, "After this ride, you can relax and get to know each other before we go out for harder trails and longer rides."

"Good," Sarah said, relieved at the thought of a short ride, still apprehensive about going anywhere on a moving horse. Her solace came when she remembered that Matt said he would ride with her. Her only confidence came at the thought of his words that the horse did all the work. She hoped that would be so. At her age, she should have known better.

Knees in. Heels down. Knees in. Heels down. Sarah kept repeating to herself as she tensed her entire body in total concentration on that first ride. Matt tirelessly instructed her on those important actions. Where was the truth that the horse did all the work?

Lou and other riders were strung out in front of her as they followed Buck and Steve down a winding trail among the Ponderosa pines and high desert brush over the rolling hills. They had ridden across the empty hillside separating them from the ranch buildings.

Matt often dropped back to chat with Dirk and Jane, a sales team for a company specializing in electrical appliances, who handled their mounts with ease.

"These are better trained than other horses we've ridden," Jane remarked, riding easily in her saddle. She stabled her own horse on a farm near their condominium. Her dream was to own a piece of land large enough to have her own barn but so far that was only a dream.

"These horses are foaled and trained right here on the ranch, ma'am," stated Matt, "These folks take a lot of pride in raising them."

Any further explanation was interrupted by racing horses and ear splitting yells.

The only two children among the guests at the ranch this week belonged to Dirk and Jane but neither gave them much attention. The teenagers traded blows whenever they came close to each other, an occurrence they precipitated often. They were at it again.

"Keep away from me," shouted the skinny brown haired daughter over her shoulder to her brother who sat his horse with greater ease than she did as she tried to outdistance him.

"Somebody's got to teach you how to handle a horse," screeched the boy in the high-pitched voice of puberty.

Matt spun his horse and moved to intercept the arguing teenagers.

"Hold on there, young man," he called, planting himself in front of the boy effectively pulling the horse to a sudden stop.

"The young lady will do fine without your badgering."

"She ain't no lady, that's my dumb sister," was the information hurled at him as Matt cantered past, leading the boy's horse to the waiting girl who willingly halted at Matt's insistence.

"What makes that boy think you need instruction, young lady?" Matt had shown no criticism of the girl's actions.

Bright eyes turned to glow on Matt at his 'lady' reference, but the eyes snapped as she replied, "My arrogant brother is afraid I'll do something better than him."

The young girl tried with difficulty to relax in her saddle.

"You're Terry, aren't you?" Matt waited for the positive nod he knew would come.

"You're really doing fine. If you straighten your back and put more of your weight on your stirrups, the ride won't be so bumpy. And I'll put that brother of yours - Pete - isn't it? up with Buck at the gate so he won't bother you."

Terry's adoring look followed Matt when he spoke to Pete as he had suggested, waiting only until Pete followed his directions.

"You ought to spend more time instructing my dumb sister than that old lady," Pete mumbled to himself as he pushed his horse ahead to the gate.

Matt rode along side Buck to explain what was expected. Sarah gripped the saddle horn and compared the two tall men. Buck's cotton shirt covered muscled shoulders tapering to narrow hips that set easily in the saddle. His jeans were worn as were his scuffed riding boots, boasting no distinctive pattern. He responded with an affirmative nod acknowledging Matt's order and swung around to wait for Pete.

Buck flashed a tight smile at Sarah with the touch of his finger to the point of his hat brim. He dipped his head and straightened his mouth, giving a kick to his horse. Pete followed him to a gate that blocked the trail.

Sarah pondered the subtle exchange between the big cowboys. Matt held a mysterious control over Buck, far more than an equivalent ranch hand, far less than a top foreman. She couldn't account for the puzzled frown that flashed across Buck's face earlier when Matt placed a mounting stool beside the red mare and stood aside for her to mount.

Matt continued checking on the riders down the line. He paid particular attention to the way each person handled their mount. The purpose of this short ride was to acquaint the ranch hands with riding ability of each guest, techniques each used in handling their horse, and their compatibility as a group.

He touched his hat in passing Arlys and Norm. They were good riders in spite of their extra pounds. Norm came to the ranch to revitalize himself and get relief from the tension of upper management. He was responsible for a large division of a major telecommunications company, which he controlled with intelligence and skill.

Arlys, planned their vacation at the high desert ranch where they could enjoy riding but also find relief from the dampness of the city that aggravated her husband's asthma. She was unhappy with their childless state, a condition to which both were resigned. Arlys volunteered many hours in a children's hospital. She watched Matt interact with the healthy vibrant teenagers with more than a little envy.

Not distracted with excessive attention to their horses, the corpulent riders were content to converse with each other regarding the climate and scenery, avoiding any mention of city and the tension from which they sought a brief escape. They smiled a greeting as Matt passed them on the trail.

"Nice ride," Norm called and his wife nodded with a bright smile. They were friendly but not gregarious. Even at home they chose friends carefully, not having much spare time for socializing and having even less desire to participate in unnecessary parties. They looked with anticipation toward the forested hills into which they would ride in the future.

Matt returned to marshal the riders through the gate, holding his horse in check until everyone passed. When Sarah came through, he directed, "Relax in the saddle and keep your back straight."

Her body tensed instead, rebelling at his constant correcting her posture.

"Keep the reins loose and your hands on the mane. That horse will follow the others."

Sarah wished Matt would spend more time helping those others. She thought he spent too much time criticizing her and wondered if others noticed his undue interest as much as Buck had. They should be getting helpful riding pointers from him, too, although in observing others, she suspected they didn't need instructions.

Lou picked up easy conversation with each rider as she passed back and forth among the riders. She explained to Ray, whose horse kept up with hers much of the time, "Sarah is totally inexperienced and needs a lot of instruction. But I understand horses and make friends with them easily. I've been riding for years." She reached out and affectionately patted the neck of her mount.

Ray's posture and riding skills were good but his wayward horse had a mind of its own that he was not able to control. He was a retired executive who went on vacations for the adventure or change of scenery, not particularly for horseback riding. His horse bumped into Lou's.

"These two animals are either best friends or friendly enemies. My gray wants to hang around your spotted pony. He doesn't believe in obeying my commands." Ray was unsuccessful at getting his horse to canter away from Lou.

When his horse nipped at Lou's, she yelled, "Here, stop that," and raised her hand menacingly toward the offending animal, which immediately shied away and cantered ahead as Ray wanted.

Sarah only noticed the other riders occasionally. To her, "Sit back and relax," was one of the many things she was unable to do. Yet she tried to obey because that was the only positive statement Matt made that wasn't underlain with criticism.

Sarah shrugged at the preposterous idea.

Sit back and relax.

If only she could relax! All the guests were rocking with their horses in a way Sarah envied, but no matter how she tried, her body was jolted mercilessly. She attempted to hold the reins as she had been instructed but the flies buzzed around her so thickly she couldn't blink without getting them entangled in her eyelashes. They hovered around the corners of her eyes and crept over her bare arms, although they didn't bite. She constantly brushed the pesky insects off with one hand and then the other, sometimes using her shrugging shoulder to dislodge the creeping insects from her cheeks.

They buzzed industriously and settled down as quickly as her hand pushed them away. When they got into her eyes she stuck out her lower lip to blow out air, sending them away long enough so she could blink. She couldn't remember ever being so uncomfortable.

Would the flies be left behind if she cantered? She kicked her horse to find out.

Dust raised by the pounding hooves of the riders ahead masked any pleasant thoughts Sarah had towards viewing the scenery. Hot and sticky feelings were all the more noticeable with the dust and flies. Sarah's patience grew thinner with each layer of dust and every creeping fly. She was ready to quit. More irritating than her own discomfort was the fresh and excited look of the other riders. The swarming flies weren't annoying to any of them.

Straining to keep her heels down and her knees squeezed in, Sarah managed to keep her body raised just slightly off the saddle. This didn't stress her muscles differently than some of the exercises she did at home but under the prolonged tension her muscles were beginning to stiffen.

And Sarah's whole body rebelled. She felt like she had been tortured for an hour, which the ride was in truth less than half that. Her original tolerance for the ride was waved away with every swat at the insects. She considered getting off to walk.

Lou was curious about Sarah's progress and kicked her mount into an easy canter, moving back to the end of the line where Sarah's horse swung its head patiently under Sarah's sporadic guidance.

Lou pulled up beside Sarah and threw out hurried questions, "What do you think? Isn't it fun?"

But Lou caught Sarah's tired and impatient expression and decided not to wait for the grumbling answer that was sure to come. She spun her horse and rode away.

When the horses finally came to a halt at the barn, Sarah had little strength left to dismount. But she wasn't going to let Matt, or anyone else, see how tired she was. Swinging her right leg stiffly over the saddle, Sarah dropped her feet to the ground, holding the horn and leaning heavily against the saddle. Her knees melted under her weight. She grabbed the saddle to keep from falling.

She clung to the saddle until her legs filled with the strength needed to hold her weight like the newly opening wings of a butterfly must fill with fluid before they contain power for flight. She felt more like the helpless calyx than an unfolding butterfly. Constantly pressing against her horse during the ride, Sarah's knees took most of the punishment and the sides of her legs pained her beyond description.

"Tired?" Matt's question so tantalizing close to her ear stiffened her spine.

Tired knees, tired legs, tired back. Not an inch of her wasn't tired - except her heart. Matt's husky voice was like high octane fuel to a fine machine, causing her heart to accelerate with a frightening beat. She struggled to keep her body from being carried away with the reverberations. She managed to maintain an outward calm.

"Not at all," she retorted, quickly tossing her head to cover her electrified reaction. A covert glance at his face caught a twitch at the corner of his mouth.

He saw through her bravado and she filled with tingling excitement. He locked his eyes on hers compelling her to return his gaze. A palpable communication flashed between them, strangely unique and wonderfully disturbing.

She grasped for a definition of the expression she saw.

Suggestive, hardly.

Provocative, not quite.

Seductive, conceivably.

Expectant, maybe. Expectant of what? She clung to his gaze, wondering what to expect. Friendship? Admiration? Seduction?

She thought she saw all these things. Perhaps in her starstruck condition, she only wished to see them. Confusion washed over her. Had some crazy dormant desire crept out of her eyes without her knowing it? This can't be happening to me, she thought. I'm too old for this sort of thing, for criminny sake. A feeling of disconnectedness swept her longings aside as she took control of her emotions. She must put down those errant feelings.

She glared at him and let out a short indignant breath that resembled a dainty snort.

"Then we'll see you in the ranch house for dinner at seven." Matt elbowed her aside and loosened the girth on her mare's saddle. His taut strong jaw clenched, activating a tiny pulsing muscle that she shouldn't have noticed. The corner of his mouth twitched. Was he trying not to laugh at her?

"I'll expect you to loosen the girth each time you get off your horse from now on. Good riders take care of their mounts," he taunted as he carefully lifted the reins over the mare's head and tied them to the rail.

A good rider she would never be, she knew, but she set her jaw in a smug smile and kept her mouth shut.

Lou came limping up and grabbed Sarah by the arm, "Let's get changed."

"Changed?" Sarah responded with tinkling forced laughter, "What a marvelous idea. Mind if I change into a pumpkin so I can set still for the next two weeks?"

"Oh, c'mon now," chuckled Lou, "A big seedy thing like that only puts out roots and you've got too much adventure in your heart for that."

Sarah noticed the speculative look Matt flicked her way at those frivolous words. She was curiously mindful of his covert scrutiny.

"A short walk will limber your legs. Then a bath will make you feel like a princess." Lou wouldn't put up with any complaints.

Sarah moved her legs gingerly. "I'm fine," she lied. Her knees hurt. Her ankles hurt. Everything hurt. But everything was still well connected and the most affected parts of her body seemed to be regaining strength. She pulled herself together, tediously and painfully. She wasn't going to show any weakness if she could help it, no matter who was watching.

Matt's eyes were still upon her.

Pretending to stroll calmly along, Sarah assumed a distracted air. She finally noticed Lou's faltering gait.

"Why, Lou, are you limping? Surely your legs don't hurt. Don't tell me you got stiff from riding." Sarah found it hard to believe that Lou hurt, too.

" I haven't ridden for many weeks, so of course I'd get stiff the first time out," Lou retaliated, as if Sarah's ignorance was uncalled for. "I'm going to get into a warm bath."

The thought of a bath and the awaiting dinner began healing Sarah's aching body. Her spirits lifted and her limbs carried her along the flower-lined path with renewed strength.

While she waited for Lou to bathe, Sarah rinsed out her blouse and underwear, carefully hanging her split skirt to wear another time. She grinned as Lou curled up with a paperback novel when she left with her towel and cotton cover-up to take her turn in a bubble bath.

Several hours later with her good spirits and normal vitality restored, Sarah sunk into a cream colored leather chair in the lounge with a drink of orange juice over peach schnapps. Her chair faced the bar across the room and she noted the drinks accepted by her fellow guests. It was an excuse to casually observe the sun baked cowboy who poured them.

Matt's hat hung on a rack beside the door. A light band of his forehead shone above his tanned face. Hair the color of weathered wood clung to his head where the hat band usually rested but fluffed up in slight waves on the top where she glimpsed a bit of scalp showing through when he leaned down to retrieve a full bottle of liquor from the base cabinet. A liberal splash of white at his temples stopped abruptly at his jawline, giving him a scholarly look. He was the most appealing male she studied in a long time.

He was competent, an experienced rider, riding instructor, host to the guests. He was good at his job, good with people, good with the other hired help. She studied him all too intently and he caught her staring.

When Matt's gaze locked on hers, she lowered her eyes and gulped her drink, worrying again he could read her thoughts. Nearly choking on a misdirected swallow, Sarah closed her eyes while she recovered, searching for an appropriate diversion.

Western music seemed appropriate and she took out her CD player, placing it on the sideboard by an accessible outlet. She inserted her latest disc, searching forward for the special song she favored to get the reactions of others. She would prove to Lou that others shared her taste in old western songs. She looked around for approvals. No one in the room seemed to notice the song. Her gaze returned to the bartender.

Through lowered lashes Sarah tried to decide what it was about Matt that hooked her emotions. She saw him staring toward her CD at the first strains of the song. He was alert and thoughtful, almost disturbed at the song. So he didn't like it either. Too bad, she thought. She wanted to hear it again, and continued to listen.

Ray rattled his scotch drink in his hand as another was handed around him to Lou who would strike up a conversation with anyone. He caught Lou unawares when he managed to speak first, "This reminds me of the time I was with a tour and we stopped at a lodge in Timbuktu. You should've seen it. Beamed ceiling, tin roof, open fire pit. Smoky place."

He paused to take in Lou's reaction but she averted her eyes to avoid his gaze. What an opening, she thought. This room was pure luxury, no smoky atmosphere in this place.

Then he sipped his drink and continued, "But the people were very friendly. Good local liquor, too. Sure hit the spot. Just like this. Isn't that right, Vic?"

Ray nodded to his traveling buddy since Lou had summarily dismissed his bragging.

"This is by far the best lodge I've seen. But we've been in some doozies, I can tell you," Vic emphasized the 'tell'. He went on to list some he remembered. The two retired men often traveled on tours together. They came to this dude ranch at the suggestion of their travel agent when their tour of a thoroughbred farm was canceled due to a fire. They had recently taken interest in polo, and considered investing in ponies, which were really thoroughbred horses with a natural ability to 'turn on a dime' like good western cow ponies.

Lou carefully sipped her drink and walked away unimpressed with their descriptions of faraway places. She winked at Sarah and they clinked glasses, "It seems to me I've heard that line before.'

Fellow travelers often talked a tall tale to 'one-up' each other with their trips. Lou wasn't in the mood to participate at the moment.

"Not a bad first ride, huh, Sarah?" Lou's statement brought a smile to Sarah's face that radiated her charm from her round chin to her twinkling eyes. Lou grinned back.

"I told you the horses would win you over."

"At times I almost believe you," Sarah answered, her gaze darting around the small animated groups that raised the noise level to an uncomfortable din.

Two women in their early forties - anyone under fifty looked young to Sarah - appeared to be professional artists. She heard them mention some related field as they chatted by the massive stone fireplace.

They moved over to the chair Sarah occupied. The youngest of the two with a heavy braid of mahogany hair down her back asked, "Are you an artist? I saw you with a sketch pad." She didn't wait for an answer.

"I'm Marianne from Denver. I have an art gallery."

At the mention of her sketch pad, Sarah remembered leaving it in the barn and wondered when she could get it. She decided it would still be there in the morning. Tonight she wasn't going out of her way for any more horsey encounters.

Marianne held out her hand and Sarah smiled as she took it firmly in her own. Marianne's companion ran her fingers through her short blond hair as she hovered close behind.

"This is my partner, Sally," Marianne added, turning to acknowledge the stout young woman packed snugly in designer jeans, who nodded with a friendly grin.

"Won't you sit down?" Sarah curled her legs under her and offered the young women the matching leather ottoman on which she had been resting her feet.

Curious about the young woman for whom Buck had mistaken her, Sarah said, "I'm just learning to sketch. So tell me about your gallery."

Marianne and Sally settled themselves hip to hip on the soft ottoman and Marianne bubbled with promotion of her Denver gallery.

"I feature new artists in all media but the gallery is mostly advertising for my own work. I do portraits in oil."

She went on nonstop about celebrities she painted after achieving success with portraits of relatives and friends.

"We sponsor an annual talent search," she continued and explained how that unique marketing technique opened untapped areas for her own work. She sought talented artists, Sally managed the gallery and the sales.

They were proud of the artists who had experienced success in various fields as a result of the recognition received in the contest and the visibility given in their gallery.

The lodge door flung open.

Sarah turned with a frown at the clamor when Pete came racing through with Terry clutching at his shirt.

The glass was knocked from Ray's hand, the liquor splashing on his jacket. The glass bounced on the carpet unharmed, spilling ice in the deep pile.

"Give that back," Terry shrieked at Pete's retreating back.

Matt latched grimly onto Pete's left arm with his own left hand, effectively stopping his forward motion.

Pete's gangly arms and legs swung around like the appendages of a dancing marionette as he stopped abruptly on the end of Matt's arm.

"There'll be no running in here, young man."

Terry clutched at Pete's shirt with both hands until Matt caught her arm and pulled the two children too far apart for contact.

The shirt slipped out of Terry's hand as she slowly released her grasp and stood contritely in front of Matt, who searched the room for the kids' parents.

"I won't allow this kind of disruption in this lodge. You settle this quarrel elsewhere." He marched the rebelling youngsters toward their parents.

"But Pete took my shirt without asking," Terry appealed to Matt as if he were the judge and this was a formal hearing.

"It's just a dumb ole shirt that's too big for you anyway," Pete countered.

Dirk and Jane, the teenagers' parents, marched the kids out of the lodge with Dirk giving his apologies, "We'll have this straightened out in a few minutes." He remained nonplussed, familiar with his children's behavior and confident of his ability to handle it. Jane followed with the confident air of an experienced supporting actor.

"And Steve wants to have kids," Melanie said, rolling her eyes toward the ceiling as the door closed behind the family. She scooped the fallen ice into the glass. Melanie and Steve Brown operated the ranch, a full time job that Melanie didn't want to compromise by having children.

"It's perfectly normal to want kids," Steve defended as he spread cheese on a wheat wafer with an eye to the darkening spot on the carpet.

"A few quarrels have to be expected," he added, before popping the loaded cracker into his mouth. He brought a bar towel and mopped at the spilled liquor.

"I can't think of anything worse than facing rebellious teenagers," Melanie countered, "and that's what little kids grow into."

"And for that we can be grateful," Matt interjected, much to the surprise of everyone. He had been firm in squelching the sibling quarrel for the second time today.

"It's the rebellion in people, especially the young, that accounts for the progress of civilization. If not for normal rebellion and testing of their limits, we might still be living inside caves. Did you ever think of that?"

"That's right," Ray agreed, "but you were plenty quick to stop those kids from fighting. You aren't lenient towards rebellion."

"There is a difference between rebellion, disruption, and disagreement," Matt hastened to explain.

"Those kids had a disagreement. That is their business. They disrupted our 'happy hour' and that is my business. Neither action can be classified as rebellion." He carried a freshly opened bottle of wine to the table and Sarah noticed how effectively he stepped out of a debate after getting his salient point across.

Small pockets of conversation erupted around the room. There was more than one opinion about rebellion.

Lou gregariously moved from one guest to another. Trust her to turn the conversation to her favorite subject. "We should go on an early morning ride tomorrow." Lou searched for an agreeable nod.

"People don't go on vacation to get up earlier than they do at home, Lou," Sarah said softly, her eyes looking for agreement from the others.

Lou continued to press her point.

"It would be cooler and certainly more free of insects." The guests simply ignored her.

"Maybe they don't want to get up for a rigid schedule." Sarah didn't care much for schedules either but she woke with the first light or the first bird call, whichever came first. Committing herself to an early ride wasn't on the tip of her tongue but she wasn't going to disappoint Lou.

"Wake me when you get up," Sarah grinned at her friend, knowing from past experience that waking would not be very early.

As if pulled by a magnet, Sarah's gaze slid past Lou's shoulder and met Matt's curious eyes. His bearing was conspicuously bold and challenging. Did she imagine the intimate message in his gaze? He seemed to dare her to get up early. His left eyebrow shot up quickly and relaxed. His mouth spread in a thin line and turned up at the corners in a sly smile. A hooded look overtook his narrowed eyes before he turned away.

Introspection held Sarah breathless for no apparent reason. She must be careful not to read emotions in that man's features merely because her body had reverted to acting like a teenager. She did not like the depth of the disturbance that insisted on erupting within her at his every glance. No, she thought, she could avoid looking at him if she must to quell the disturbance.

But there was nowhere to turn from the inner upheaval that occurred at every thought of him.

Chapter Five

When it's springtime in the Rockies

Sarah stood, jerked indignantly and turned her back to Matt. That put him out of her vision. But, as much as she intended to ignore him, it didn't work. His features remained indelible on her mind.

Melanie pushed 'play' on Sarah's CD to repeat the western favorites and waved the guests to seat themselves at the dinner table.

Marianne and Sally sat on either side of Sarah, across from Norm and his wife, Arlys, with Matt beside them. Melanie and Steve sat at either end, others taking the chairs between. The noise of scraping chairs dominated the air for a short time, briefly drowning out the western music. Strumming guitars beat out a pleasant atmosphere, soothing enough to allow conversation, rhythmic enough to set an upbeat mood.

The conversation was subdued while the fresh garden salad was consumed. Babs and Tad removed the plates and discussion resumed. The background music was unheard, or so Sarah thought, until her favorite song began. Sarah was alerted for reactions to the tune.

Melanie stopped so abruptly in mid sentence that the guests looked toward her to question the cause. Melanie's eyes ricocheted to the guests around the table. She asked, "Where did that come from?"

Sarah shrugged. "I got the CD at the variety store on the way here." She wasn't sure that was the answer Melanie expected. She continued her interest in the response of others, wholly tuning her own heart to the melody

"It's quite moving, don't you think?" Sarah asked, her eyes darting to receive immediate impressions from the guests.

"Umphh."

"Mournful."

"The guy's got a real problem."

"Crude."

"A real oldie."

Silent faces contorted in critical thought while the lament filled the air. Steve and Matt were the only ones showing continued interest in eating. Melanie directed Babs to serve the next course.

"I'll probably wear it out playing it," she continued.

Matt bent his head over his cup, sipping at his coffee, showing undue interest in the dregs at the bottom.

"You can't wear out CDs," Pete announced with great authority. He was a bright teenager who absorbed facts like a blotter. His blue eyes reflected his intelligence. His modern haircut and designer clothes placed him in the class of the privileged. He learned quickly and related his knowledge with the same speed in such a gregarious manner that he rarely offended his peers and never insulted his parents. Other adults thought he needed more restraint.

"She just means she likes it very much," Arlys corrected Pete's erroneous impression in her patient motherly style. She smiled at him when he dutifully sunk back against his chair and accepted her modification.

"She told me she'd meet the singer in the moonlight and console him," Lou grimaced, "Can you imagine that?" She rolled her eyes at the ceiling.

Matt choked. He caught most of the exploding coffee in his hand. He covered his mouth with his bandanna, coughing uncontrollably. Concerned attention went to him and the remainder of Sarah's song played out to his spasmodic coughing. His face was reddened from the exertion and his watery eyes blinked as he regained control. His mumbled apology went to no one in particular, yet was addressed to everyone with much chagrin.

"Goes to show how terrible your song really is, Sarah," Lou insisted. She had the right to tell Sarah her real feelings and Sarah took it with a grin, playfully batting at the air toward Lou with her open hand. With the crooning strains of The Sons Of The Pioneers, eating resumed. Tumblin' Tumbleweeds restored harmony to the diners.

Plates of beef and asparagus were set before them and the delicious aroma was too enticing to ignore. Broccoli in cheese sauce was passed in a serving dish followed by corn relish. No one was quick to interrupt their meal with heavy conversation.

Sarah took up a discussion with the young artist beside her.

"Is this a working vacation for you?" Sarah asked Marianne as she put her fork into her broccoli and stirred it in the melted cheese.

"I didn't intend to work," Marianne answered, her eyes sliding, in turn, over the people sitting around the table, "but I made some charcoal sketches for portrait considerations. There are some character studies here I shouldn't pass up."

"Like who, for instance?" Sarah inquired, her interest piqued. She savored a mouthful of tender roast beef while turning her full attention to Marianne's answer.

"Like Norm, for instance. He has the features of a first class manager always in competent control. And Arlys. She has the face of a Madonna with the mischief of a kitten in her eyes. And Buck,"

Marianne looked into Sarah's eyes, "Have you met Buck? He doesn't eat in the dining room but he was on the ride. His eyes hold the pain of the world."

Sarah stared at Marianne, amazed at her perception, curious about others.

"How about Matt?" Sarah saw a lot of character in the lines of his face. She studied him covertly now and again, thinking back to his coughing outburst. Was it his response to the song? The song was playing for a chorus or two.

She choked sometimes after some startling remark when liquid passed the open epiglottis. Matt's misdirected swallow happened during her favorite song. Some related remark must have done it. Matt took particular notice of the song when she first played it at the bar but the look he had then was one of disapproval. Come to think of it he choked after Lou remarked on Sarah's willingness to meet the singer and console him. After Lou's reaction, Sarah was ready for his rejection. What did Marianne think about his characteristics?

"He's got a confident arrogance in that guarded air about him that's too complex to capture in this limited time," Marianne mused.

Sarah ate the remainder of her beef without another word but she studied many faces around the table for the impressions that went deeper than skin.

Unobtrusively, Babs and Tad cleared the dinner plates from the table and served a light dessert of mixed fruit.

Sarah watched them return, tease for tease, Matt's joking straight-faced banter, always in good clean fun. He was their friend. They respected him, too. He maintained a pleasant rapport with the ranch regulars, except for Buck.

Why she noticed that or even cared she couldn't imagine, except to agree with Marianne's remark of his complexity. She didn't like the mark of mystery about him. Or was that what intrigued her?

Sarah hoped to quell the constant brooding on her giddy feelings toward that cowboy. She forced herself to focus on the words of Melanie and Steve, who kept conversation on the light side from each end of the large oval dining table.

"Remember those first guests, Steve?" She looked from her husband to each person at the table to assure herself of their interest before continuing.

She got high marks in her college psychology classes. For her social work degree, Melanie interned at several social agencies for the state. She added a minor in hotel management after meeting Steve in a required biology class at the University of Iowa when he began working toward his degree in Animal Husbandry. She constantly reminded herself of her good luck in finding Steve and making their life together on the dude ranch.

Melanie was born and raised on an Iowa farm and was discontent with life in the cities where she had first found work. She was completely happy with her management of the dude ranch, matching wits with the guests to encourage their participation in ranch life.

"They swam and sunned themselves every day and didn't want to come up for dinner. We finally showed them how to set up a barbecue grill under the trees and made them eat right there," she remembered.

"And ever since, we made a stream side barbecue a regular feature," Steve added proudly. He loved the high desert and never ceased devising ways to help the guests enjoy it, too. He was away for the years it took to get his degree and more than his education, he regarded Melanie, whom he met in the course of his studies, as the ultimate force in shaping his life. They had worked and played together on this ranch for almost ten years. He regarded her with a quiet love, forgetting his line of thought.

"You have a grange dance on the schedule, I noticed," Vic was always ready to fill in any short opening in the conversation with his observations.

"That's right," Steve agreed, "and we take you to a local rodeo, as well."

"But most of our guests just simply like to help with the ordinary chores on the ranch," Melanie reminded them.

"You'll get a taste of a cowboy's life out on safari. When you get back you'll have a chance to gather cattle."

"We tried to keep a couple of cows for milk but couldn't get any guests to do the milking so we gave that up," Steve laughed, "I wasn't going to be around twice a day for the job."

"And none of the ranch hands would either," Melanie grinned at Matt, deepening the dimples in her cheeks.

"That's Terry's speed," Pete said derisively, "She's always pulling at my shirttail. She outta be put to milking cows."

Terry's mouth dropped open and she bolted upright in her chair poised for an ensuing fight, her words halted by the determined look on her father's face. He put a staying hand on his son's shoulders, murmuring admonition quietly in Pete's ear. Then Dirk turned to Steve. "I'm sure Pete would tell you how to do everything around here if you'd ask. He's quite sure he has all the answers, especially if they torment his sister." Dirk's eyes swept around the table with a knowing shrug.

"I think everyone goes through a stage when answers seem so clear," Sarah put in quickly to cover the embarrassed silence that threatened.

"We don't have children," said Arlys, "do you?"

"I have a daughter," Sarah answered, with a nostalgic smile, "but she's grown up. She once accused me of depriving her of a brother. I don't know how much that influenced her decision to marry a man who already had two children. She considers them her own."

"I know there's too much involved in raising children," Melanie said, "that's why I'm not in a hurry to have any."

"We'd like to adopt a child," Arlys said, lowering her eyes after a darting a secretive glance at her husband, Norm, sitting at her right.

"I've heard it takes a long time to find a baby to adopt and then you never know what you get," Melanie said, "I'd just as soon have my own - start from scratch - if you see what I mean."

"That isn't always wise," Arlys said, nervously adding, "I'm willing to take my chances with a child who needs parents and a home." She raised her chin and drank the last drop of her wine as if to emphasize she meant what she said and put an end to the subject.

Matt, half rising in his chair, offered to refill her glass. At the negative shake of her head, his analyzing gaze dropped from Arlys to his plate, as if thoughtfully meditating over her remark.

Melanie tapped a spoon against her wine glass for silence. When all faces turned toward the head of the table, she referred to a list of house rules on a green sheet of paper she held in her hand about mealtimes and trail rides.

Steve announced, "The three day safari into the National Park will start the day after tomorrow. I'll brief those who sign up for that after dinner. I trust all of you are excited to go."

None of the activities were mandatory, but they were planned because of past success. Approval buzzed around the table and all rose to have coffee in the lounge.

"Lou, are you going on that three-day ride?" Sarah whispered to her when she caught Lou's arm.

"That's what I came for," Lou nodded.

Sarah groaned inwardly. Three full days of riding and camping. She recovered from today's ride but how would her body react to such punishment, day after day? She wondered again if her decision to come here wasn't a colossal mistake. She took Lou by the arm and together they walked outside.

House finches twittered impatiently about the seed containers, gaily attending to the last feeding for the day, flitting from ground to tree branches, far too animated for the still life study that suited Sarah's mood.

Swallows and night hawks plied the air, snatching up the airborne insects. Ravens called far overhead, flapping their way to their nighttime perches. The clouds stringing out above the horizon orchestrated a stunning sunset. As the sun slipped below the horizon the late spring day still held some light. The cooling air was inviting. From across the yard, the scent of lilacs came and went on small bursts of breeze.

"Shall we walk down the driveway to the main gate?" Sarah asked, "or did you just want to get away from the crowd?"

"You know I like crowds. Besides the gate's a long way off," Lou countered, remembering the drive in. "We won't get back before dark."

"I don't think we can get lost. Let's start out and go part way at least." Sarah liked the solitude of the evening, the edges of piling clouds turning from bright red to orange. This was the first opportunity she had to view such a wide expanse of uninterrupted sky. She had no time to notice it on the afternoon ride, let alone appreciate it for the awesome view that it was.

Lou was unimpressed with the sunset and disagreed, "It's desolate and lonely if you ask me. I'll take in a little fresh air, then go back." She impatiently urged Sarah back towards the lodge. Through the windows of the lounge Sarah could see guests in animated conversation. That was what attracted Lou.

"I've got to see what's going on," she said, heading up the steps. Everywhere she went she was drawn to the action that centered around people.

"Not me," Sarah answered, "I'm going to enjoy the quiet evening a little longer before I go to bed. I'll leave a light on for you."

She went in to the lodge and got her Cd player. Alone in her room she could listen to any song she liked as often as she liked.

The wide expanse of sky was appealing and Sarah hesitated to go inside. From her view in the drive, there was so much sky to see, more sky than she had seen in one place, so open, so wide, so inviting.

The security light flooded the walk leading to Sarah's room. Buck stood in the path with a sketch pad in his hand. She was surprised that he showed up nearly everywhere except in the lodge. Perhaps there was a logical explanation. It was of little consequence and Sarah didn't think much of that. It was the unspoken exchanges between Matt and Buck that aroused her curiosity. In light of Marianne's take on his character Sarah looked at him with renewed interest.

He touched his hat and pushed it toward the back of his head as he bent his face down to look at her.

"This belongs to you, doesn't it, ma'am?" Buck asked as he held the pad out to her.

"Why, yes, I left it in the barn. Thank you for bringing it." She reached for the pad but he didn't release it into her hands.

"Beggin' your pardon, ma'am, but from those sketches you started, I think you need to look closer at horse's legs," Buck said, hesitantly. He nervously leaned from one foot to the other, uncomfortable as a critic.

He pointed at the sketches and explained, "I noticed you have some good starts but..." He flipped open the pages and pointed to the conglomeration of forelocks, forelegs, and bent knees Sarah had drawn of horse legs on several pages. "This should curve in more here and the tendon comes straight down here," he expertly pointed out.

His eyes avoided hers and he continued, "It might help if you look at muscles and tendons close up."

He withdrew his hand and held his breath anxiously awaiting her response. "I apologize for being so forward, ma'am..."

"I won't listen to another word unless you stop calling me ma'am," Sarah admonished. "Please. I'm Sarah."

She knew her drawings left much to be desired. She wanted to get them right. It surprised her to be criticized so accurately and succinctly by this young man. She accepted his judgment without resentment.

"I'm sorry, ma'am - I mean Sarah. I apologize for bein' presumptuous but I've been around horses a lot and I draw a bit myself. I'd like to help."

"Thank you," she smiled, "I'd be glad to observe horses from some other vantage point than a saddle. What do you suggest?"

"Watching the legs in motion is important," he countered.

Sarah forced a laugh and shook her head, "When I rode I didn't have time to consider any legs but my own. I couldn't think about anything except staying on the horse. I'd rather observe the motion without worrying about riding."

Buck shrugged and remained silent. He wasn't at a loss for words, simply aware that he might have already said too much about her drawing.

"I noticed you had a tense time of it today," he remarked.

"That's for sure," Sarah conceded, "I didn't enjoy the ride very much. I'm not surprised you noticed. Matt's a tough teacher."

"Matt's trying to do right by you. He put you on a good horse. And that makes learning easier. I thought he should let the horse teach you. He tried too hard, seemed to keep harping on the obvious."

"I felt like I was picked on," Sarah agreed.

"No, he wasn't picking on you. He wants you to learn the right things, wants you to like riding."

"So does my friend," Sarah sighed, "I don't think I'm the type." She was afraid of that before she came, and after the grueling ride, she was almost certain she would never enjoy it. Her discomfort spread from her negative thoughts on riding to the work needed to improve her drawing and she wanted to shut off the conversation. She held out her hand for a departing shake and Buck took it in a firm grasp with his smooth supple fingers, different from the hard calluses so apparent on Matt's.

"Thanks for your suggestion." Sarah stepped back, dismissing him to resume her walk.

"Don't stay out too long. There's a storm coming," Buck nodded as he pressed his hat solidly on his head, touching the point of the brim in a solemn salute before he disappeared into the shadows.

In the darkness Sarah could not verify Marianne's description of Buck's *pain-of-the-world in his eyes* but she heard an echo of pain in his voice. She reflected on his defense of Matt's bothersome training method. She didn't expect Buck to champion the man who constantly admonished him. She watched him melt into the darkness, thinking what a strange gesture for the big young man.

Buck's footsteps faded into the night. Sarah turned toward her room, deciding to immediately go to bed so she could go early tomorrow and observe the horses. She looked over the rough sketches she made on the plane before seeing the horses, agreeing with the constructive criticism, dwelling not too much on the puzzling man who made them. She resolved to work diligently on her sketching.

Thunder rumbled in the distance. Lightning flashed, harshly defining the edge of the horizon and she watched the eerie lights bounce about the sky. Flickers of light darted across the black clouds, jabbing and fencing with the shadows below the trees. A storm was closing in. She pushed aside the thin filmy inner curtain to better enjoy the oncoming storm.

Rain would fall before morning, Sarah thought, which she hoped would cancel tomorrow's ride on which she hesitantly signed to go. At any rate, she wasn't going to ride all day. Her body had not taken kindly to the half hour in that saddle this afternoon and maybe never would be fit to take a full day of riding, even if she practiced every day for the next two weeks.

Sarah liked Buck's idea of observing the horse anatomy more closely, and in her view, that observation should take place from a comfortable position on the ground.

Her body was weary and sleep came almost as soon as she crawled into bed. She turned her face toward the wall away from the lamp she promised to keep on for Lou, whose normal noisy ablutions made no impressions on her sleeping form.

Distant cackling of geese eased Sarah into consciousness before the dawn fully awakened her the next morning. She didn't hear Lou come to bed, so soundly had she slept. She sat up and looked at Lou's sleeping figure. She smiled, thinking how Lou expected to wake her for an early morning ride.

Rubbing the sleep out of her eyes, Sarah pulled aside the tightly-woven sage-green fabric that shut out last night's lightning display and looked into the bleakness of the early light. She couldn't tell if the sky was overcast or if it was simply the colorless air caught between night and day. It was bland, a little on the milky side - the buttermilk sky Hoagy Carmichael wrote about for the movie *Canyon Passage* fifty years ago. The shrubs beside the window were wet and the drops fell off the leaves as they swayed with the faint breeze. She grinned, expecting the rain to cancel the day's horseback ride she had signed on at Lou's insistence.

Splashing cold water on her face, she decided to go for a walk without waking Lou to remind her of an early ride. She dressed quickly and slipped her windbreaker over her shoulders to ward off the morning chill.

Rain dripped off the leaves in big single plops with an occasional splash hitting the top of her head as she walked under the trees. The air held the scent of lilacs and other blossoms she could not identify. Spots of water huddled in depressions among the stones of the walk but other than the allover wetness there was no indication of how much rain fell, although the sidewalk was cleared of the traces of geese. At least it wasn't raining now for which she was grateful. At a juncture, the path led in two directions. One way would take her to the lounge and she was in no mood for breakfast, aware that there would only be coffee at this hour.

She turned on the path that led to the barn and the smell of sage dominated her senses. Drawn in that direction anyway,

Sarah remembered Buck's suggestion that she look more closely at horses before doing more sketches. She didn't bring her sketch pad but she could have a look anyway. At this hour there wouldn't be anyone around.

Sarah peered cautiously into the barn, surprised to see two saddled horses relaxing three-legged in the aisle. They perked their heads and pointed ears toward her when she stepped inside. Pleasure flooded her to think the horses she worried over before she came watched her expectantly in welcome with large luminous eyes. As if by radar, she knew the horses' welcome was intended for her movie cowboy as well.

Through the door on her right, Matt came leading the blood red mare. He carried a bucket just out of reach of the mare's nose. Saddling the willing mounts was a routine requiring no conscious thought and his mind wandered over the upcoming ride. He huffed when thinking of last night. How the conversation between the blustery Petrosky and the prickly Nelson woman unnecessarily dominated his inner vision. He didn't seriously believe Sarah would meet his challenge to go on an early morning ride. Did he want her presence so much he conjured her image? When his eyes set upon her he stiffened and his body thrummed. Her appearance surprised him with delight. He should not have welcomed her. What was he thinking of? Being pleasant to all guests was part of his responsibilities but is this all that it was? Good public relations? He could not stop his features from softening at her approach. His entire body filled with energy.

Trying not to be unduly ingratiating he touched the brim of his worn hat and greeted Sarah with a pleasant, "G'morning."

She came to see the horses but had she really expected Matt to be there? That he made a note of her rejection of an early ride last night in the lounge she felt a challenge and made only a half hearted effort to waken Lou when she dressed earlier. Had she wanted to go to the barn on her own? Her heart leaped and she swallowed, clutching at her lurching stomach in an effort to slow her breathing. Would she ever be able to control her wayward body when this model movie cowboy came into view?

Matt tied the mare to the post at the end of a stall and set the bucket of feed down within its reach. A throaty nicker thanked him pleasantly. He pushed his hat toward the back of his head to reveal the lighter band of forehead below his pressed hairline and hooked his thumbs into his jean pockets. He made an unabashed study of Sarah's entire trim length. He made no effort to hide the fact that what he saw pleased him.

That unnerved her more than the first surprise of his presence with her unsaddled horse.

"I'm glad you came," he said quietly with an intimacy that brought out the wariness that plagued her and made her doubt her own ears.

Being frivolously pleased that he was glad, unnerved her even more. Oh, how easily this movie-type cowboy could turn her bones to jelly! She totally forgot the horse's legs she came to study.

Sarah looked from the mare to the other saddled horses, nervously trying to think of something appropriate to say. She ran her fingers through her short gray hair smoothing the unruly waves in an unconscious check on her appearance.

"You look fine," he assured her, gratified at the feminine gesture, pleased that she would preen for him.

"The ride isn't canceled then. I didn't know you saddled horses this early," she said, covering her nervous display with banal conversation. She couldn't bring herself to say she was glad she came to the barn but her hammering heart told her that she was.

"Yep, and I welcome any help," he leaned down to retrieve the empty bucket the mare was pushing around with her grasping lips in search of the last kernel of grain.

"Do you want to try saddling your horse?" he asked. His face moved perilously close to Sarah's as he held the empty bucket away from the nuzzling horse's chin. He looked at Sarah steadily, waiting for her answer. He absorbed her with his quiet gaze, exciting her every time it poured from his sun-squinted eyes, more than any other gaze she'd ever encountered. Too damned much more.

His steady gaze raised her hackles in a strangely perilous way she couldn't understand. She liked the man. He was personable, polite, and certainly not condescending. But she put up a barrier of dislike. She needed something to protect her from the scurrilously sexual feelings that instinctively invaded her deepest core. She was unable to control the way her skin goose pimpled under his scrutiny.

"And I suppose you're willing to teach me?"

"I'm willing to try. Here." He handed her a brush. There were a dozen things he was willing to try with her and he quickly acknowledged that not one of them involved the horse.

"Brush the back while I get the saddle." He put a small scoop of grain in the bucket and carried it away.

Sarah placed her hand under the strap on the back of the brush, gripping it tightly. She stroked the backs of cats and dogs many times and supposed the brush ought to be used in the same way on the back of a horse. She raised on tiptoe and even then she couldn't get the same perspective she had with dogs or cats. She experimented with short brush strokes in several directions. It was easy to tell which was right by the way the hair laid flat and smooth under the brush.

The horse approved of her brushing, she could tell. It leaned into her strokes. Its head remained forward but the convex shape of the large eye enabled it to watch every stroke.

She thought, then, of sketching, and bent down to stroke the foreleg. She felt the tendon Buck mentioned and traced it from the fetlock to the joint, understanding the bones, not knowing the terminology. Self-consciously she jerked back to brushing when Matt came up beside her. He brought a blanket to the left side of the mare.

"Why brush before saddling?" Sarah asked as she came around to watch Matt, "I would think the horse needs brushing after the saddle is removed."

"Yes, that's important, too. This brushing is just a precaution. Makes sure there's no burrs or dirt on the hide and straightens the hair. Also gives the horse a special feeling about its rider."

Sarah understood that perfectly now that she had observed the animal's appreciation of the brushing for herself. She glanced at the saddles on the railing. She recognized the one Matt had adjusted for her yesterday and wondered what the purpose of the doodads fastened to it. Large portions of the leather showed evidence of hand-tooled vines of leaves and blossoms worn down from long and heavy use.

Matt smoothed the blanket across the horse's back. He folded the far stirrup back on the saddle and lifted it off the rail holding it out to Sarah. She gamely tried to heave the saddle up on the big red horse.

"You're strong," he said, and watched her lift the heavy western saddle above her head, not quite high enough to slide it into place on the saddle blanket. He leaned close behind her and added the length of his wiry arms to hers.

"Yah, for an old lady," she finished.

"I didn't say that," he admonished, his hands near hers gripping the saddle, his body deliciously brushing against her back as he helped lift the saddle above the horse.

"Everyone usually thinks it," she admitted, nervously. She pressed close to the horse, unable to avoid Matt's body as he settled the saddle on the horse's back. She had released her hold on the saddle the instant he lifted it to avoid contact with his body but the slightest move only crowded her back closer against his body. She was not going to shove at him the way she did in escaping the geese. She waited for him to finish arranging the saddle while she frantically tried to think of what to do next.

"I think you lied on your reservation request anyway. Nothing about you says you're over fifty." Matt was in no hurry to move away. His hands were on the horse's back keeping Sarah loosely between them. He twisted his torso just a fraction and leaned to peer into her face.

"Well, I am. To add years would be dumb. Why would I want to lie? I can't see any point to that," she countered with a look of incredible defiance. She wondered at his age, scrutinizing the leather-like features. Her appraisal was slow and complete. Not exactly that she delved for his age but she was curious.

As if he read her mind he said, "I was fifty-eight last March and if it did any good I'd lie about it all the time."

A shield fell across his face masking all expression as he flipped the near stirrup up on the saddle and stood toward the rear of the horse.

"You did good. Be careful in reaching under the horse for the cinch straps. Keep all your movements slow and careful."

When Sarah had the cinches pulled as tight as she could, Matt gave them another tug and tightened the front cinch two more notches.

"You'd better cinch it closer to her front legs. Sometimes she holds her belly full of air and then when you mount she'll let out the air and the saddle slides down her side."

"That makes her a real individual, doesn't it," Sarah marveled. "Do horses really think that much?" She didn't find that hard to believe after observing the horse while brushing.

"Some do a lot of what appears to be thinking. I guess it depends on how well a person knows a horse. Riding the same horse often helps the relationship."

He looked at her for a thoughtful moment, then asked, "Would you like to go for a quick look at the sunrise?" An intriguing look of pride filled his eyes and they begged for her acquiescence.

Sarah's heart jumped. "Don't you have to saddle the other horses?" And just as quickly she could bite off her tongue for throwing up a barrier to his invitation. Not that she was anxious to ride, but to be treated to a sunrise was exciting. Last evening

Lou refused to share the sunset. His expression displayed a particular delight in sharing. "I'll have time to finish." He bridled her horse and put the reins around the horn. Sarah sensed in him a desire to move quickly and her submissive heart urged her to comply.

Chapter Six

Makin' believe

Matt laced his fingers together and leaned down to offer his hands for Sarah to use as a step and reminded her, "The stirrups are already set for you. C'mon, we have to hurry."

Quickly, she swung up and took her stirrups, pleased he had given her the same saddle she used the day before. No significance to that, she shrugged. Probably every saddle was designated for a specific horse anyway. They rode out of the barn at a slow walk.

Matt kicked his horse into an easy canter to the far side of the corral where he opened the gate and waited for Sarah to pass through. She kicked at her mare but only got a teeth-rattling trot out of her. When Matt closed the gate behind them, he came up beside her.

"I'll get your horse to gallop. You grab the mane and hang on."

He waited until her hands grabbed hair and wheeled his horse behind hers.

Before the full meaning of his words cut through to her, Sarah was braced in the saddle. Matt slapped her mare and the horse nearly surged out from under her. Sarah had no time to search her brain for the correct instruction from yesterday's riding lesson. She was tense and rose slightly in the stirrups. How smoothly the mare moved beneath her. No teeth rattling. No punishing jolts. Her body swayed with the animal's stretching gallop. The gait was even and steady.

She leaned forward, eyes wide with suspense, as she kept a death grip on the mare's mane. The horse was moving swiftly and she wasn't falling off. She didn't think of how far were they going nor why they didn't have much time. She was caught in the panic and excitement of the exhilarating ride.

Matt stopped at the top of a rise and turned to grin as the mare came to a prancing stop beside him. Sarah was jolted the moment she settled into the saddle and she grimaced. He reached over to quiet the blowing horse with an assuring pat on its neck, nodding toward the eastern sky. A brightening sunrise enveloped the world in washed pink colors on distant clouds. The morning air was thoroughly cleaned by the overnight rain. The smell of freshly washed sagebrush filled her senses and settled around Sarah with the arousing effect of an extravagant perfume. Her head rotated slowly so her eyes could take in the sky that filled the whole world.

More subtly than the storm clouds in the sunset of the night before, the stringy clouds lay spent on the horizon like colorful rags wrung dry. They reflected a serene color spectrum. Pinks and the palest yellow spread across the limitless horizon before them.

"Wow. It's beautiful." She breathed the words with quiet homage, not differentiating between the visual impact of the sunrise, the fresh scent of sage, or the feeling of suspense shared with the rugged man. All three combined to stun her senses with the reverberations like those of a giant drum roll, issuing a humming echo through her inner faculties, leaving her trembling in awe.

For unmeasured moments she sat transfixed absorbing the beauty into her consciousness. Sarah wondered if she would be able to recall in her memory those colors if, when she got really old, her eyes failed and she could no longer see this beautiful part of nature.

"Yah. It is beautiful. And I want to see as many of these as I can just in case I loose my vision in my old age."

She looked at him sharply, concerned again that he could read her mind. He's not the only one who thinks about getting old, she thought. He was stripped of a part of his mysterious aura. For her, aging was no mystery, but a reality she was willing to meet head on.

"Just watch," urged Matt, "You'll see the crack of dawn."

As trite as it sounded, the proverbial crack did appear to open just a moment before the brilliant edge of the sun's orb was visible at the horizon and the sun stealthily slipped into the new day.

Colors flowed imperceptibly, subtly changing in tone and depth on the fringes of the stringy clouds. Sarah smiled at the remarkable spectacle. Matt's appreciation was like her own. She cast a sharp curious glance in his direction, catching him staring at her with introspection. Their eyes clung for an eternal moment. But it was not to last, that moment of intimacy. A shade slid over his expression and he quickly turned while pulling his hat more firmly down on his head. His face seemed to close up, his mouth took on a familiar hard line.

" That's it. There ain't no more, as the saying goes" he said abruptly. The time they had to see the spectacle was short. No wonder he wanted to hurry. Only a few minutes later they were touched by the full morning sun.

He gently flipped the reins of his grazing mount urging it back to the trail on which they came. Sarah turned to follow his easy canter on the return to the ranch. She jerked in the saddle when her mare jumped ahead to keep up with Matt. Her hat fell back and caught on its chin string to bounce against her back.

Squeezing her knees she leaned forward and hung on to the mare's mane. Valiantly she tried to recapture the smooth rocking ride she managed on the way and for a time it worked. Rising above the saddle, she welcomed the fresh morning air that brushed her skin with a vital freshness. And suddenly, unnecessarily, she began to worry at the sudden speed of her horse. Not at all secure in her saddle at such a pace, Sarah's hesitation was transmitted to her mare. She soon found herself jolted to a walk, desperately trying to remember the correct position of her knees and heels for the best control.

Matt was trotting ahead, widening the distance between them.

On the edge of a ridge, he suddenly halted his horse, making a more careful study of the scene below him. Just as suddenly he swung and kicked his horse to the right, heading downhill, definitely off the trail to the ranch.

Leaning forward in curiosity, Sarah's knees pressed in, a clear signal to her mare, a signal she was unaware of giving. The horse broke into a trot heading after Matt's horse as if it followed her wish. The jarring trot jerked her entire body and she stiffened in the stirrups. With a terrible effort she was able to land once for every two times the horse's back rose up to slap at her backside. That did not fill her with acceptable triumph.

She remembered Matt telling her that in horseback riding the horse did all the work.

No doubt it could be that easy. If only she could learn how to tell the horse what she wanted it to do, she would feel better about the arrangement. But she worried about Matt riding off without her.

What kind of trick was he playing, pulling away at a hard gallop beyond the hill? She hung on as her horse followed at a faster pace, up and over the hill. Clutching the mane to stay on, Sarah dared not look around for Matt. He came within her vision when her horse turned in his direction. At the foot of the hill, he was spinning a roping loop near the wide place in the stream.

The target of his loop was a calf whose head was just out of the water. A nearby cow foundered frantically in the mud appearing distraught and silently imploring the calf to save itself from the quagmire, where last night's rain turned the churning loose sand to gummy sucking mud.

Sarah's horse jogged stiff legged down toward Matt's horse. She watched the cow and calf struggle in the mud, relaxing her grip on her horse's mane, straining back to remain upright on the downhill trek. It was an easy descent. The gradual slope slowed the horse naturally because its anatomy became an awkward vehicle while going downhill.

The ride went well, even if slightly rough, until the blood red mare stumbled to its knees. The whole scene went spinning before Sarah's eyes. She saw the ground coming up to meet her and she tightened her lips as a fearful gasp escaped her. Sarah bounced once. Her shoulder took the brunt of the fall and she rolled forward in a somersault under the momentum. For a moment she lay stunned.

Although she knew she was falling off before it happened, she could not avoid tumbling over the horse's head to land in a sideways sprawl on the ground still soft from rain. Sarah gasped for breath while the impact of her fall kept her senses reeling. The alluvial silt and clumps of bunchgrass were saturated with water, cushioning her fall to some extent. Cool wetness crept into her clothes and finally her consciousness. Her body rebelled at the contact with the wet ground. She took a deep breath. Her inner eye looked over her sprawling figure. No serious harm done. No bones broken.

Her breathing became even and steady. She struggled to sit up. Her knees trembled at the thought of the disaster when she tried to put her weight on them. She settled back in a crouched position patiently allowing her body to regain strength. Her eyes widened with embarrassment as she worried that Matt may have seen her fall.

Through her stunned awareness she saw a muddy calf gasping white-eyed at the end of Matt's taut rope. He extricated the exhausted animal from the mud and pulled it to solid ground. The wary cow's hooves sucked at the gooey mud as the animal heaved itself jerkily to the edge of the mire. The desire to join its calf shown in its eyes. It was propelled by thrusting shoulders and nodding head. The frantic cow succeeded in its extraordinary struggle to join the calf on solid ground.

From her grassy vantage point, Sarah watched Matt flow from his saddle to remove the rope from the resisting calf that stood stiff-legged and trembling. She watched as Matt ran his hands over the back and legs of the calf, wiping off the excess mud in the process. Sarah's brows wrinkled and her face twisted in distaste at the action. Handfuls of pulled grass became his towels as he sponged the wobbly calf. The calf strained against him, pushing toward the cow for reassurance. It was sturdy and not unduly harmed by its misadventure. The calf wobbled haltingly toward its mother and Matt stood aside, confident that he had done all he could. The maternal instinct and nature took over.

Matt coiled his rope. He hung it on his saddle, watching the cow urge its rescued offspring to suckle. The calf accepted the assurance of safety it found and nudged at the cow in the primal quest for food. The cow's long pink tongue roved carefully over the wet shiny coat of its suckling calf, an action that seemed to wind up the string the miniature animal boasted for a tail. The straggly appendage went round and round, as if generating the energy the calf needed to press and pull at its milk supply.

Knowing that was a scene she would love to capture in sketches, Sarah again considered her own condition. She tried to rise. Unsteadily she watched Matt contemplate the reunited animals.

With a determined shrug acknowledging he had done all he could, he put his foot in the stirrup, and as if he came to a certain conclusion about them, he mounted and swung his horse back toward the trail to the ranch. He was going to go back after Sarah. It was then she came into his line of vision and he frowned at her position. She was poised with her knees bent and one hand on the muddy ground, pushing her body into an upright position.

She nervously stood up, brushing uneasily at the soil absorbed into the brightly flowered print of her overshirt at her shoulder. Fully aware that Matt's attention was on her as he urged his mount towards her with kicking heels, Sarah could see his frowning question. Her embarrassment grew, not from having fallen from her horse as much as from the wet soiled appearance of her clothes. What a mess she must be! Reddish brown mud adhered in clumps to her graying hair. Her hat hung limply, squashed out of its shape during the brief roll between her back and the wet ground. A smear of the desert soil darkened the tanned skin of her cheek. A wave of uncertainty spread through her trembling body. Nervously she sought a distraction.

"Hail the hero," she called, extending her arm in a wide salute. "Great job you did there." She babbled to cover her discomfort with the hope of staving off an explanation of her disheveled appearance. Then she promptly felt more uncomfortable for making such a frivolous statement. But it was true. He saved the small animal so recently birthed.

The closer he came, the more Matt became aware that Sarah had not been sitting on the hillside merely as a spectator to his actions. He brought his horse to an abrupt halt, swiftly bouncing off, adding an anxious step that brought him to her side.

"What the hell happened?" he demanded. With an impatient look of unexpected concern, he stared at her muddy face.

With his hands spread wide waiting for an explanation, Matt leaned back and crouched to inspect Sarah's unkempt figure. Not a bit escaped him, from the top of her head down past her soiled shirt and mud-spotted jeans to her muddy shoes. He grabbed her shoulders. He squelched the urge to run his hands over her body to examine every inch for damage. She was wet and muddy. She appeared unhurt. She was not trembling but she was very unhappy.

"What happened?" The pressure of his hands relaxed on her shoulders, the cupping grasp became caressing, his voice concerned.

Sarah caught her breath and closed her eyes thinking this was no time to worry about the mud. The flush of color in her face enhanced her deep tan in the rosiness of the early morning sun. Her eyes, snapping open with indignation, were clear and sparkling.

Straightening her back carefully so as not to dislodge his hands, she placed her hands on her hips, defying his concern, establishing her well-being. It was her balance she must think of. Her knees wobbled slightly. His approach brought a recurrence of the strange feeling she always had in his presence. It was not a repercussion from her fall.

His entire body warmed at her indignation. He cupped her chin in his hand and wiped a lump of mud off the corner of her mouth with his thumb.

"We can find better stuff for breakfast than this."

Sarah wiped at the dirt she didn't know was there. Her chest rose with a deep intake of breath and her eyes flashed resentment.

"I was thrown off that horse." She wasn't playing games. It wasn't as if she committed a capital offense, either. It was an accident. In spite of that her eyes closed tightly in shame and guilt. She still felt trauma from whatever happened. Matt pinned his gaze on her closed eyes. He should hug her but he didn't dare. He might never let her go. He let his hands slide down her arms. He had better lighten up.

She felt his hands close on her elbows. She looked up into his face, his slitted brown eyes sparkled mischievously. A widening grin erupted in a deep chuckle he could not contain.

"Was that fun?" he laughed, "Rolling in the mud?" His breath warmed her forehead so unexpectedly that she found it difficult to realize he was laughing. His mirthful eyes receded further into crinkled cheeks. He was laughing! And he was laughing at her condition!

He sobered slightly and his piercing gaze dove into her depths as he leaned down to her face with his more burning statement, "You are all right."

Hesitating at her silence, he shook her imperceptibly when his hands tightened on her elbows. "Well, aren't you?" Matt's arms supported her weight leaving her the strength to glance down and gain time to compose herself. Sarah's knees felt as watery as if she was on the deck of a ship instead of a muddy hillside.

It was the fall that made her tremble.

Certainly.

"Did that mare really throw you?" Matt didn't entirely lose his mirthful expression. He wanted a negative answer to his statement.

That was clear.

He forced her to look up at him by the forward pressure on her elbows almost lifting her body off the ground. He couldn't believe the worst of the horse and that made her angry.

Defiantly she stuck out her chin. It wasn't her fault. But then again, it wasn't exactly the horse's fault either. "Well if I had dismounted on my own I'd have stayed on my feet, I assure you," she snapped. She struggled against his gripping hands. Trying to twist out of his grasp only brought her body fully against his. Too late she realized she made the wrong move if she wanted to avoid his touch.

She had to avoid his touch. That was the only way to erase those silly feelings tossing about in her stomach, sending her pulse into a breathtaking race. Foolish uncontrollable reactions only occurred in youthful bodies. She stiffened before deciding how she could extricate herself gracefully without looking more of a fool.

Her knees still trembled.

Her ragged breathing was the result of the muddy tumble. Certainly.

Matt accepted her hesitation as surrender. And his defense crumbled. His hands slipped behind her back and he pulled her against his full length. He could give her a moment of support for her weakness. Strangely, this gave her strength. Stranger still, she enjoyed his arms and decided not to pull away at all.

A comfort spread through her like the warmth of a hot drink. She relaxed against him fully, enjoying his embrace, denying her hands the power to go around his neck. What a wondrous feeling.

The touching of one body to another.

Worry tweaked her conscience. Had she become so vulnerable she welcomed any body's touch?

Better to get her body touched by a hug from Lou. At least it would be safer, considering the longing Matt's embrace dredged from depths she didn't know she had. She unwisely stayed close too long in the doorway yesterday. She must not let that happen again. Sarah placed her palms against his chest and pushed away.

Matt was the ranch's "reel" cowboy and was available to comfort and care for all the guests.

The time and place put her with him when it might have been any other woman in his embrace. She didn't really want to believe that.

Her resolve strengthened when she remembered his laugh.

"I'm sorry," she apologized. She had no reason to be angry just because he laughed at her, although nothing about it was funny to her. He laughed before, at her fear of the geese. Laughing must be his style. No wonder he remained a bachelor.

Being the brunt of laughter stung her deeply. She burned with embarrassment and it renewed her anger. But it was herself she was angry with, she realized, now that she gained control of her emotions. She tested the stability of her knees before she stepped away on her own power.

"The mare stepped into a hole and I wasn't prepared to hang on." Trying to distract herself from her wayward thoughts, she looked at the mare munching contentedly on the grass not too far away.

She paused. Then with a careless toss of her head ventured another thought, "Maybe I would have fallen off even if I had anticipated it."

She hugged her arms across her stomach feeling a chill replace the warmth of Matt's body. He had embraced her. She pushed him away. Too bad she wasn't more seriously injured. Then she wouldn't have felt self conscious about his surrounding arms. She would have accepted as much solicitation as the muddy calf.

At least she wouldn't have earned a laugh.

Sarah rubbed at her elbows where Matt's hands left sand from the wipe-down. It was his touch, not the sand, that burned her bones. The delicious thought of his hands rubbing all over her body ran through her mind. She must stop enjoying such fantasies. The way he read her mind was annoying and she grasped for a denial.

"I don't know why I keep pretending I can ride."

"I don't think you should keep pretending a lot of things," he said cryptically. His eyes held hers for a piercing instant before he turned away.

"What do you mean by that?" Sarah glared at him, fearing again that he could read her mind. She suspected his accusation had nothing to do with her riding, but his real meaning was precisely what she didn't want to deal with. She didn't trust herself to look any deeper into their relationship.

Matt made no attempt to clarify his statement. His terseness rankled her more than his laughter. His refusal to answer her question left her at a loss for any other.

Walking slowly toward the mare and talking softly, Matt picked up the reins. He examined the front legs carefully before leading the mare to Sarah. Studying him with narrowed eyes, Sarah avoided his direct gaze as he approached. She hesitated to take the reins.

"Are you afraid to get back on?" Matt asked with a slight twist of his mouth. "If you stay on the trail you won't find any holes."

He turned the horse and offered his hand to give her a leg up. Sarah fairly stomped on his hand in mounting, if one can stomp on anything as unstable as a hand held out some distance from the body.

Matt's thrust at recovery of her deliberate weight threw Sarah higher above the mare than necessary. She settled down awkwardly on the surprised mare and gained the stirrups as she grabbed the saddle horn with both hands to avoid going completely over the opposite side.

Matt handed her the reins and watched her with a stiff impassive face. She was a touchy one. What was he ever going to do with her, he wondered? After holding her so close he had a wealth of fantasies to consider with her. He closed his eyes in denial.

"I'm ready when you are." Sarah straightened up with a haughty shrug. How could he be so implacable?

In seconds Matt was in his saddle, urging his mount up the slope and back to the trail. Why did she get so cranky? Neither spoke a word although Matt stayed close by and Sarah knew he watched her and the big red horse from the corner of his eye.

Try as she would, Sarah could not relax in the saddle the way she was instructed to do. Every nerve and muscle was much too tense. She wanted to get away from this unsympathetic man that set fire to her soul.

Leaning forward with the intent to get back to the ranch at the same moment Matt's horse broke into an easy canter, Sarah squeezed her knees and her horse followed smoothly back to the barn. Once again in her wayward innocence, she succeeded in giving a correct command. She was delighted and her features glowed at her success.

Dropping to the ground beside the corral, Sarah felt elated. She was getting the hang of riding. She was sure of it. She clung to the mare for a moment, gingerly trying her legs to make sure they would hold her weight.

The girth. Loosen the girth. She raised the stirrup to get to the buckle. Matt looked on with a raised eyebrow. He was surprised and very pleased to see she was not too shaken to remember the task.

He gripped the strap, grazing her fingers, removing it from her hands. His touch sizzled as it stroked her skin and she withdrew as if contacted by a bare electric wire. The charge nearly overwhelmed her. She failed to notice Matt's equally stunned response to the touch.

He had important things to say to her but she was too riled to be receptive so he kept his remark simple. "You'd better get cleaned up for breakfast," he suggested, his tone speculative as he tied the reins to the rail.

She bit back a retort. She did not need to be told something so obvious. Sometime she might insist that he stop giving her orders but not now. He was not serious enough to listen to reason.

She stomped off toward her room confused at the speed in which he changed expressions, brushing frantically at her muddy clothes, unable to accept his mischievous teasing in the intimate manner his smile implied. He was goading her and enjoying it. She took his attitudes at face value, not able to decide if he was joking or if he was sincere. She took his thoughtfulness far too seriously. And she couldn't imagine how she could stop.

The trouble was, she wasn't sure she wanted to.

Chapter Seven

Oh, lonesome me

Sarah grabbed her bath-towel and hung it by the shower. Everyone was at breakfast so she had the community bathroom to herself. She peeled off her clothes and rolled the muddiest garments together, the drier surfaces to the outside of the roll. No need to smear the mud around.

She turned to the shower and was shocked at the disheveled picture staring back at her from the mirror. Her hair stuck out ridiculously like unkempt strands on Pappy, the sidekick of a cowboy movie hero. Actually she looked more like she was thrown from the strawberry roan, where she collected a few square yards of churned up dirt. Brown streaks covered her cheek, a smear easily tracing the path of Matt's thumb. Sand lay on her shoulders, the residue from his hands that briefly caressed her neck.

She touched the corner of her mouth where he brushed the mud away, playfully reminding her to find better stuff for breakfast. She wanted him to hold her then, to console her, to tell her it was all right, to assure her she wasn't the only person who ever tumbled off a horse, to rejoice in her luck she was not seriously injured, to give her at least the same consideration he gave the muddy calf.

Instead, he interrogated her, refusing to believe the horse had thrown her, laying the blame for the foolish fall on her ineptness. He laughed at her, made light of her predicament, made fun of her appearance, as if her tumble was of little consequence. She relinquished her immediate hope of consolation, stung with the knowledge he preferred to laugh at her messy dilemma in the aftermath of an accident that had shaken her regardless of the fact that it had no critical outcome.

Her stomach knotted in anguish when he showed no sensitivity to a mood she thought they shared after the intimate appreciation of the sunrise they recently viewed.

She recalled the elusive emotions that skittered across his features when she caught him studying her in the rosy dawn light. She couldn't identify them then, and admitted she didn't want to believe they were the pleading invitation and the desperate longing they appeared to be at the time. She wondered if those were emotions she could expect from a seducer, a man who would ravish any female that came within his grasp.

She shook her head in denial. She wasn't a typical female likely to be ravished. Even if she was, he didn't act according to her concept of a seducer. His expressions were too agonized to be contrived. He had shown a deep sorrow, a profound yearning. He had also turned away at her glimpse, too quickly for the moment she needed to set those impressions in her mind for later scrutiny.

With the associated confusion tearing at her when she caught him laughing, she lost her temper. The moment his arms surrounded her after he rescued the calf, she pushed him away, refusing to give in to instinct, unrelenting in her goal to remain a detached independent woman. She wished she hadn't done that. There would have been no harm in a prolonged embrace. Her inability to make up her mind was disturbing. What did she want? An affair, as Lou suggested? A roll in the hay with a movie hero?

For heavens sake, not that, Sarah, she scolded herself, and furthermore you do not want a serious commitment, and don't you forget it.

To think she had expected a man, and a handsome virile man at that, to fawn over her. Over a face like that? She looked down at the pile of muddy clothes and shrugged. She shook her head in disgust and turned on the water.

The shower head sprayed strong and hard and she welcomed the liquid attack. Sarah soaped her body until it was sleek with creamy suds from her oval bar of soothing cosmetic soap. She squeezed a dollop of green shampoo fragrant with fresh spring flowers into her broad palm and spread it around the top of her head with one quick circular motion leaving it to soak into her scalp.

She adjusted the temperature of the water down a few degrees to prevent her skin from turning as red as a scalded lobster. The pressure released tiny streams that felt like storm driven sand and she turned into them with the hope of cleansing more than her surface skin. The hot pelting water washed away the streaking mud but the abrasive action only magnified and spread the delicious tingling Sarah felt where hard calloused fingers grasped her shoulders and touched her cheek. The cleansing water did not curb her desire to languish in Matt's wiry supportive arms.

Clamping her eyes shut against the foaming shampoo, Sarah raked her nails viciously across her scalp. She was angered at the visions in her traitorous mind, confused that she wished for more. Her body insisted on betraying the intentions she set our for her life pattern. She was appalled that her thoughts became such willing accomplices.

In clean blue jeans and a peach colored knit shirt, she declared herself ready for breakfast. She walked resolutely to the lodge. Facing Matt wasn't going to be easy. The fragrance of fresh coffee drifted from the kitchen and bolstered her resolve. She took a deep speculative breath and stepped into the dining room. She anticipated the usual casual morning greetings but she did not expect to be the center of interest for the entire breakfast crowd.

Lou was her usual loud self full of excitement. Chewing around a mouthful of jellied toast she burst out, "Where have you been?"

Sarah did not expect the forthright demand to give a public explanation.

Lou washed down her toast with a gulp of black coffee and her incriminating tone continued. "I thought you came early for coffee but Melanie told me you went riding off with Matt over an hour ago."

Inquiring eyes waited silently for a description of the unscheduled ride. Forkfuls of syrupy pancakes were raised to open mouths, eyes never wavering from Sarah's scrubbed figure. She held back an inward twinge at the depth of their examination, knowing they couldn't see where her skin still warmed from Matt's touch, feeling somehow guilty that she monopolized him at their expense. She saw the empty chair with the cutlery reserved for her and she concentrated on even steady footsteps to take her there.

Lou didn't let up.

"The folks know you consider this ranch a movie setting and I suggested you play a part to suit your mood. Are you a neighboring rancher or a cowboy's sweetheart?" Either one implied a love affair.

Sarah felt betrayed that Lou would bring up the fantasy they discussed when they first came into their room. Frustration and irritation filled her deep intake of breath as she pulled out the empty chair. Lou swept her gaze around the table assuring she held the attention of the others.

"We know what you're up to, don't we folks?"

At Sarah's innocently raised eyebrows, Lou went on, "Going off with Matt before the rest of us get up is pretty suspicious."

Lou clucked and shook her head, raising an accusing eyebrow. She was at her best when she was teasing and she knew that her friend would take it in good humor. Sarah slid into the chair and reached for a glass of orange juice, hoping the cool liquid would squelch the rising heat in her cheeks.

"You wanted to go riding early so I was planning on it," she retorted. She hoped the others would remember Lou's attempt last night to raise some interest in an early ride. Behind lowered eyelids Sarah recalled the innocence in which she took the ride and decided she had ample reason to defend herself.

"I tried to wake you but you grunted for me to go away. You should have come with me. The sunrise was lovely."

Under the amused eyes of the other guests, Sarah requested hash brown potatoes and eggs over easy. A plate of warm fragrant toast was placed before her with a carafe of steaming aromatic coffee. She felt a sympathy emanating from all but Lou and she was puzzled by her friend's attitude. Perhaps mentioning the saddling and riding instruction would take the edge off Lou's insistent teasing.

"I asked for a riding lesson and that was quite fortunate. As it turned out, Matt saved the life of a calf. It was mired in mud down by the river. It would have perished. Maybe the cow as well." Sarah convinced herself the ride was of economic importance and far less personal when she thought of it that way. She relaxed at the thought. The significance of the special riding lesson was not lost on the others.

Sarah didn't realize how defensive she became. If she had taken Lou's first statement as a joke, no one would have given it another thought. She could see the smug reactions around the table, as if they accepted and approved.

No one believed for a minute that the ride was an innocent lesson and in a secret way she was pleased. Her own attempt at saddling the beautiful horse was an unexpected maneuver and Matt's deliberate moves to be close at the time was exciting as well as confusing. She could not explain why she so willingly accepted his plea to go quickly with him. In fact the need of an explanation did not occur to her until the mystery of the dawn confronted them as they sat mesmerized in its beauty.

Then she considered Matt's request intensely personal, accompanying him a special privilege. His manner implied as much until she caught him contemplating her, a moment before his eyes shuttered, when his mood changed, his attitude cooled.

Sarah tried to understand the mood of those seated near her, her lowered lashes covering her covert study. One corner of her mouth turned up slightly as she noted their indifference. A ranch romance was an interesting sidelight but of no real significance in the guest schedule. Sarah was no longer the prime subject for discussion. Separate conversations erupted around the table, essentially accepting her status without criticism. The ride in the fresh morning air sharpened Sarah's appetite and she concentrated on the hash brown potatoes in a crispy pile on her plate. The eggs were done to her liking and she ate with a smugness that surprised her.

Something about the morning left her with a pleasant residue that overpowered her confused emotions toward Matt. He was not at the table and she found it easy to push romantic thoughts of him away. She renewed her intention to stay clear of the implied relationship.

"I think I'll stay here and practice sketching," she announced quietly to Lou, who glared at her.

"How can you do such a thing? I'm going to change into my boots for the ride," Lou announced, setting her cup down, "How much longer are you going to be?"

"Just a few more minutes," Sarah answered, "You don't have to wait for me. I'll catch up, but I really don't want to ride all day."

Lou walked out and so had the other guests, creating an unusual quiet in the large dining room. Only a muffled scraping of dishes and pans came from the kitchen.

Melanie's voice broke through the metallic noises as she instructed the kitchen workers about the schedule for the remainder of the day.

A young voice interrupted Melanie with a demand, "Where's Matt?"

"He went to get the packhorse," Melanie answered, "Wait... Tad...tell him the sheriff wants to talk to him before he goes out."

Tad was a kitchen helper, young and eager to learn his way around the ranch as well as the kitchen. He had been at the ranch for three years, choosing household work over barn chores. Although he enjoyed riding horses, he did not have the dedication to work in raising or training of them. He willingly filled the need in the lodge.

Sarah heard Tad shout an okay and closed the door. She remembered today's ride was to be for the full day and she had to act on her announcement to Lou. No all day ride for this old lady, she declared to herself. She would tell Melanie right away. On second thought she might as well go to the corral and tell Matt she wouldn't be going. Her body quickened at the prospect of seeing him.

Maybe he would let her unsaddle the mare and keep it in the corral for a model. On second thought she didn't want to face him. It might be safer if she simply didn't show up at the corral at all. Lou came rushing up to Sarah before she crossed the veranda.

"Yoo hoo, Sarah, what's going on? There's a pile of muddy clothes at the foot of your bed," she called.

Matt came riding along the side of the building with a pack horse in tow. He gave Sarah a thin crooked smile that evaporated as quickly as it came. He touched his hat to Lou then turned to Melanie, who rushed up beside him, to contest his declaration.

"I have to go over there right away, you know that."

"How long will it take?" Melanie was asking, not pleased with the development.

"I have no idea. But Buck can help Steve handle the trail ride. The lunch is already packed. I'll send Jerry and Eddy over as soon as I can." Matt spoke with final authority. He touched his heels to his horse and trotted off toward the corral.

Matt spoke with final authority. He touched his heels to his horse and trotted off toward the corral.

By the time Sarah got to the corral, all the time refusing to answer Lou's incessant questions about her muddy clothes, Matt was striding toward the ranch pickup.

Sarah found Buck, whom she now knew was in charge of today's ride.

"Buck, I'm not going on the ride," she announced, "I had more of a ride this morning than I bargained for."

"Yes, ma'am, Matt told me. I reckon he expected you might want to stay at the lodge," Buck replied. "I'll take the mare's saddle off and leave her in the corral for you...if you'd like."

"Thank you, Buck. I'd appreciate that," Sarah gave him one of her biggest smiles. Lou caught that friendly exchange without knowing what brought it about. Lou caught Sarah speaking frequently with him, always snatched conversations about sketching, usually guarded, and those secretive moments brought on more teasing. Lou expected the conversations really were innocent. She honestly thought Sarah would be lonesome if she stayed at the ranch but found more fun in teasing.

"Sarah, will you quit making time with the cowboys long enough to tell me what's going on," Lou insisted.

Sarah didn't remind Lou about playing a movie role but it was often in her thoughts. Acting the part of a cowboy's sweetheart around Matt was appealing. Trouble was, she didn't have a script to show her how she fit into the drama. Her association with Matt wasn't going the way of a movie romance. At least he wasn't using the same script she was. None of the action appeared to upset him the way it was disturbing her.

"Buck is in charge of the ride so you can't monopolize his time. You haven't told me how you got mud on those clothes.

You weren't romping in the grass with that skinny galoot, were you?" Lou kept pressing the issue.

Lou didn't let up on Sarah for a minute. She couldn't accept the association that developed between Sarah and the men as simple camaraderie between staff and guest, no matter how innocent Sarah pretended it to be. Lou was more than a bit envious that the most visible bachelors showed more interest in Sarah than Lou thought was fair. But she enjoyed riding and visiting too much to dwell on it for long.

"Matt's around here somewhere. He'll come up with something to interest you." Lou set her chin with a characteristic snap.

"Lou, I've been laughed at and made fun of more than I like for one day. Just go ride and I'll tell you all about it when you get back."

"You mean you're not going?" Lou watched Buck remove the saddle from the mare Sarah was to have ridden. Lou looked across the ranch yard and saw Matt driving away in the pickup.

"If that cowboy wasn't driving off, I'd think you were going to spend the day with him."

"Lou, that's foolish. Matt's got better things to do than waste his time with me. Not that I wouldn't enjoy spending the day with him minus the horses. Sometimes he's rather nice."

"Oh, c'mon Sarah, he's a poor excuse for a man. Skinny legs and arms and he's got an awful looking jaw. His hair is thinning out on top of his head. Didn't you see that last night? He's getting old."

Sarah stared at Lou with an open mouth. She had seen every one of those things and came up with an entirely opposite evaluation.

She laughed, "Here's a pot calling a kettle black. Lou, you get out of here before I tell everyone how old you are."

Lou raised her fist in a feigned blow, "All right. All right. But you've just gotta come with us, you'll be all alone at the ranch if you don't."

"Not really. There's always someone to do the chores," Sarah declared. "And I won't be idle. I'll work on my sketches. You should see how many I've made." She didn't have her sketchbook to show Lou. "And with more time I can sketch cattle, too."

The suckling calf with its winding tail intrigued her. She hoped she could capture the essence of cattle more successfully than she had of horses for all the time she'd studied them. Sarah hoped her sketches would improve. She must work to capture the proportions. If she failed to make any real progress with her skill, she suspected it might be simply because she had no talent. She found little incentive to ride horseback. During the short time she spent with Matt she did experience a thrill in the ride. But the horse responded more to him than to her direction and she fancied her real delight was more from his company than from riding. Deprived of his company she doubted there would be anything about a day long ride to enjoy.

What happened to her resolve? Why did she want him when he left, reject him when he was close? It was a dilemma to plague her and she looked forward to a day alone in which to search her heart and her future. The pleasure she derived from the time spent with her sketch pad was directly a result of the solitude. It was an utterly unexpected bonus of her vacation. And she was delighted to exploit the opportunity to continue her solitary days. The concept was one Lou could not understand.

"I like to be around people. I don't enjoy being by myself, even on horseback," Lou chided, "At least you've got the good sense to keep company with a nice horse, but I think you just plain enjoy being all by yourself."

Lou shrugged, giving up to the extraordinary concept. "And don't forget. You're going to explain everything when I get back."

Sarah always enjoyed company but wasn't adept at making small talk. Strangely enough, she found there were some people whose company she appreciated without any conversation at all. Lou rarely gave her the opportunity to be one of those.

"Well, I consider a vacation to be a unique experience," Sarah said, a smug smile breaking her serious expression. She waved Lou off with best wishes for a wonderful ride.

Buck turned the blood red mare into the corral and tossed her a chunk off a bale of hay.

"She's all yours, Sarah, and she'll be glad for your company," Buck touched his hat and went about the business of getting the ride under way.

Sarah watched the mare follow the corral fence to keep up with the departing trail riders. The horse nickered with longing at the disappearing riders and Sarah hurried back to her room for her sketch pad.

Buck was right. The mare was unhappy to be left behind and eventually responded to Sarah's call.

"I think I'll call you Red," Sarah announced to the blood red mare when she put her foot on the bottom rail of the corral and laid her sketch pad on her thigh. The mane and fetlocks were black but every other hair on the horse's body was a burnished red that took on an underlying intensity of crimson in the bright sun. The horse moved to the water tank and back to the far end of the corral.

For nearly an hour Sarah watched every movement of Red's legs and hooves, noting each change of line as the tendons and muscles bulged or receded. She sketched quickly with bold strokes and filled pages with repeated drawings.

Needing to change her position from time to time, Sarah finally slid between the corral rails. Her body quickening momentarily, recalling the instant Matt dragged her from the stall that first time she touched the horse. Red turned dark questioning eyes toward her as if to monitor her actions. The eyelids drooped and the horse continued to grind bites of hay. Sarah considered the movement an approval, stepped slowly forward and sat down gingerly on part of the hay that Red did not want.

More primitive sketches flew across the paper from the point of Sarah's soft lead pencil. She valiantly made an effort to improve her drawings, her eyes moving intensely from the anatomy to her paper. Putting down her pencil, Sarah arched her back, now weary from concentration on her drawing. Flies that she hadn't noticed before crawled over her face, so engrossed was she in her work.

The red horse pointed its ears forward and raised its head toward the barn. Sarah turned to follow the horse's gaze but saw nothing nor did she hear a truck's motor when it came into the ranch yard.

Only at the faint sound of voices was Sarah cognizant of what Red already knew. Matt had returned to the ranch. Tucking her drawing pencil into her pocket, Sarah stood up and brushed the hay from her jeans. She breathed deeply and hesitantly waited for the lean cowboy, her heartbeat increased in tempo with each passing second. Before she took one step toward the barn, the hum of voices turned into audible words and she stood stark still at the angry sounds.

"I won't and you can't make me," were the first angry words she could discern.

"You are. But I'm not going to make you. You're going to do it yourself," Matt's harsh, stern voice declared, "and Buck is going to help you."

Silence followed.

An ominous silence, pregnant with hostility. Sarah held her breath in expectation of a further explosion.

Red trotted to the barn door and Sarah caught a ragged breath, almost sucking in a fly. She immediately clamped her mouth shut with a shudder. Sending a furtive glance toward the barn, she felt a pang of guilt at eavesdropping, however inadvertently.

In a moment of quiet discretion, Sarah walked quickly around the barn toward the ranch house when she heard a painful cry. She hurried into the lodge. What a coward she was! If kids were being mistreated by the cowboy any decent person would go to their rescue, but not Sarah.

In the large dining area no one was about. She numbly poured a mug full of coffee and stirred in sugar and cream.

Sarah started at the sound of Melanie's voice, "I know that. He told me before he left this morning."

After a long pause, "You know he has no control over that, Sheriff."

Melanie's voice sounded plaintively defensive, "I know. I'll tell him."

Sarah heard the phone crash into its cradle and imagined that Melanie swore softly as she came tearing out of the office, which was a small room tucked into the corner beyond the bar at the kitchen end of the lounge.

Melanie's worried expression changed to cloaked surprise at the sight of Sarah with the coffee mug to her lips. "Oh, Sarah, I didn't know you were here. How's your drawing?" She only asked with feigned interest to cover her surprise, her thoughts on something far more pressing because she didn't wait for an answer. Melanie stopped at the swinging door into the kitchen and thoughtfully looked at Sarah.

"Did you, by any chance, notice if Matt brought back the truck?"

"I saw it in the yard just a few minutes ago," Sarah could honestly say. She hoped she didn't have to admit she knew where Matt was or what she thought he was doing.

Melanie rushed to the door and raced across the veranda to head in the direction of the barn.

Sarah's heart was in her throat. The hot coffee stuck like molten lead but her mind raced.

Sheriff.

The sheriff wanted to talk to Matt early this morning, preventing him from going on the ride at all.

No control.

Over what? What was Melanie going to tell him?

Sarah looked toward the kitchen. She pushed against the swinging door and slowly peered along the counters, looking for someone to whom she could talk. Did she dare to ask the questions on her mind? They burned on her tongue as surely as the hot coffee did a moment before.

She took a step into the kitchen and as calmly as she could, called, "Hi, is anyone here?"

The young woman who had served last night's dinner turned from the salad greens she was cutting, "Just me, Mrs Wilson. Do you need something?"

"Will I bother you if I stand here and talk?" Sarah asked in a meek voice she hoped would help get her the invitation she sought. "And please call me Sarah."

"No bother," the young woman hesitated over calling the older woman by her first name, "Sarah. I'm Babs." You're supposed to get a salad and sandwich at noon and it's almost ready."

Babs seemed friendly enough but Sarah wasn't sure how to approach the subject closer to her thoughts right now than lunch. "Do you always work the kitchen by yourself?" Sarah asked as she sipped slowly at her coffee.

"No. Tad went along to give Buck a hand on the ride until Matt sent over some extra help."

Sarah refused to admit the real reason for her curiosity about Matt was not his whereabouts as much as it was a disappointment that he wouldn't be around for an accidental encounter. She shouldn't try to keep track of him but she was driven by an inner desire to know.

Babs smeared butter on two slices of bread and reached into the refrigerator for a plate of sliced ham.

"Everything is under control here," Babs assured her.

"Matt didn't expect to be called away. Where did he go?"

Sarah considered the question innocent enough - until she met Matt's glaring eyes across the kitchen.

"That, Mrs Wilson, is none of your business."

Sarah cringed at the ominous tone he used on her name. The formal emphasis he put on it frightened her.

Matt picked up a half loaf of bread and swooped up some ham slices with a piece of plastic wrap. The lines around his mouth were harsh and a grim expression settled across his eyes. He moved like a man possessed.

The conversation at the barn flashed through Sarah's mind. Shame and embarrassment flooded her face.

"Of course...I'm sorry...I didn't..." She whirled away and left the room, her vision of a fantasy cowboy evaporating in a cloud of anger.

Chapter Eight

Why, oh why, did I ever leave Wyomin'

How could Sarah admit her attraction to Matt after that outburst? He was mixed up with the law. Or worse, he was a party to child abuse. She wasn't exactly ashamed of him. She was ashamed for him, and confounded by her deep feelings for him. She had to muster some defense against those feelings. She must fight them all the way. She was determined to avoid him. That was the place to start.

Sarah shouldn't have worried about that. Matt granted her wish. He never came in the barn or the corral where Sarah went after lunch.

Nor had she again seen the boy he spoke with in the barn. She hadn't really seen the boy then, she reminded herself, but he sounded younger than the boy seen on the veranda when she and Lou arrived. The boy Matt sent off hadn't been around since then, either.

Sarah did enjoy the solitude, but try as she might, she could not keep her mind from wandering. The pencil stroked the paper with sharp lines and subtle shading, usually moving without conscious guidance. A tall hat with curled edges appeared beside the bits of horse anatomy. A tall slim figure walked among the quickly sketched horses. Matt was materializing before her in shades of black and gray. She looked up to see if he was near.

She would be embarrassed to meet him after his rebuke, but she looked for him at every turn. His whereabouts were none of her business. He was a ranch hand and she was a guest. What else could she expect?

What more could she have?

What more did she want?

Her confusion annoyed her at the same time it puzzled her. Hard concentration on sketching did not succeed at keeping thoughts of him away. She flipped over to a fresh page and started over. She had to concentrate harder if she was going to prevent his image from flowing out of the lead of her pencil. It took hard conscious effort to reproduce only the lines of the horse. Every pencil stroke of a knob or tendon of Red's legs brought a recollection of wide hands cleaning mud off legs of a spindly calf. Every line she drew of Red's shoulders was overlain with Matt's gentle soothing fingers. Vignettes of horse's shoulders and withers were interspersed with those of powerful shoulders and rugged masculine jaws. She couldn't shake away Matt's image.

She sighed with a resigned thrust of her shoulders. Rotating her head and flexing her neck, she got up from the upturned feed bucket and walked briskly to the lounge. But a drink of coffee wasn't what she wanted. She felt the urge to put her sketching aside and walk the trail taken earlier by the horseback riders.

With her light jacket tied by the sleeves around her neck, she asked Melanie for directions to the river. She wanted a destination for a hike. And she was going without her sketch pad. For an hour she was going to walk in the fresh open air.

She passed the barns and gazed at the jagged peaks, a dramatic backdrop for the hilly terrain racing away in the distance. The light brown hills curled with somber clumps of brush dotting the slopes like dark freckles on tanned cheeks. Outcroppings of weathered rock stood at attention like sentinels guarding hills in the near distance, pointing to the majestic mountains piercing the sky beyond. Horses in the pasture raised their heads curiously from their scattered positions on a hillside as Sarah slowly jogged the first thousand yards down the trail. Soon she was breathless and slowed to a stiff legged walk.

She had been sitting around too much, she reflected, she was short of breath too quickly. She forced herself to keep up a steady pace. She wiped her sweaty forehead with the sleeve of her jacket. She did not expect the sun to be so hot. A hawk circled lazily overhead, its head turning, eyes alert, searching, searching, searching... The sky beyond was a hazy blue without a cloud. Hopping insects flitted out of the grass, disturbed by her footsteps.

Dark sharp points of pines put jagged profiles on the contours of the lower hills. Hoof prints vaguely marked trails branching off at random. There were many more unmarked trails than she was told and she chose a path without really knowing which was the one she should follow. From the description Melanie gave her, the river was in the general direction she was heading. The river must flow somewhere in the dips between the rolling mounds of waving grasses.

All around her, the hills rolled, hiding canyons and gullies. Rocky outcroppings punctuated the landscape with rugged contrasts, accentuating its compelling beauty. The divergence of the scene stirred a profound satisfaction within Sarah. She was unaware of any particular dissatisfaction in her life. Yet here, somehow, she felt relieved of a burden. She couldn't remember when she ever felt such intense peace. The air was clear and fresh, although warming far more than she expected. She puffed, determined to keep up a fast pace as the incline of the slope increased to challenge her. She searched for a familiar landmark, vaguely recalling the ride toward the sunrise. When she reached the top, she was treated to a view of lush green foliage in the fold of the hill below.

This was not the place from which she had watched the sunrise with Matt.

Matt.

For a few moments her thoughts of him were peaceful and tender. But she couldn't escape reviewing his every facet. His angry censure was far too vivid in her memory. She had thoughtlessly severed any cordial relationship between them. She wouldn't watch a sunrise, or anything else, with him again. He was angry at her intrusion in his business. The bubble of fantasy she wove after their shared ride to the sunrise was brutally burst by her own tactless curiosity. Her shoulders drooped with sadness.

What was done was done.

Finished.

She put aside her amorous thoughts of that cowboy. The whole idea was ridiculous anyway. A romance at her age was preposterous, Lou's reference to frisky feelings aside. This dude ranch interlude began as a vacation and that was what it would continue to be, with or without a movie set romance. And she was going to do her best to enjoy it.

The satisfaction from the seclusion of the past few hours began to make itself felt. The prospect of two weeks of this was exhilarating and wiped away the disappointment of the lost friendship. Maybe, if she stayed out his way, Matt might accept an apology. It was a good thought and worth a try, if the unlikely chance occurred.

From where she stood, the hill rolled over and dropped into a valley with tall silvery green cottonwoods and drooping olive green willows snaking along an irregular line. The domain within the thick growth looked darkly mysterious and drew her with its quiet solitude. The tall trees, thick with underbrush, beckoned with a cool invitation like a welcoming neighbor. The river must be close, if not hidden within the trees in view. Melanie said other guests found a place to swim on the river. Perhaps here was access to the stream where she could cool off sticky perspiration. The thought was exhilarating.

She moved swiftly toward the trees, with little effort required by the down sloping path, finding the distance further than she first thought. This wasn't the only time distance in this open country fooled her. The hillside flattened into a small valley that rolled on toward higher hills and towering mountains. Ragged outcroppings of weathered rock jabbed into the deep blue sky, shielding dark mysterious openings at their base. Gray green shrubs, tangled and untamed, tumbled down the slope toward the more vital green of lush trees.

Tall branching trees stretched high above a one story wooden building nestled among dense shrubs. A screened porch with a latticed base ran along the side Sarah approached. She scanned the front of the house for signs of occupants. Hesitating, Sarah surveyed the variety of buildings that spread out behind it, not entirely visible through the haphazard arrangement of overhanging trees and spreading shrubbery.

A low, single bark swung Sarah's attention back to the house where a big black dog, with the white markings and shaggy coat of a collie, limped out of a hole in the decaying lattice. The dog's attitude held no menace. At Sarah's hesitation its tail waved a friendly welcome. Marking the dog as aged by the graying of the its muzzle, Sarah smiled at the hospitality it offered with its wagging tail. Its steady limping approach with upraised snout further verified Sarah's impression of an aged animal. She extended her open hands, palms up, for its inspection.

After a thorough sniffing, the dog sat down and looked toward the porch. Sarah considered this an invitation to continue up the path to the door. Still no one came to greet her. Across the screened porch and through the open front door, Sarah peered into the house, seeing an overstuffed chair and an armless rocker. Beyond that, through a narrow arched doorway, cupboards surrounded an open window. Knocking gently, Sarah was hesitant to disturb the pleasant tranquility. Her rapping knuckles produced a hollow thumping of the loose screen door. She knocked more vigorously and called out.

Disappointed that no one answered, Sarah suppressed the notion that she could walk in. It was contrary to her training to explore a stranger's house unless invited. She shrugged, turning to leave, thinking no one was inside.

Until she heard crashing pans and dishes. Instantly concerned that someone was in trouble, Sarah tensed. She called, "Is something wrong?"

No answer.

Absolute silence.

Anxiety rose in Sarah's breast and she strained see the cause of the noise beyond the shadows through the open doors. Was someone stricken with a stroke or heart attack and fallen against a sharp counter in the kitchen? Was a person lying wounded and unconscious?

Childhood training aside, she opened the door and rushed across the porch, uncertain of the cause of the noise, poised to help a fallen victim. With a rising fear at what she might find, Sarah stepped into the kitchen, eyes searching for the source of the crash.

A hostile round-eyed youngster in dirty clothes glared at her in mortal fear. His beautifully childish face was topped with an untamed mop of golden hair. His jeans were green stained and stiff at the knees, his black tee shirt blotted with a masked trio of upright green turtles, weapons and shields at the ready.

Sarah let out a tense breath and her apprehension vanished, replaced with stunned surprise. She studied the startling cause of the clattering which had brought her so unerringly inside.

He looked to be less than ten years old, his defiant mouth distorted by a glob of peanut butter. A smear of jelly laid on his cheek like a bloody wound. Drooping with the weight of the thick oily spread, a slice of half-eaten bread hung from his hand. A plastic bag with bread and the jars of peanut butter and jelly was clutched against his heaving chest. He eyed her warily.

To give him space, she retreated a step toward the living room door, relieved there was no fallen body needing CPR as she feared. She tried to judge what kind of emergency aid would serve him best.

No restraint, no salve, no bandage, no resuscitation would treat his invisible problem. She puzzled as to what his problem was.

The child, a frightened cornered child, surveyed his only escape route. With frantic eyes he measured, for intended flight, the space across the narrow kitchen from Sarah to the outside doorway. His darting eyes sought her face and his eyebrows pinched above his nose while his frightened eyes narrowed as he watched her retreat. An elusive pain flashed across his features, quickly replaced with a willful boldness.

"I'm not going back." He spit out the words with venom and determination. The expression echoed yesterday's statement Sarah heard in the barn.

Reacting to his banty-like contempt, she took a slow step backwards as if driven off by his words. What had Matt said? *You're going to do it yourself.*

She relaxed her arms to look as unthreatening as she possibly could. This wasn't the first time she was confronted by a angry child, although the first who was so mortally frightened. He stood immobile a long moment, his wide fearful eyes begging for her answer.

"I'm not going to make you go anywhere," she said, quietly. Her heart wrenched at his momentary relief. Terror dominated the boy's features and, although Sarah had no notion of how to comfort him, she sensed his yearning.

As if he divined her thought and rushed to deny it, he scrambled to the door. She lunged forward and caught him in her arms, flipping the bag of food against her back. She held the struggling body with the sticky bread pressed against her shoulder, his face smothered against her warm neck, one arm lashing at her chin, knees digging into her stomach. Animal grunts punctuated his frantic jabs and Sarah winced at the fragile covering on his bones. He kicked and flailed, his eyes tightly closed, his strength matching hers. She pushed his body aside, jerking her head back to avoid his blows. His wiry muscles became inert and for a second the struggle stopped. Sarah looked into his face in surprise, curious that he should give up so easily.

Except he did not give up. He twisted the second she hesitated, elbows jabbing, breaking free, racing for the door, slamming it outward with an open palm, whacking it back against its spring. He stumbled down the back steps, falling briefly on one open hand, holding the plastic bag of food aloft with the other while he gained his balance, whipping dirt around his feet, recovering frantic irregular steps, struggling upright, regaining his speed, flinging himself across the narrow back yard, bolting behind the leafy bushes.

Sarah watched him disappear like a pursued rabbit, as the screen door slapped against the frame, relinquishing a hollow echo splitting the empty house. She had no reason to capture him. Pursuing him was useless. He knew where he was going and she did not.

She was reminded of the moment before his terrified flight, staring at the smeared peanut butter and jelly that marked his passing. She peeled off the mangled slice of bread plastered to her shoulder and tossed it on the kitchen counter. She unwrapped the sleeves of her light jacket from around her neck and wiped at the stain left on her blouse, rolling the offending peanut butter inside the garment. She stood rethinking the past few moments. She had entered a stranger's home, accosted an emotional child, raised more questions than she answered. Although she entered with good intentions of saving someone's life, she was really an intruder. She mutely retraced her steps through the living room she so rudely crossed in her misguided errand of mercy.

A burst of breeze through the open window billowed the crocheted curtain panels into the room, breaking beams of yellow sun into shards that lifted and fell through the moving lace, casting a kaleidoscope shadow, turning against the wide pine board flooring. The sunbeams lost their yellow brilliance in the undulating waves of dark-tipped hairs swelling on the fur rug that once adorned a coyote. A surging response shivered through the flourishing green streamers of a Christmas cactus spraying out in such profusion they hid the source of the plant and the surface of the wicker stand that held it. The armless rocker nodded in the breeze to show off its dark green paint worn dull on the contoured wooden seat. In a nearby slatted rack, assorted magazine and newspaper pages ruffled carelessly.

Beside the overstuffed chair was a glass covered maple table on which rested horn rimmed glasses and a string tie with a silver longhorn steer head clasp. A man lived here. A woman, too, judging from the plant and the lacy curtains. Standing on end against the table was a guitar, its case open on the floor as if it had been hurriedly set aside. All this Sarah noted in a glance, as she pondered those parts affected by the sudden breeze that brought life to the deserted room. It held a vitality, as simple and spartan as the furnishings were. It salved the melancholy brought on by her encounter with the child.

She must tell someone what she found. Melanie? Steve? Matt? To relate the incident she would also have to admit she went inside without invitation. She would have to describe the place and what would she say? "I found a hidden ranch and frightened a young thief?"

Regardless of the story she told or whom she told it to, she had to go back. She trudged along the trail on which she came, her earlier tranquility replaced by apprehension. The uphill walk made her puff and she paused to catch her breath, admitting she was not as fit as she boasted to Lou. She wiped her perspiring face on the jacket wadded in her hand. Looking back, the ranch lay nestled in the valley, once again obscured from her view by the towering trees. It was a hidden ranch, an oasis. She had violated someone's personal space and was at once guilty and thoughtful.

She veered toward a rock area searching for shade and rest, with steps slow and soft to avoid the tumbled rocks strewn in the fresh spring grass. Sinking wearily on a jutting rock, she closed her eyes and leaned back, more disheartened from the unpleasant experience with the boy than tired from the uphill struggle.

The absolute silence was astounding. It was like the moment after the crash in the kitchen, a moment beyond a climax, an instant held without breath, poised for disaster. Yet, when she reconciled herself to the deafening silence, Sarah relaxed and was content. As she let herself appreciate the newfound pleasure, far off sounds invaded, making her intensely aware of the world of cattle ranching. Horses neighing, cattle lowing, hoof beats somewhere in the distance and excited calls of riders. Nowhere before in her life, at work or at home, had she been able to appreciate a tranquil moment as she did now. A strange whispering swish filled her senses, washing over her like water pouring continuously without obstruction over small rounded boulders, soothing in its constancy. Too real to be her imagination, she opened her eyes in wonder at the illusion.

Hundreds of bats emerged from the cave, whispering wings. Not her imagination. Not an illusion. The boy smeared with peanut butter clutched his arms and hands protectively over his head as he propelled his crouched form out of the dark opening in the rock, fleeing with the nocturnal mammals he disturbed. Sarah watched him go, under the dark cloud of small brown bats, then studied the cave, the boy's hideout, the bats' roost. She was at once mystified and curious.

Bats were the only mammal that could truly fly, although some squirrels glide long distances when leaping from great heights. Bats do not have feathers, but hair, give birth to live young, and feed them with mammary glands. Sarah disbelieved stories of bats becoming tangled in people's hair, although that must have concerned the boy. Night fliers have an infallible echolocation system from which radar and sonar systems were developed for human navigation.

Sarah also knew bat wings were tough durable skin, thin enough to see through. Bats' scientific name, *Chiroptera*, came from Greek words meaning hand wings because the connected webbing contains a bone structure similar to human fingers, allowing aerial acrobatics matched by very few feathered fliers. Holding herself silent and still, Sarah waited until the boy stumbled beyond the rocky outcroppings and disappeared in the trees upstream of the buildings from which she came. Waves of bats whispered through the air. The novelty of bat lore tugged her senses. She had never been inside a bat cave.

Stay out of this, she told herself, as she rose up and stepped cautiously toward the very cave her conscience warned her to avoid. Large rocks obstructed her passage, confronting her with a hazardous climb which should have further deterred her, but she picked her steps carefully and continued on. The rocks were large and she found them solid, making progress much easier than it first looked.

Until she slipped.

In less than a hair's breath, the rock collapsed beneath her foot and her leg followed into the void. Normally very agile, she was unable to recover her balance and prevent herself from falling deep between the rocks. Amid grinding and grumbling of other rocks misplaced by the collapse, Sarah found her right leg held fast, immovable.

She groaned, pulling futilely to free herself. Not crushed - at least she felt no sharp pain - her right leg was pinned between rocks, aching under heavy pressure. Her first thoughtless impulse drove her to grapple with the oppressive weight as if the rock was simply an unworthy adversary to be summarily shoved aside. She pushed at the offending rock, not budging it in the least, then ceased her struggle, seeing its displacement for the impossibility that it was.

Now she really was in a fix!

A strong lever could dislodge the weight of the rock that pinned her. But there was no such tool within reach. She wouldn't have the strength to use it if it was. The reality of the situation hit her with the force of a crushing blow. Fear swept her into catalepsy, muscles unable to move, overwhelmed with hopelessness.

But her mind did not go into suspended animation. She controlled her panic. She must find a way to free herself and, for this, she must consciously attend to her leg, consider exactly how she was stuck and how badly she was injured. The very thought of searching for answers gave her hope, and hope brought action. Instinctively, her leg convulsed, not impossibly wedged between the rocks, after all. She moved it again to verify that fact. Her knee was bent but her leg was not intensely pinched full length between rocks.

But something held her fast.

Sarah pushed the last of her fear back and concentrated on the situation. Her left foot perched on a rock which she tested for solidity. It held firm. She steadied herself with her hands and began to pull her right leg up. She was able to lift it a very small distance between the rocks. It was the material of her jeans that was caught, not her leg. She might be able to pull her leg out of the pant-leg. Intent on testing the possibility, she unsnapped her waistband, and straightened her left leg as best she could, to slide the zipper down and push her jeans below her hips. Getting her left leg out of her jeans was the hardest part. There was no freedom of space among the rocks for the simple gesture and she was awkwardly posed with her pinched leg so much lower. Moving her torso freely brought a jab of pain to the confined leg. The numbing shock of bruising was wearing off.

But with the expectation of freedom close at hand, she did not give up. She struggled and managed with some contortion to pull her left pant-leg down to her ankle. It did not go over her running shoe so she stripped that off and pulled her foot free. The air struck her naked thigh. The coolness made her aware that she was undressed. She was unprotected by private walls and concerned about being seen in her bright blue satin panties, lacy and scant, never intended for observation under sunlit conditions, except perhaps pinned upon a clothesline to dry

How silly she was to be concerned in this vast emptiness. The obsession for privacy was onerous, a socialization she could not escape. Hurry, then, she urged herself. Get out of this position. She braced herself with her left foot, protected only by her sweaty cotton stocking, her hands tentatively against firm rocks. Slowly she began to extricate her pinched appendage from the pant-leg, moving her hands to other rocks when needed for better leverage. The struggle was tougher than anticipated. Her skin scraped when her muscles twisted and she gritted her teeth against the pain as she worked through the space where her knee was bent. Even then the material of the jeans bound her passage and threatened to prevent her freedom.

Her running shoe was caught on the rock edge, holding her foot captive. She hated to leave the shoe behind. It was a struggle to wrench her foot from it. The shoe clung stubbornly to her heel. She twisted and kept the pressure on. A speck at a time, the shoe began to release her foot until her heel almost popped out in a gust of relief like a ripened seed exploding from a pod. With a grimace, she kept pulling, hard and determined, skin scraping the gritty rock. The strain was intense but the cotton material protected her from the nastiest abrasions.

And suddenly, her leg was free!

Sarah surveyed her leg with wonder, rubbing her hands up and down the length, assuring herself it was all there, marveling at her good fortune. Her injury could have been far worse. She could have been crushed, her leg broken. For a moment she was immeasurably pleased. The rough grit of the rocks through her satin panties as she shifted her weight, reminded her that she was still undressed.

She must get her jeans. She must put them on. Grabbing the waistband with grim determination, she yanked hard. Knowing they might get torn no matter how careful she was, Sarah pulled at them with a vengeance. Only the leg would be damaged. Torn off completely, a missing pant-leg would not be as embarrassing in her reappearance at the lodge as no jeans at all. The pinching rocks did not yield the material easily, nor without exacting a toll, but they grindingly surrendered the jeans under Sarah's insistent pull. The rip was minor, a wearing of the threads rather than a blatant tear, but the jeans came out in one piece. Hugging them to her chest, she sank back on a rock in weary gratitude, resting from her struggle, relieved at her success. She would not go back unclothed after all. She gave them one more thorough appraisal before she prepared to slip them on.

Sarah shook her jeans, arranged them by the waistband, tossed the ends of the legs in front of her feet, poised to slip into them, when an apparition in the corner of her vision caught her eye.

Matt stood silently immobile, with his thumbs in his pockets, watching every move she made.

Chapter Nine

I want to be a cowboy's sweetheart

For an instant Sarah was too mortified to move. She was embarrassed at being caught in her underpants, magnifying the thought of exposure that flashed in her mind when she first shed her jeans. Quick as she could, with her knees trembling, she scrambled to her feet and held her scarred jeans in front of her bare legs. After experiencing Matt's anger just hours before, she was not surprised to see him grim and unmoved. He might have felt she deserved the humiliation. She felt unjustly punished.

Matt stood with his arms loose, elbows out, thumbs hooked in the corners of his front pockets, feet spread, evenly holding his weight in an accusing posture. His rugged face held no discernible expression, his eyes shadowed and unreadable. His voice was low and demanding.

"What were you doing in the cave?"

"That, Mr Bannister, is none of your business." Indignantly Sarah mimicked his rude answer to her earlier question at the lodge. He had no right to interrogate her, the impertinent ranch hand! His arrogance solidified her decision not to reveal the recent episode in the hidden ranch kitchen. She resolved to tell everyone but him.

"You are a guest of this ranch," he stated, emphatically, his voice menacingly quiet and authoritative, "Your wellbeing is our concern." He made no move, no indication that he cared about anything but an answer to his question. He appeared unmoved by her discomfort, unfeeling in his perusal. To the contrary, his unhurried demeanor showed he intended to prolong it. He did not appear to breathe.

"Turn around so I can get dressed" Sarah insisted. Then her eyes narrowed with speculation. She had not heard a footstep or any other movement to warn of his arrival. She had no idea how long he watched her. But he asked about the cave. He must have seen her struggle in the rocks. She glared at him with renewed loathing.

"How long have you been standing there?" Matt did not move so much as an eyelash. He kept his eyes on hers with such unseeing intensity, it was obvious he was memorizing her entire image in an effort to conjure her reason for being there. His stillness defied her.

"Why are you here?" Sarah shook her jeans to emphasize her demand. She watched him glance toward the cave, a movement of his eyes that required a minimum of surrounding muscles, nothing else.

"I saw the bats. Unless disturbed, they don't fly out before dusk." His elbows flared, just a little, and his eyelids dropped. Agitation seemed to sweep through his frame, but otherwise he remained unmoved. Matt immediately regretted his explanation. He did not have to answer to her, yet he wanted to mollify her with every fiber of his being. He searched for a way to mitigate the bad feeling he left her with when he growled at her earlier in the lodge. He was discouraged at the turn of events and yelled in frustration, his anger not particularly directed at her. He never vented his frustrations on the ranch workers. They were already too involved.

He only meant to keep her from becoming involved, too. And here she was, in his territory. That meant she was already involved. How much, or how innocently, he had to know. That first morning he expected empathy from her after she rode with him to enjoy the sunrise. He sensed a kindred spirit in the way she shared his appreciation of the inspiring panorama. Maybe she wasn't sharing. She may have only shown a universal respect toward nature, not exactly something to be compared to his personal circumstance, nowhere near to his desires. Desires that were becoming far too passionate and surfacing far too often.

Other things about her, like her response to his horse, her determination to practice proper riding habits, and her persistence in quietly entertaining herself with sketching his horse, usually without disrupting the ranch routine, indicated a serious minded independent woman that piqued his interest every time. What was more disturbing to his previously contented bachelor status, she kept invading his thoughts and he found every thought of her inexplicably warming his loins.

He was surprised to learn how deeply his singing voice touched her and nothing else could have so intimately bound him to her. Her response to his singing voice gladdened him more than he could explain. But that was a superficial affinity, one that probably wouldn't actually affect their relationship. There was much more to his character and his life than his past success. She knew nothing of his present business, how one ranch intimately depended on the other. She showed an unquenchable curiosity about everything but maybe she was just curious. When it came to the nitty gritty problems of his domain, maybe she wouldn't want to know.

Still, she did ask about him and the thought that he was on her mind pleased him even more than her response to his recording. He was immediately ashamed for losing his temper, but couldn't back down about that. Guests were seldom privy to his activities. He had directed his staff to reveal only unavoidable facts of the interrelated operation and his involvement, consequently his first reaction was to tell her to butt out. An apology for his outburst was out of place. Maybe even too late.

He was stimulated in a deep primal way by her outrage, and the pleasure that flooded him softened his features. Her anger was embarrassment at being caught undressed but that didn't cross his thoughts. His concerns for a boy and the bats had long since slipped out of his mind. She stood indignantly before him in the prettiest underwear. He couldn't keep his soul from soaring in response. Just looking at her always made him feel so good, better than a sunrise, or the sweetest fruit. He wanted to hug her. Each time the opportunity presented itself she appealed to his chivalrous nature but he refused to hold her, refused to get involved. He yielded to his more sensible nature and remained stoically impassive, on the surface at least. On the inside he was tied up in knots and was at a loss as to how he could untangle them. He held her gently after her fall from his horse but she wasn't a clinging vine and didn't lean on him for long. Maybe at another time she would let him hold her longer, maybe even hug him back. He pushed his hands deep into his pockets at the exciting thought and hunched his shoulders apologetically.

"I stopped to enjoy the view," he said, letting a knowing smile steal across his lips. He should remain grim and serious but that was more difficult than herding the flock of bats back into the cave. Once he let his emotions loose, he couldn't stop teasing. She didn't take kindly to that teasing but somehow he felt closer to her so he forged ahead.

"The unusual color made me forget myself." His head dipped and his eyes sought a view of her hips showing slightly behind the jeans she held to her front.

"Get how of here and forget the whole thing," she insisted, acidly, shaking her jeans indignantly in front of her, impatient for him to turn around so she could get dressed.

"Well, I can't do that, ma'am," he said, refusing to leave or turn around. He had a legitimate reason for being here and had no intention of leaving without her. Any excuse to remain close to her was better than none. Turning his back was out of the question.

"Melanie figured you'd been gone too long and put everybody on the lookout for you. I have to take you back so she'll know you're unharmed." He was so matter of fact about his mission, he managed to look disinterested in her circumstance. Sarah gave a quick snort of indignation. He withdrew his hands from his pockets and leaned forward. His eyes warmed with desire, open hands outstretched.

"You are all right, aren't you?" He couldn't help but repeat the concern he had when she stood muddied before him at the calf rescue. He wanted her to be all right. He could see she was all right. He was relieved and disappointed at the same time. If she was injured and helpless, he could be more intimately attentive. As badly as he wanted her in his arms, he rather liked her strong and indignant.

"You watched long enough," Sarah snapped, "You know very well how I am." His posture was not intimidating, his attitude not demanding, his features not disparaging. He was handsome and in control. If he had appeared when she first fell he could have helped her remove the rock, saved her the embarrassment she now felt. She was sure he would have done just that.

She glared at him, confused at the changing message she saw in his eyes. Now there was not the impassive indifference she first saw. She dropped her gaze. Her impression of nakedness when she first removed her jeans was a general discomfort at being vulnerable in the open space. Strangely now, before him, she felt no embarrassment in her nakedness, only a peculiar apprehension, a prickling arousal. His sudden appearance brought an ambiance of security. He made no swift move, no hasty response to her outrage. His voice remained powerful and sweetly robust.

"I'm not at all sure how you are." He tipped his head and appraised her thoroughly before continuing.

"I do know some things. You're beautiful, strong, and resourceful," he recounted, lifting his shoulders, his hands still stuffed stiffly in his pockets, adding lightly, "with a delightful taste in undergarments." He couldn't tell her how pleased he was to know she didn't restrict her curves in anything more confining than those shimmering blue panties. His glance narrowed briefly on her rounded breasts wondering if there was a matching garment under that peach blouse of hers.

She should be incensed at being undressed for his viewing, but she was not. He saw her underpants and obviously wasn't going to turn his back. He made it clear he enjoyed looking at her but made no further move to jump her bones. Sarah swung around with a haughty breath, lowered her jeans and jerked them on.

Matt's rumbling tone continued, "Unless you bruise easily, the skin abrasions will disappear in a few days and no one will ever know you got into an unfortunate situation."

Sarah was incredulous. Men often got a miserly satisfaction out of telling tales on women, elaborating on the descriptions to the detriment of the object. He could make a lot of seeing her like this if he wanted to.

"You aren't going to tell what happened?"

"That you stripped for me? Why would I want to admit a personal privilege like that?" His tone was husky and intimate, his thoughts far from ridiculing. And he had no intention of sharing his visions with anyone - except her. Especially if he could make his erotic ideas come true.

Sarah gaped.

"But I didn't strip for you!" She huffed with all the wrath she could muster, her gaze raking his tall thin frame. Of course he was teasing her, bating her. She tried to quell her anger, face the truth of his amusement.

A peculiar change took place in his demeanor. He suddenly displayed signs of discomfort, alarmingly out of character.

"I investigated the disturbed bats and found you with torn jeans," he shuffled as he described his future explanation. "It is up to you to explain what happened before that." He shuffled nervously. "Get your shoes on and I'll take you back."

She swooped down to grab her shoe, slipping awkwardly into it from a one legged flamingo position.

"The other one is stuck," she explained, pointing to the offending rock in a helpless gesture. She realized he hadn't been watching all that long if didn't know she lost her other shoe between the rocks.

"I'll come back for it," he assured her. He reached a helping hand toward her in agitation. He couldn't help his impatience with her. She acted so wary. She never seemed to feel the same heat of eagerness that swept him. Sarah accepted his hand, dropping her eyes to watch for unstable rocks, choosing with care where she put her stocking foot. She idly glanced up his frame. She fervently hoped he didn't see the emotional response to him that swept her from head to toe. She nervously dropped her gaze, instinctively memorizing his entire physique. Her gaze flicked back to the bulge in his pants and dawdled for a surprised moment.

So that was what agitated him! His arousal interfered with his teasing manner, disturbed him to distraction, mortified him with uncharacteristic apprehension. His reference to personal privilege illustrated what had not occurred to her in the aftermath of his earlier anger. He was annoyed at his own unbidden physical response.

He was not as indifferent to her as he tried to pretend with his impersonal surveillance and recurring flippancy. His unbridled carnal response put an entirely different perspective on their relationship. Her grip on his helping hand reflected her awareness. Matt noticed her expression change, her gaze soften, and contemplated where it lingered. He led her carefully across the rocks to the grassy area where his horse was ground hitched. She was surprised to see the horse she had twice ridden. Only the saddle was different, larger, more ornate.

Without letting go of Sarah's hand, Matt picked up the reins and turned to help her mount his horse. Sarah hesitated to double with him on horseback. When she looked at him, he was staring at the smear on her shirt, disbelief and fierceness hardening his features. She was astounded at his changing attitudes.

"That looks like peanut butter." The sparks of outrage fairly singed her, "How did that get there?"

"None of your business," Sarah muttered, jerking recklessly to free herself, suddenly astonished.

Peanut butter? Sarah heard of allergic reactions to taste and smell, but the sight of peanut butter? She was caught in both his hands, forearms imprisoned in viselike grips.

Matt slammed her body into his hard full length in a forceful jerking shake. He pushed her back and glared at her with eyes darker and wider than those of yesterday. His fits of temper were too easily ignited, he was frighteningly volatile. But as she stared at his expression, it wasn't anger she saw, it was desperation. She found it impossible to be indignant. She even lost her fear.

"It is my business," he growled bluntly, his tone less harsh when he peered into her face, his grip less severe when he realized she no longer struggled.

"I...I..." she stammered, swaying away from him.

"Don't lie to me, Sarah," he warned in a menacing tone. He grasped both her wrists and held them firmly up between their bodies, insulating his tense form from her quivering vigilance. Even the menacing tone became endearing when she realized that Matt used her given name. In his anger before he had called her Mrs Wilson in a most derogatory tone. Minutes before he addressed her as ma'am.

"Somebody took mine...and you're..." Matt whispered the incredibility of it, shaking his head in disbelief, "but how can you be?"

He peered into her eyes for an answer and his grip on her wrists intensified.

"Tell me...have you seen one of my boys?" Sarah's eyes were big and round and truthful, but she murmured not a sound. Her mind raced with his words: one of 'my' boys. What did that mean?

He shook her by the wrists, "Tell me. I've got to find him."

She jerked her fists, failing to gain her freedom. She quelled her initial insolence and rebellion, maintaining the pressure against his vehemence. An inner strength welled up within her, matching his power and conviction until a strange premonition stilled her action. She curbed her resistance, caught in his examining gaze, impaled by an intense demanding glow. Her heart melted and drowned in his dark depths.

A fierce tension catalyzed and held them spellbound for an eternal second. It was an alarming emotion outside themselves, yet enveloping them both, an anxiety that drew back in separation, then drew them together, uniting them with an undeniable force like the unrelenting attraction of a powerful magnet. A strange understanding replaced their hostility, hovered like a humming bird above a lovely blossom, anticipating a sweet reward.

Her voice was controlled and confident, "A boy left with the bats." Her eyes darted toward the cave and back to Matt's face, without a turn of her head. "Could that be 'your' boy?"

Matt released his iron grip on Sarah's arms but he didn't let her go. He studied her eyes, her face, her stature, with eyesight that didn't see her at all. Behind the glazed look, his thoughts raced and various emotions flooded across his face. He blinked and focused on her eyes once more.

"I'll take you back to the ranch. Come on. We can ride double." He helped her mount and swung up behind her.

Sarah burst with curiosity. Many isolated instances connected Matt with boys and she wanted to know what the connections were. Each time the circumstances appeared ominous, almost illegal, perhaps punitive. Did she dare to ask? Did she want to know? Would the truth shatter the movie image she built around this cowboy? Sarah's feet didn't begin to reach the stirrups on

Matt's saddle. She wanted to take charge and control the position of her body but she was only baggage, an extra load placed in front of the rider. The saddle confined her hips and when Matt slipped on behind her, his body molded against hers in a warm comfortable fit. His arms took control, one firmly curled around her, the other gently against her side holding the reins.

She gripped the saddle horn and held herself straight but it was impossible to put space between them. Her back moved loosely against his front with each rocking step and the swaying of his rigid body against hers was erotically tantalizing. During the first few moments of the ride she wildly fantasized about his reaction to the motion considering how aroused he was to see her underwear. Her interior temperature rose to the danger point and she tried to release the steam through short quick breaths. She simply had to control herself.

She tried to relax and flow with the movements of the horse, and succeeded with much more confidence than she had when her own feet were in the stirrups. She thrust her titillating visions aside and sent out radar to read his thoughts. She was disgruntled when she decided his mind was far removed from the personal chafing of their anatomy. She suspected Matt's thoughts were not on her at all. He was a complex individual, aloof yet appealing, with an extraordinary depth that caught her as if she were but a piece of flotsam, drawn into a whirlpool. At the outer edge she had resisted with all the strength of her logic but the pull at the vortex was too great and she was sliding into the exciting abyss, not entirely against her will.

Disjointed pieces of his life and character shown all around her, enticing and intriguing. She had a yen for putting puzzles together. The puzzle he presented was not one she chose to leave untouched on the flat and solitary surface of this ranch adventure. His angry and frustrated moments were only a few of the tempting pieces. Not always had those emotions been directed at her although he was particularly volatile in her company. His eyes held a soft yearning when she demanded him to turn away so she could dress. At the time she shunted his reaction off as a lecherous act of a man, but he liked what he saw and simply told her so.

Nothing in his posture now indicated anything but concern that ceased to center around her, at least not concern about her injury. He had a wall of mystery around him and she groped for a weak spot through which to reach. Prying was not her style but she felt an unconquerable urge to know more about his life, to be involved with his problems, perhaps be a party to his solutions. Her motive escaped her. She was here and it was now and what she struggled to do was play a harmless part in this fantasy western. She groped for a script. The silence, though not uncomfortable, demanded to be broken.

"I was lucky you came by," she ventured. It was a weak effort to thank him and she turned her head to catch his response, some acknowledgment of her appreciation.

"I have twenty boys," he said, implying that his absorption with peanut butter had its source in human bodies, "at *The Singing Ranch*." His voice was deep, his tone even. Silence followed. He seemed to think he'd said enough.

Sarah's head came to attention, her eyebrow arching in question. She thought of the two she'd seen and asked, "Troubled boys?"

Matt's arm tightened around her and he leaned to peer into her face. "Did someone tell you that?"

"I saw the shoplifter and the peanut butter boy," she said, adding no other adjectives, twisting to press her shoulder hard against his chest so her uplifted face met his eyes with a sideways glance. She couldn't keep her eyes on his face. His jaw was so close. His skin like smooth soft leather. His scent masculine, completely enslaving her senses. She straightened and looked ahead. At her remark, his arm jerked reflexively, and she felt his hard eyes on her, his swift breath on her hair. She waited for his response, watching the plodding head and black mane flowing before her for a long silent moment.

"So you jumped to your own conclusions, is that it?" he accused. He did not hurry to get Sarah to the ranch, as he first intended. He slowed the horse, prolonging their time together, exaggerating their rocking movements. He had difficulty focusing his thoughts on his lost boys. Sarah had more of a story to tell about the boy at the cave. He hoped she would tell him willingly.

"How did you get peanut butter on your blouse?" he insisted, "Don't tell me you were in that cave with Eric." His tone dared her to tell the truth.

Without understanding why she trusted him, she began, "I saw him at The Hidden Ranch."

"Where?" he interrupted, "What hidden ranch?" When Sarah raised her thumb and gestured behind them, Matt turned Red around and halted the horse, facing in that direction.

"Down among the trees below the rocks." She went on with the episode, aware of his avid interest, conscious of his tense embrace, absorbed in the intimate position, determined to enjoy it as long as the circumstance allowed. "When the boy disappeared in the trees I gave up and started back to the lodge. I intended only to explore the cave when I came upon it. There was no boy until he came out with the flurry of disturbed bats." To underline her last words, she placed her hands on Matt's embracing arm and leaned back to twist her face and meet his eyes. His attention was on the cave, a muscle pulsing in his jaw. She was puzzled at his concentration. She wanted to read his expression, no longer trusting the inflection of his voice.

Even as he listened for fabrications in her story, Matt knew it was the truth. Guarding his private life from curious dudes as he had for years was successful but the innocent involvement and genuine interest by a guest was a new and welcome feeling. The barrier he kept in place was his choice and no one have ever come close to invading his privacy. Now that Sarah had intruded or rather came inside that barrier he felt the flood gates of the desire for privacy breaking. A yearning swept through his heart to pour his life's secrets upon this solitary woman. She tugged at his heart, like none other ever had. He wanted to trust her, desperately wanted her to trust him, too. His arm braced her hands when she gripped him and his chin lowered to meet her cheek when she turned. Her clean feminine scent drifted to his senses, pleasantly restful compared to the cloying perfume worn by other women he encountered.

He was not immune to the fair sex but avoided entanglements, even minor associations with guests, because of the unfortunate experience that tore his family apart so many years ago. In his arms was a different kind of woman, causing him to waver. The horse impatiently stomped and tossed its mane, throwing Sarah hard against Matt and he stiffened in the saddle. His firm jaw pressed against her cheek, the corner of his mouth determined to protect her and simultaneously retain control of the rebelling horse. Under double weight the horse no longer responded meekly to Matt's uncertain hand or repressive knees.

Matt's arm came up tighter still against Sarah's breasts to balance his weight and hers, countering the prancing movements of the horse. His knees tightened, pressing his thighs closer to the horse, embracing Sarah's hips more tightly between his legs. His full attention was on the reality of her position. He was wrapped, arms and legs around her, and he thought of nothing else. His directive to the horse faltered, as his logic dissolved and all his senses responded to a primal urge.

Sarah was captive in his arms and he pressed his advantage. He wanted more than the embrace required to retain Sarah in the saddle in front of him. She could not escape. She couldn't even fight if she chose and he was immensely pleased when she made no move to resist. His heart swelled in triumph. His right hand cupped Sarah's head and he kissed the corner of her mouth. Stark still, he held his breath a moment, awaiting her response. Sensing no rejection, but cautious that her reticence came from the fear falling to the ground as she had once before, he lightly tucked a feathered kiss beyond the corner, again shyly concerned about refusal.

To his stirring surprise, Sarah brought her mouth fully to his.

He took it. Happily. Delightfully. Hungrily.

He could have devoured her completely, no questions asked. Matt clung to the saddle with the instinct of a professional rider, totally accepting his good fortune. For a thrilling moment, Sarah clung to his lips with the confidence of a circus performer doing a back flip on a great white stallion, her heart totally enjoying the performance. The horse was not in a circus. It felt overburdened and impatient to put an end to such dallying.

The big red horse felt a slack in the reins and seized the advantage. The bit was grasped between its teeth and it stretched triumphantly in a gallop toward the barn. The fantasy of rapture could not compete with Sarah's fear of riding and she broke the magic moment, curled her hands tightly on Matt's arm and hugged it securely to her stomach tense that disaster was in the making. Red came to an abrupt stop at the corral, where an expert kick of Matt's toe unlatched the gate and swung it open for their passage. Her heart beat did not settle down. What brought on that passion? The restless horse. Matt was trying to make some sense of her meeting with one of his boys and the horse almost humanly wouldn't stand for it. She was not surprised that an animal would put two and two together before she could.

He told her nothing more about '*The Singing Ranch*' or 'his boys' after his first statement. Sarah wondered after his objection, if she was ill advised to think of them as troubled. The conversations she overheard were most certainly troubling. What was she to think? The opportunity for questions passed.

Matt regained command of his wayward horse and directed it toward the lodge, turning into the path toward Sarah's room. For a person on foot, the maze of overhanging branches was a protective canopy, for horseback riders the outstretched limbs became giant rakes, threatening to sweep them to the ground.

Matt wrapped his body protectively around Sarah, a position he found intoxicating, one he would willingly become addicted to. With an outstretched hand he fended off the converging limbs. Sarah's heart beat wildly. Unlike the old memories stirred by Matt's body when she backed into him in the doorway, his enveloping body now inspired nothing but visions containing him in extended fantasies. The fact that he was a willing accomplice in her desire to keep the misadventure secret added a mellow depth to their conspiracy.

"I want to talk to you after dinner," he said, intent on getting Sarah to her room before her stocking foot was noticed, insistent on getting her out of his arms before he grew impossibly hard again. He stopped the horse at a secluded juncture of the path. He hesitated to remove his arm, which thrilled Sarah until she realized it was she who refused to let go. She released him, lowering her eyes to cover her culpability as he helped her dismount. She glanced up then, looking fully at his face. She saw no apologies, no explanations, no regrets. Expectations and questions crossed his features. A traitorous muscle convulsed along his jawline. She swayed unsteadily for a moment, found her land legs, then stepped aside.

"Report to Melanie," he ordered. He backed his reluctant mount and rode away.

Sarah did not understand what caused him to initiate that elusive kiss on horseback. She did not hesitate to affix a full hard kiss of her own, not thinking about the consequences. She hurried toward her room, floating in a romantic euphoria, reflecting on his request, his forceful statement, to talk to her after dinner. What did he want of her? Was this the onset of an affair? Her heart flipped at the thought of it, not without a passing reference to Lou's remark on frisky feelings.

The thought sent a thrilling jolt though her stomach.

Chapter Ten

Welcome to my world

A talk after dinner was what Sarah needed, although not entirely what she wanted. The revelation of Matt's boys at the hidden ranch was a new concept. She hoped for an explanation that would clear away the mystery, unsatisfied as she was with what little information she had. All she really knew about the dude ranch was what Lou showed her in the brochure, describing the ranch in general and guest activities in detail. There was not the slightest hint of anything out of the ordinary, certainly not sordid nor criminal and no mention of another ranch nearby. Unusual drama unfolded, nevertheless, at this ranch, unprecedented in any vacation. Her emotions, entangled as they were with Matt, entitled her to know more. At least she thought she deserved more information.

Management, competently handled by Steve and Melanie, held another aspect of mystery. The instant silent communication between them at dinner during the first strains of Sarah's favorite tune harbored a secret alarm they set quickly set aside in favor of harmony at the table. Did she remember an apprehension hovering there? She forgot to consider it in the ensuing coughing spasm that came over Matt at the time. It seemed absurd to have been caused by the strains of her song. Until Matt mentioned 'his boys' Sarah considered him one of the ranch hands, about the same as Buck, a step below Steve in authority. He apparently held another status in the community and now with his urgent stolen kiss, his status catapulted into new heights in her life as well.

Where that was going was something else. At the thought of the kiss she hugged her stomach and closed her eyes to recapture the feeling. Her heart fluttered like a teenager and she suddenly felt foolish. A teeny bopper she was not. And even when she was young she had not felt like this. Could nor recall ever feeling like this toward any man.

She was attracted to him at the first meeting, annoyed at his fun at her expense, thrilled at the attention he lavished on her. Exactly what those moments meant to him, she couldn't guess, although he was not shy about accepting her kiss. But the moments of intimacy meant more than a serendipitous pastime to her. To expect more may be a serious mistake, she thought, considering the drift of his attitudes. She remembered the scenes clearly. He displayed courtesy at her introduction, arrogance at her fears, anger at her questions, humor at her expense, persistence at her shortfalls, curiosity at her calamity.

And suddenly he kissed her.

The passion on his part was reticent, actually shy, to begin with, a gentle caress of a kiss, hardly more than a touch. His lips got braver and when they tugged the corner of her mouth she lost all common sense and seized the opportunity to taste him fully. He responded like one addicted, the craving intensified at her behest. He may have initiated it but she encouraged it. Looking back, she realized, she had demanded it. He did not begin with great amorous intentions, although she sensed his earlier teasing was a cover up for his shyness. She was at a loss to explain why he waited until riding double before he kissed her, an action

that might have resulted from the residue of his arousal at the
rocks. He didn't appear to be a passionate man, only volatile in
his reactions to some background spectacle he usually managed
to hide. In his previous actions she saw empathy toward animals,
concern for the workers, nothing of compassion. Maybe he saved
his compassion for his boys. His character was complex and the
baffling conglomeration left her confused.

She hurried to change into tidy clothing before she
encountered anyone. No one must see her messy blouse and dirty
jeans. She found a plastic bag on her bed in which to hide the
offending garments. Explaining the soiled and damaged clothing
to Matt was necessary. And as he suggested, she saw no need to
explain to anyone else.

She thought of the day-long ride undertaken by other guests
when she came out of her room and wondered if it was over.
Unusual activity emanated from the front of the lodge. Not all
the noise could be a result of her tardiness in spite of the concern
that Melanie expressed to Matt. Her absence would not have
created such a stir. Slamming doors and loud voices aroused her
curiosity. Through the trees beyond the flowers, she saw a car
that was not there earlier. Perhaps other guests arrived, although
she couldn't imagine where they would stay. All the rooms in
the guest cabins were filled with the people she knew. A car door
slammed as another car was added to the parking lot.

At first she hesitated, thinking she would be intruding, but
quickly shrugged that feeling away. The lodge was not a private
home. It was a public place, not only a rendezvous for guests
but a gathering for local citizens wanting day rides. She went
forward, slowly nevertheless, checking the waistband of her tan
cotton trousers, making sure the brown striped shirt was tucked
properly in place. As she approached the corner of the building,
she recognized the new arrival by the sheriff's logo splashed along
the side of the car. Too late she realized the uniformed man was
looking at her and she could not retreat. He did not wear a shiny
star to identify him as a real man of the law. His sand colored

uniform held a sharp crease, crisp and clean, tightly stretched across a firm belly protruding slightly over a wide brown belt with a large agate cabochon set in the silver buckle. The man took quick steps, coming up high on the balls of his feet with each one, making his head bob up and down in a motion causing his propulsion. His hands hung at his sides, fingers clenched and unclenched as they swung in time to each step.

Sarah stood her ground, waiting for the sheriff, if indeed he was the sheriff, to speak. He obliged her with a friendly, "Howdy, ma'am. Is your boss around?"

"I'm just a guest here," Sarah stammered, not wanting to admit she didn't know who the boss was. Matt called Melanie the boss lady. Matt bossed Buck. Steve bossed the trail rides. But Sarah didn't know who bossed the bosses.

"Sorry, ma'am. I never know what the kitchen help look like. I thought the guests was all out riding." He paused when he saw her pained expression to change his explanation.

"I talked to Melanie this morning. I'll go find her." He touched his hat brim, nodded slightly, bent excessively at the waist, and jerkily took the front steps with the intensity of a mountain climber.

Sarah turned back toward the kitchen. Her ultimate goal was to report to Melanie but since the sheriff was there, no doubt on more urgent business, she could wait. Riders who had been searching for her knew Sarah was safe so her report could be made later. She admonished herself for her carelessness and the inconvenience her time spent at the cave caused the ranch routine. She was frowning and shaking her head when Tad met her on the path to the storeroom. He welcomed her with a grin at first sight that melted away when he saw her frown.

"Is something wrong, Mrs Wilson? I didn't think for a minute you were lost, or that something bad happened to you. Are you all right?"

Sarah realized she must look wretchedly tired and shook her head. "No. No, I'm all right." She couldn't think of anything to say that wouldn't lead to relating her part in the bat cave adventure which she was determined not to discuss. She noticed Tad was on his way to the storeroom.

"Can I help you get something?" she asked.

"Yah, Babs needs more than I can carry in one load. I'd like some help," he agreed, hesitatingly, "but you're a guest. I don't suppose you should."

"Nonsense. Guests are supposed to help with the regular chores on this working ranch," she argued, and at his quick approval of her logic, nodded toward the storeroom with a wave of his open hand. She remained silent, letting Tad mentally check off the items he was to retrieve: several marked packages from the freezer, for tomorrow's breakfast and tonight's dessert, and a gallon can of peaches from the open shelves. He put those things in a plastic carrying carton and handed it to her.

"Think you can handle this? I've got to take a sack of potatoes."

Sarah took the carton easily and went to the door before he could have second thoughts. He came with a burlap sack of potatoes balanced on his shoulder, his longer strides taking him to the kitchen door before her.

Babs was not surprised to see Sarah entering with Tad. "Trust Tad to commandeer a helper," she chuckled, relieving Sarah of her load.

"You were out a long time on your walk. Melanie wanted to be sure you were okay. Were you sketching again?"

"I walked for a while, but -" she could truthfully say that much, "But I'm disappointed with my drawing. I'm not very good and I don't see any improvement."

"You ought to get Buck to help," Babs offered, unwrapping the rectangular freezer package to reveal a carrot spice cake.

"Buck already made some suggestions," Sarah said, surprised that he was mentioned, "but that doesn't make my drawings any better."

"I don't suppose he should do them for you." Babs chewed at her bottom lip, thoughtfully. "He could, you know. He's very good," Babs insisted, setting her lips in a thin line to emphasize her commitment to Buck's talent.

At seeing Sarah's surprise, Tad added, "He's shy about his talent. Matt doesn't encourage him much, so he won't show his stuff around."

"What's Ma..." Sarah started to ask what he had to do with Buck's talent when she saw Babs shoot a warning look at Tad. Curiosity about Matt Bannister wasn't allowed. She learned that earlier.

Sarah looked around the ceramic tiled counter and quickly repeated, "What's for snack?" Dinner was hours away and her walk used all her reserved energy. The cooking odors honed her appetite.

"Cream of broccoli soup in the deep cooker," Babs replied lightly, nodding at the covered container on the electric range, "and if you're really hungry I'll make a sandwich of roast beef, ham, or cheese - your choice."

"The soup sounds good, and a beef sandwich on wheat," she ordered, grinning comfortably at the transition to a safe subject.

"Can I eat it here in the kitchen? It's lonely by that big table." She nodded toward the dining room, and pretended timidity, not certain her request would be approved.

"Sure, Melanie would rather not be interrupted anyway. It's all right, if you don't mind eating at the breakfast bar with us."

Sarah didn't mind at all. The last thing she needed was to alienate Melanie any more than she already had. The boss lady was unapproachable as it was, leaving Sarah with a constant underlying feeling that she was intruding with any approach, no matter how guest-related her question might be. Sarah slipped on to a tall stool beside Tad, who was spooning soup into his mouth like a starving orphan. Babs carried two bowls of soup to the bar, placing one in front of Sarah. She put hers on the other side of Tad and sat down.

"I'm surprised you didn't go on the ride," Babs said, looking sideways at Sarah. "Everyone is always included at least part of the way on the first day long ride.

"Matt told Buck to encourage her to stay and draw," Tad said, crumbling a handful of soda crackers into his soup. "He said Sarah took a nasty spill off Ruby and ought to rest for the day."

Sarah looked sharply at Tad. Oddly, the accident referred to was her spill off the horse after watching the sunrise. No one was yet aware of her brush with Matt at the rocks. The best thing to do was not mention it at all. The bruises on her leg were not debilitating. Somehow the incident seemed unrelated to the dude ranch and she decided to hold back every bit of it.

It amazed her how the news of her earlier accident got worked over, at the breakfast table, in the barn, and now in the kitchen. But all she could say was, "Ruby? Is that the name of the red horse?"

"Yah, isn't that cool? The reddest horse on the ranch. Matt's favorite, too." Tad managed to spoon up the remainder of his soup between those revealing sentences.

"Tad, you talk too much," Babs warned, "Melanie wants those potatoes scrubbed and ready for the oven in an hour. You'd better get started."

Sarah's eyes remained on her soup and she continued to eat slowly and thoughtfully. The startling things she was hearing only raised more questions. Her intuition warned her to proceed with care, if she was going to pick up valuable details about the mysterious life of the big cowboy from these loyal workers. Melanie had closed off explanations to her and she didn't want to stumble foolishly and chance losing the opportunity to win Babs confidence. Matt yelled at her once and she was ready to overlook that after today's development. She was doubly careful not to act like a busybody again.

"You have a lovely kitchen to work in," Sarah said, looking at the large cooktop, double ovens and other electrical appliances interspersed on long counters of light green ceramic tiles.

"It was designed like a commercial restaurant especially for the lodge," Babs said, carrying the empty soup bowls to the dishwasher.

Tad went to work on the potatoes and Babs laid two slices of wheat bread on the counter by the refrigerator.

"Do you want a two slice sandwich?" Babs asked, "Or just one?"

"One is fine."

"Good. Then I'll have the other," Babs said as she proceeded to bring out butter, mayo and sliced beef and efficiently arrange them in order to prepare the promised sandwich.

Sarah's gaze wandered again over the kitchen appliances, noticing a movement of the swinging door that led to the dining area. It was hinged so it hid the incoming traffic from the breakfast bar and she couldn't see who was coming in. The sheriff entered the lodge and at least one other stranger had been there as well. Sarah tried to listen for an indication of what was going on beyond the kitchen but all she heard was a closing door and returning footsteps. She had no business being preoccupied about Melanie's visit with the sheriff. She felt like an intruder when Melanie walked into the kitchen, her features grim.

Sarah got up, "I'll leave."

"No. Finish your snack. It's no secret. The whole county knows by now," Melanie said, as she took a seat at the bar.

Sarah froze.

The whole county knows? Knows what? The vision of Matt describing her unclothed body in vivid blue panties flashed through her mind. He promised not to tell!

"Matt usually manages to keep his problems from the guests. This one got out of hand." Melanie must be referring to the sheriff's visit and was about Matt's boys, a subject more elusive than the bats. Sarah decided she could breathe again. She looked forward to talking with Matt about his problems tonight.

Around a mouthful of sandwich, Babs curiously asked, "Which one of his hopefuls is it this time?"

Babs was born and raised on a ranch near Idaho Falls. She heard antidotes of Matt Bannister's successes at *The Singing Ranch* most of her life. She did not have the opportunity to go to college and worked for years in hotel dining rooms and cafes. She enjoyed being a sou cook and waitress so when the opening occurred at the Bar X, she discussed her experience and her aspirations at length with Matt and Melanie and took her present job which she found both challenging and rewarding. Her attraction to Buck developed into passion they had not yet revealed. She recently heard Bucks concern about the two boys worrying Matt at the moment and remarked on his escalating problem.

"Don't be disrespectful!" Melanie sent a disproving glare at Babs' remark then dropped her eyes in apology, "It's not one of his at all. A young kid was dropped off and before Matt could figure out what to do with him, he disappeared." Babs and Tad stared at their lunch, knowing that much, expecting more details. Melanie stood up, unwilling or perhaps unable, to offer more. She looked down at the young people until they raised their attention from the unfinished snack.

"It's time to get to work on dinner preparations," Melanie said and she went into the office.

Sarah kept her eyelids lowered and concentrated on her own sandwich but forgot to eat. She left the kitchen and the sandwich behind. Matt usually kept his problems from the guests, Melanie said. Ongoing problems? Questions kept chasing through her mind, whirling around Matt, his association with growing boys, his boys on *The Singing Ranch*, and his run in with the sheriff. What kind of a man was he? He led too complex a life for her liking, whatever he was. She better rethink her attraction to that cowboy. She got up and left the kitchen by the back door to be out of Babs way and not delay dinner. She strolled toward the corral disturbed what she learned about Matt from Melanie. Dinner was some hours off and a chance to look beyond the buildings would give her the opportunity to think.

What was there to think about? Her mind was already in turmoil. The mysteries at the ranch did not make for a pleasant vacation but she was here and the stable soothed her nerves. What a change from her earlier feelings. She had never thought much about horses before. Now the scent of hay and horses were not only pleasing but just the diversion she was looking for. She felt removed from Matt. The open stalls reminded her of Red and the welcome she felt the moment she stepped into the dark interior the first day she arrived. Yet here in his domain her ambivalence returned. Perhaps she shouldn't meet him after dinner as he requested. But he did not make a request. He simply said he wanted to talk to her.

Wanted.

The tone she recalled was more of a command. She had the impression he got what he wanted. Did it matter what she wanted? At the moment she wasn't sure just what that was. She wondered if she could prevent herself from becoming involved. But her inner voice posed an impertinent question. Wasn't she already involved? He was attracted to her. But his subsequent hostility, and above all, his uncanny ability to arouse her own passions confused her. Sarah went to the corral looking for Red - Matt called the horse Ruby - when she remembered it was Ruby she and Matt had ridden from the cave. Tad said Matt favored the big red horse and he went to get, then had ridden off to continue his search for Eric.

She heard hoof beats and looked in the direction of the main trail. In a flurry of dust Buck and Pete came tearing over the rise, returning ahead of Steve and the guests. How quickly the soil turned to dust after the night's rain. Buck waved to Sarah before pulling his horse to a stop with a wry smile of triumph. He was two lengths ahead of Pete and dust flared up in big puffs around the stomping hooves.

"Aw, you cheated," Pete yelled, jumping off his horse and nearly running into the rail, "I coudda beat you easy if you hadn't got a head start."

"No, Pete, you couldn't. I didn't cheat. You're not a champion rider and that is no blue ribbon horse," Buck reasoned.

"You could only win if I let you. Would you be proud if I did that?"

"Course not," Pete grumbled.

"There's no shame in coming in second. You rode well and handled that horse as good as anyone," Buck said, as he let the girth out a couple of notches. "Loosen that girth and cool down our horses. And I'd like to have your help in brushing and feeding the other folks' mounts."

Pete's chest swelled with pride at Buck's request for assistance. The big cowboy understood the young man's needs very well. Sarah smiled, noting Matt wasn't the only ranch worker to discourage undesirable traits by instituting positive action, bringing out the best in the young man. She glowed with admiration.

Buck handed his reins to Pete and turned to Sarah, surprised and pleased by the high regard in her eyes. His two fingers touched his hat brim as he spoke, "Howdy, Sarah. How was your drawing session?"

"My drawing is hopeless. I couldn't do anything right." She was relieved at telling the whole truth for once, but she avoided looking at him. From the corner of her eye she watched him settle his hip against a rail and wondered if he was going to pursue a critical discussion.

Buck's gaze narrowed on the approaching riders when he spoke, "Got a congenial bunch this time. They got along real good. We'll have a nice safari into the forest." Sarah glanced up at him then, and he caught her eye, held it for a moment before he looked away.

"You coming along?" he asked. His nonchalance covering what was a loaded question. He hadn't figured out why Ruby became Sarah's horse.

"I don't want to but I suppose I'd better get into the dude ranch mode," she said, reluctance in her voice as well as her words.

"You ought to," he insisted, "if you expect to get your money's worth out of your vacation."

He didn't wait for a response. He wondered at the significance of Ruby's part in Sarah's day of leisure as he strode toward the returning riders to care for their horses. In the flurry of dust and excited riders, Sarah considered Buck's withdrawal unnecessarily hasty. She looked around to see what influenced his retreat but Matt was nowhere around. Buck's approval of the group's compatibility made Sarah rethink her opinion of the three-day ride into the national forest. No doubt she would enjoy being with the other guests. She agreed that they were easy to get along with. She could talk with Marianne for hours about the art in her gallery and she had only begun to tap the depth of knowledge Arlys possessed. She hadn't broached the subject of child raising with Jane. No one's personality grated against her own. It was the thought of a long tiresome ride that brought a twinge to her stomach. She clutched her fingers and joined Lou in the walk to their room.

Lou was dusty and tired but loudly talkative as usual, especially graphic about hours of sweaty riding, lunching among the rocks, uncovering scorpions, and constant pointers on riding skills. The very things that highlighted the exciting trip for Lou would be for Sarah uncomfortable, if not downright unpleasant. Buck was wrong about joining the safari to enjoy her vacation. What Lou described did not sound enjoyable at all.

"Are you going to tell me how your clothes got muddy? You promised," Lou reminded Sarah when they got to their room. Lou unbuttoned her shirt and cocked an expectant eye at Sarah.

"That big red horse stuck its foot in a hole and stumbled. I didn't know how to hang on so the sudden stop threw me."

"You got thrown from a horse?" Lou stared wide eyed but she didn't remain silent.

"No wonder you don't want to ride again. I wouldn't either. But your clothes were full of mud."

"It rained hard last night and the ground was wet. I just didn't have the good sense to pick a grassy spot."

"All the trails have been wide and solid. How did that horse find a hole?" Lou had a suspicious gleam in her eye.

"Matt went off the trail to pull the calf out of the mud and I couldn't keep my horse from following his. I tell you, Lou, I just can't handle a horse."

"You expect to learn everything in one ride? My dear, you're good, but not that good. Give it time. You'll see. You're going to fall in love with horseback riding. I just feel it in my bones." Lou was out the door before she finished the last sentence.

"Yeah, sure," Sarah called. She might fall in love with horseback riding if there were more episodes like the one this afternoon. There ought to be places more conducive to loving than the back of that big ruby red horse. She didn't mention the incidents that led up to that and felt a little guilty for not taking Lou into her confidence. But so much was made of her intentional rides with Matt, she grimaced to think of how much Lou would make of Matt catching her without her jeans on. It seemed more prudent to forget the boy at the hidden ranch as well as the bat cave. Matt didn't want it spoken of at any rate and Lou wasn't exactly tight lipped about anything she learned.

Sarah examined her injured leg through her cotton slacks while Lou was out. The bruised part of her thigh was tender but so far the muscle didn't ache so Sarah expected it to heal quickly like Matt suggested. It was one more good reason for her to insist on staying behind when the others went on the three day ride into the national forest. She wouldn't be able to describe her injury as the reason but that would make her more stubbornly persistent about wanting to improve her sketching. She left the room before Lou returned. A drink before dinner sounded like a handy form of medicine.

One by one the other guests drifted in and settled on a comfortable chair with a cool drink. Sarah listened to their refreshing comments about the afternoon ride. They were pleasantly weary but in good spirits with big appetites. The uncomfortable parts of the riding experience never came up during the animated talk at the dinner table. Everyone found humor and excitement in the ride.

"Weren't you scared going down that steep trail?"

"Didn't Sally nearly fall off?"

"Wasn't she looking for the deer?"

"Did you see the deer on the ridge?"

"What deer?"

"How could the trails be so dusty after last night's rain?"

"Wasn't my horse just the best?"

Sarah thought there was a little too much Mary Poppins in every one who sat around the table. They laughed lustily and ate heartily, appetites honed by the day-long ride. Split baked potatoes were heaped with sour cream and chives. Large mushrooms were rolled in thin roast beef and garnished with red cabbage and caraway that gave way to expressions of appreciations from all the guests. But Sarah had no appetite. She pushed her food around on her plate, listening to conversations about the ride, wishing the talk could include some insight that would lead to the solution to her dilemma. Matt's boy wasn't her problem. And Matt wouldn't be either. Unless she let him.

During a lull in the table talk, Lou called across the table, "Sarah, you'd have more of an appetite if you quit eating peanut butter sandwiches between meals."

"What are you talking about? I didn't." Sarah started to deny the accusation when she realized that Lou must have seen the blouse and jacket smeared with peanut butter and, being an avid between meal muncher herself, Lou jumped to her own conclusion. The heat of embarrassment crept up Sarah's face and no doubt she looked guilty to inquiring eyes around the table. Everyone believed Lou's accusation about snacking between meals and Sarah was amazed. Let them believe it. Then Lou would forget it. Sarah managed a weak, but slightly guilty, smile.

"Where did you get peanut butter?" Melanie asked. "We don't buy it. Nobody around here will eat it."

"It's my favorite," Terry admitted, proudly.

"Yah, she even spreads it on her Ninja pizzas," Pete scoffed.

"Matt has a fondness for it," Steve mused, offhandedly, his eyebrows crinkling a bit, wondering how there could be a connection between Matt's favorite peanut butter showing up on Sarah's blouse. He saw no relevance in either fact.

"Where is Matt anyway?" Ray asked, "He hasn't been properly bartending if you ask me. I had to make my own drink tonight."

Sarah was off the hook to defend herself. The spotlight that paused on her momentarily, passed on. She felt so relieved she put a forkful of beef into her mouth and actually enjoyed the succulent taste of it. Everyone was more interested in Matt's whereabouts and looked to Melanie to enlighten them. Sarah added her mumbles as she shook her head, encouraging the distraction, if possible.

"He had business in town," Melanie's excuse for Matt's absence sounded too pat to be thoughtful, one used quickly to put a stop to further inquiries. That was Melanie's specialty.

"He'll be back later, I'm sure." Melanie's fork clattered to the floor and she smoothly retrieved it, going into the kitchen briefly for a clean one. Table talk resumed in small groups while they finished eating. Sarah ate out of habit, as difficult as she found to concentrate on the taste. When Arlys and Sally refused dessert, Sarah did also, but as she stood, her muscle cramped and a piercing ache shot through her injured leg. She told Lou she was going to her room.

So far Matt had not returned. Her weariness was brought on by her confusion. She was excited at the prospect of seeing him and perplexed at her concern over his passion. His swing of moods was swift and radical. Her earlier excitement over the horseback kiss tapered off. Her eager response was foolhardy and brazen. Matt would have every right to consider her a presumptuous female and keep his distance. No matter how she castigated herself she didn't believe she was totally responsible, nor was she a frivolous wanton female. She felt abandoned and depressed. If he wanted to talk at this late hour he would have to come for her.

As she passed the kitchen, the door swung open and Matt stepped out. He tightened his mouth and glanced meaningfully at the side door that led to the guest cabins. She caught her breath and continued on favoring her leg. Without a word, he fell in step beside her until they were outside. He took her elbow and stopped her.

"Your leg was seriously injured. We'll have it x-rayed tomorrow." He looked her up and down.

"It's all right. Really. The bruise runs the full length. But I don't think it's serious." If heat was healing, the bruise would heal in minutes the way her body caught fire at his show of compassion.

Matt was not convinced. Judging from her limping gait, the injury was greater than she let on. He would have to look after her if she wouldn't do it for herself and it was not out of concern for ranch liability.

"Shall we sit in my truck?" he asked, indicating with an open outstretched hand the path they should take. Sarah followed his directive. He opened the passenger door and helped her in. The bench seat was smooth artificial leather she knew as naugahyde, a durable expensive covering for any furniture. Was it put on car seats? She had no idea. The interior was clean and well kept, not expected after the faded dusty look of the exterior. Some men were more meticulous about their vehicles than others. It had been her responsibility to clean the Wilson family car. But for her the interior probably would never been cleaned. The drive-through a carwash only cleaned the exterior. She turned to Matt with admiration.

He liked the glow he saw radiating from her sweet round face. Her very presence made him content and his mouth widened in a tight grin. The deep shadows hid Sarah's expression but he hoped he read compliance in the way she turned to wait for him to get into the driver's seat. He would have preferred a big smile on her face. He took a deep uncertain breath.

"I'd like to show you my place," he quietly announced when he was settled. A particular destination was not implied when he invited her to sit in the truck. Now it hung between them like a tangible thing. He did not move, his eyes and hands on the steering wheel. After a long pregnant moment, he slowly turned and peered at her in the reflected glow of the security light.

"Are you agreeable?" His voice was husky and uneven.

"I...I...guess so," Sarah answered, uncertain to what she had agreed, unable to identify a reason for his vacillating, unwilling to hope it was anything more than weariness.

"I thought you'd tell me about your boys." But the tone of his question implied more than an innocent tour of his place. Or a lengthy discourse on his boys. She sensed a promise of something else – going beyond the passion on horseback. And her pulse raced to match the throbbing engine as they proceeded away from the dude ranch yard.

Chapter Eleven

Put your head upon my pillow

Sarah sat in Matt's truck holding her breath. She could not relax on the soft naugahyde bench seat. Exciting tremors of expectation kept her on edge. Matt wanted to talk to her after dinner, he said, when he helped her off Ruby at the guest room. She floated in the afterglow of the passionate kiss they shared on the galloping runaway horse. She limped to her room not because of her leg injury but because she wore only one running shoe. The rough hard stones of the cobbled walk were harsh and daunting on her stocking foot, but did not dim her euphoria. She hurried to avoid being seen and consequently to answer for her lost walking shoe. It remained imprisoned in the rocks from which she pulled her bare leg. She feared her heart was becoming similarly imprisoned by the working ranch hand beside her, driving his aging battered truck skillfully over rutted back trails, taking her to his place.

Rational thinking was out of the question where he was concerned. A few hours of indifferent conversation and a succulent ranch dinner passed before she had time and privacy to do any serious thinking about him at all. And even then she found it difficult to settle her beating heart down to normal. Only when she insisted on reminding herself of his arrogance and his recurring laughter at her expense could she muster her contempt and view him without the silly schoolgirl tremors that otherwise overtook her. How could it be possible that she should be so affected at her age?

But she was. Her entire outlook about horses and riding underwent an immense reversal when she walked into the barn to find the source of a welcoming nicker in her first hours on the ranch. But the mind boggling change occurred when she encountered this man she now sat beside. His attitude, his personality touched her very core. His presence in the drug store could not have been more casual and the incident would not have unduly impressed her if Matt passed from her acquaintance. Instead he was a major figure on the vacation ranch. He was not only the first individual to welcome Sarah and Lou but, later in the doorway to her cabin, he became the first man ever to awaken dormant emotions that since racked her body and soul over and over again. She struggled to settle on mundane subjects to regain her sanity.

She looked at him and repeated her expectations, "You were going to tell me about your boys."

For long drawn out silence she wondered if he heard her. Or was he going to answer? He took a deep breath and over the orderly droning of the well-tuned engine Matt's story began to unfold. "As I told you, I have twenty boys. Only one is troubled by circumstances of his own making. That's Rusty, the one in the store."

"Was he shoplifting? Is that the trouble he's in?" Sarah began to make sense of the scene in the variety store. She knew he put a DVD in his pocket.

"That's the latest symptom. He is possessed with making money. But his trouble is much deeper, far more than we have resources to do anything about. He's a fourteen year old going on twenty nine. He comes up with unhealthy and unreasonable notions and tries very hard with occasional success to win the others over to his scheming."

"The others?" Sarah queried.

"The others are homeless. That is, they were homeless until they came to *The Singing Ranch*."

"What exactly is *The Singing Ranch*? An orphanage? I didn't think that kind of institution existed anymore." The idea was puzzling. The concept beyond her imagination.

"It's a working ranch where the boys learn responsibility, how to raise horses, train them, work cattle, practice whatever skills needed to be productive adults. Any craft they want to learn they are encouraged and trained. They learn to work with others and respect differences."

Sarah absorbed his description of the ranch, strange scenarios skittering through her mind. He was, indeed, filled with compassion for his boys. Not surprising there was little left for guests or strangers like herself. Where did Eric fit in? What was he running from? Why was he eluding Matt?

"How old are they? Eric doesn't look big enough or strong enough for ranch work."

"Eric is not one of my boys. He hitchhiked or was dropped off a few days ago. We don't know where he came from. Wherever it was he doesn't want to go back."

"That's what he told me." Sarah recalled the belligerence and determination with which Eric spit that bit of information at her when she surprised him in the kitchen.

"He ran away after he was told he couldn't stay at *The Singing Ranch*. I caught him in the barn and left him with the authorities to find out who he is and where he came from. He slipped away from them and the sheriff thinks I'm hiding him."

"I don't understand."

And she didn't see any reason for the sheriff's accusation, or the boy's desire to stay there, or for that matter, what he was running from. Why was he refused a stay at the ranch? Sarah had more questions than answers. Matt's hand reached toward her in the shadows of the moving truck and the action completely removed consideration of wayward boys from her mind.

"Understanding will take some time," he insisted softly, as he captured the hand she unerringly guided to his. The truck rattled over the cattle guard, the noise an ominous underlining for his words.

The simple statement held a great deal of promise and although Sarah slowly turned her palm to his, she couldn't comprehend the depth or breadth of all it implied. For over thirty years she was a one man woman. She stared into the distance where the headlights pierced the darkness with an unbending shaft of light and suspected history would read differently after a few hours spent at Matt's place. The truck headed down a steep incline. Slowly she tensed, staring with a creeping premonition at the tall trees illuminated by the bright headlights. They looked very much like those she admired just hours ago in her discovery of the hidden ranch. Tall trees everywhere would look similar with headlights shining on them, wouldn't they? The entire area looked suspiciously like the hidden ranch. Why did that bother her?

The closer the truck bounced along the gravel trail, the more familiar the trees became. The terrain leveled out and they proceeded through shadows among the mature trees and aging shrubs. Although this approach was opposite from the direction where she walked in, the shadowed yard and the advancing dog were familiar. When Matt brought the truck to a stop in front of the porch with the broken lattice, there was not a shadow of a doubt. It was the hidden ranch. He said he was taking her to his place. But why stop off here?

"This is your place?" The statement was a question, not reconciling the house with her concept of a ranch with twenty boys. In daylight or in darkness, this was where she'd found the boy in the kitchen.

"Yup. My place."

It was a positive statement made in a tone filled with pride and satisfaction. Matt shut off the motor and the lights. With his sinewy left arm he reached across Sarah to open the passenger door, bracing himself with his other elbow on the back of the seat behind them. She pushed against the seat to give him room. He hoped that's why she moved, that it wasn't a recoil from his proximity. He caught his breath and waited, puzzled at her hesitancy. Well, he didn't blame her for having second thoughts. He was more unsure of himself and what he was leading up to than he had been when he kissed her on horseback. What if she saw him for the ugly old man that he was?

"Have you changed your mind?" he asked quietly. "Do you want to see my place?"

Her face was so close he could feel her heat but she was looking toward his home so his question was directed to her profile. How sweet and pleasant it was to look at, this rosy cheeked face with bright and intelligent eyes. Her nose was straight and her cheeks round with little smile lines running like crazy rivulets into the corner of her eyes. Her cute little earlobes he longed to nip peeked out beneath her short gray hair that seemed to have a wavy phosphorescence in the faint interior light. She turned to face him and he saw her puzzling over the answer. He willed it to be affirmative, unwilling to want less, expecting a whole lot more.

"I was here this afternoon." The upturned inflection on the last words made it a question, suggesting a puzzle not an explanation.

"I know."

He pushed his hat back with his right hand, making his intentions clearer, at least making his eyes more visible and they were filled with promise. Matt's outstretched arm was almost touching her, although not nearly as closely as it did when they rode double on Ruby. His body twisted sideways and his face was so close, a more comfortable position for a passionate kiss. Could it be as good as the one on horseback? Sarah's breath was ragged and her gaze fell on the wild hairs of his sideburns, skittered along his jaw, sliding to his lips. Her breathless question surprised them both.

"Why did you have me ride Ruby?"

"What has that got to do with anything? My horse is at the ranch." He stiffened and a frown pinched his eyebrows together, making a straight dark bushy line below his otherwise smooth forehead.

"Then the mare really is 'your' horse?"

"Yes?" He gave an answer and asked a question in one short syllable.

"Nobody rides her but you?"

"You do."

The line of conversation made less and less sense, so distracting when he had more intimate plans beyond talk.

"I'm beginning to realize that is very unusual. Tell me about it."

Matt's hand fell to Sarah's shoulder urging her to get out of the truck. When she resisted, he said, "Ruby called you into the barn and you almost jumped aboard the first hour you were on the ranch. How could you expect me to do otherwise but saddle her for you and teach you to ride?"

He scooted towards her with little pushy movements and began to crowd her off the seat toward the open door.

"C'mon, it's comfortable in my place. I can tell you about it."

He would if he could find the right words to explain his feelings. He couldn't explain them to himself and lord knows he'd tried a dozen times in the past two days.

It was either slip out gracefully without stepping on the dog or get pushed out. Sarah clutched at the door handle to steady herself but Matt's arm came around her back, his hand under her arm and they slipped off the seat together, landing on the ground linked as one. He released her quickly, before she could protest. She felt a loss when he dropped his arm. She cast a surprised look at him that he skillfully avoided returning by concentrating on the truck door. The limping black dog was not to be ignored. It sniffed at Sarah, accepting her without protest, his tail a welcoming flag. Matt's legs were surrounded by a deliriously devoted animal, weaving and wagging its body around a revered master with trusting canine homage.

"Nobody here but us friends, right, Fella?" Matt ruffled the ears of the old dog as he lovingly untangled the animal from his legs. It had only been this past year that the dog had taken to waiting at the house for him. For years Fella had been his constant companion, frolicking with him from ranch to ranch, or running beside Ruby or riding with him in the pickup.

Matt took Sarah by the elbow and led her up the steps and across the porch, mindful of her injured leg. He snapped a switch inside the front room door, hung his worn hat on the wooden peg above it, and watched her intently, considering how she would adapt, really fit, into his refuge. He watched her looking at the austere furnishings as if she had never seen them. He knew she had and worried just a bit. Living with him would take some getting used to, no doubt about it, but...if she was willing.

"Where do you put twenty boys?" She didn't think there was an upstairs. From what she saw this afternoon, only a couple lived here. Matt was not married, she knew that much, but the facts regarding his living arrangements were as nonexistent as the details of his boys. She viewed the scene differently than when she passed through it twice before. The room did belong to him. She could envision him in the rocker reading in the lamplight, relaxing after a day's ride.

"I didn't say I'd take you to *The Singing Ranch*."

He could see how she might have been misled into thinking it was, in light of his obsession with Rusty and Eric. It wasn't the lives of the boys he wanted her to accept. The pattern for the boys' future was well established and controlled by professionals. It was in his own life where he was groping for a different purpose.

"This is my place," Matt repeated, turning inquisitive eyes fully to her face, realizing for the first time that she had not known that. Now that she did, he awaited her reaction, hoping it would not be negative. This was his domain, his only escape, where he could withdraw from his problems and strum his guitar to renew his fortitude to meet each coming day.

"It's what you called The Hidden Ranch," he reminded her, remembering how wistfully she had described her visit there when he held her on his horse after he found her at the cave.

"I thought a couple lived here. When Eric dropped the pans in the kitchen I ran through expecting to administer CPR, thinking someone collapsed from a stroke or heart attack."

She looked toward the kitchen, and her gaze ricocheted from one item to another that had led her to believe the place was shared. The furnishings appealed to her in a restful way for which she had no words. She would have been delighted to accept an invitation to sit that afternoon and enjoy a cool glass of lemonade and a friendly conversation. Eric spoiled that. But then the house had otherwise been empty. She couldn't reveal those intimate thoughts. She explained the confrontation with Eric to Matt before and couldn't think of anything else to add.

"I live here. Alone. At the end of my day, I sleep here. Alone."

Sarah's gaze flashed to his face and pinned his eyes for an inquiring moment. His meaning was more than a statement of fact. It was issued with an intimacy she couldn't mistake. She dropped her eyes before her own desire leaked out and gave her emotions away. She remained introspective and silent, unsure of what to do. Unsure of what she wanted to do. Unsure of the reason for his statement.

"Won't you sit down, at least?"

He trembled in fear of the refusal in her silence but he wasn't going to give up easily. His sweeping hand indicated the overstuffed chair and the rocker, leaving the choice of seating to her. Sarah settled in the chair, puzzling over the new information.

Matt read her baffled expression and pulled the rocker closer to her. He lowered himself warily as he cleared his throat.

"I bought this homestead a long time ago," he began, sighing heavily as he leaned forward with stiff arms braced against his knees, his shoulders hunching up around his neck in the process. So he wasn't simply a ranch hand on the dude ranch after all, Sarah thought. That didn't make much of an impact on her impression of his persona, or modify the pleasure she found in examining his rough features. He apparently was a real ranch hand and on his own ranch at that.

She listened as he continued. "I lived in Tennessee and decided to go west. You know, I might have been influenced by Horace Greeley's advise to young men." He paused, with a negative shake of his head. "No, it was more than that. I didn't want to go west so much as I wanted to get out of the east."

Sarah's eyebrows went up expecting a revelation. She didn't have to say a word, it was obvious he was going to explain.

" I was married. I had a son" he hesitated, groping for words he hadn't used in years. He looked into Sarah's eyes with an outward steadiness he didn't have inside. He had to put some finality on that part of his life.

"It fell apart...my life back then...they left...I drank...I had to find some other place."

He was so wrapped up in memories he read the message in Sarah's eyes as sympathy and pity. Not the kind of emotion he yearned to inspire. He dropped his chin and his gaze as well, his head receding further into the hunched shoulders, creating the image of a most dejected and unhappy man.

"I'm s..." Sarah was sympathetic. Life in her neighborhood was full of tragedy, fortunately hers was not, and she didn't think that her being sorry for his past was appropriate. She saw nothing in his present circumstance to be pitied. If that was what he was fishing for, he could forget it.

"You were successful in your move, then?" she probed, not unkindly.

"I did turn my life around," he admitted as he took a deep breath and straightened his backbone.

The details were not important now. Sarah liked his song, the rendition that made his fortune and brought his downfall, or rather, stopped his rise to fame. He was a successful cowboy singer - too successful. The honor and money went to his young head in a big way. Almost before he knew what happened he lost his wife and became a failure as a father. He couldn't say those things to Sarah. Not yet. She was too fresh an acquaintance, her acceptance untested. He loved her already and that scared the hell out of him. He wanted her approval. He thought of revealing his folly. No. He wanted her admiration for himself as a person, not as a famous singer. Could he ever win her love?

"But I didn't bring you here for a history lesson."

What an understatement that was. He relaxed his arms and dropped his hands loosely in his lap.

That was precisely why Sarah came. To get some history. So far he had explained parts that didn't seem important in the overall scheme of things, which was their personal relationship. For all his masterful ability to be in charge, he was groping for an explanation. Was he going to come right out and bluntly tell her why he did bring her here, if not for history? His story? She was too attracted to him to turn aside and walk away. She had to know more about his mixed up life. She wanted to believe that the disturbing things she found out about him were misconceptions, as some of them had already proved to be.

The sheriff's role was now clear, although apparently he was not entirely satisfied with Matt's denial of harboring the runaway. Eric's outcry in the barn took on a different, less ominous, meaning. Nothing abusive there after all. Matt's inability to control what Melanie spoke of on the phone was clearer, too, as Sarah remembered his desperation over Eric's escape. She sensed his desire to change the course of his history as well as hers. She was no more able to play some childish mating game than he was so it was up to her to press the point.

"Then why?"

"I want you to help me locate Eric."

Sarah stiffened in shock. That wasn't what she read in his eyes moments ago. What was his problem? She leaned attentively forward, agreeing with the concept. She would help him in any way. He had but to ask, but in this, not believing it was within her capability.

"How can I do that?"

She was all too willing to help Matt with anything. How could she not be interested in every aspect? his boys, his life, his sleeping arrangement? She was openly receptive to his explanation. How could she help?

"In your wandering today, you ran into him twice. That's more than I've been able to do in two days on horseback. I searched the cave and found no sign that he lives in it. I'd like you to see if you can find some indication of what he uses for a hideout."

"Of course, I'll do everything I can. But how can I find something you can't?"

She accepted his challenge to search for Eric. It held the prospect of a deeper understanding of him, which was the real goal of her involvement, her desire to remain close.

"I don't know if you can."

His tone was wrought with hopelessness. He was downhearted and discouraged. He clamped his eyes shut for a moment. Then he opened them with a startling shot, pinning her eyes with an extraordinarily intense gaze. She wanted to drown in those deep brown mysterious depths. She was drawn toward him, sensing his hunger, his desire, his passion. She tugged at his emotions, willing him to release them upon her, devour her, if that was his wish. What happened to her intent to remain alone and unattached? Where was her resolve? Why had she ever thought up such an impossible resolution?

"What I really want is..."

His eyes darkened with longing, "I mean, the boy is important, but..."

His passion had been rejuvenated since he met her and emotions dredged up for which he no longer had the right words. Silent communication was just as inadequate but that was all he could muster. He could say no more.

Sarah delved into his eyes with her own to verify what she wanted to see. His message opened a receptive shutter in her heart. It was a message Sarah understood with the undisputed clarity of a keen lens, as if she stopped in time to form a lasting picture when that message was received. She caught her breath and her features brightened. A fleeting ray of hope flashed across Matt's features. He recognized her gasp to be the enthusiastic jolt of expectant passion, the thought obviously as exhilarating to her as it was to him. His forehead beaded with perspiration. He waited with his heart in his throat.

"There's no doubt I like being with you," Sarah admitted. And as her stomach quickened with desire, she thought, I like the idea of being with you all the way. She worried at his hesitation. She leaned forward to encourage a response. How could she not lead him on when she was sure of her desire? Is that what he was waiting for?

"If I thought it possible."

Matt dropped his face in his big strong hands. So close was he that his hair nearly brushed her cheek. He was the picture of hopeless despair. She reached out to stroke his hair back from his pale smooth forehead. At her touch, his head snapped up to search her eyes. He should show more enthusiasm if he read her mind as she often thought he did. Was Matt hoping against hope that she wanted him as much as he wanted her?

Sarah put her hands lightly on his knees, smiling with encouragement, eyes bright with affirmation. His hands dropped to cover hers. The curious pleading expression in his deep brown eyes exploded in thrilling joy when he recognized his hope fulfilled.

"Will you?"

His eyes widened to verify her submission and the air was still and intense between them. He saw the message in her eyes at the sunrise. He took on her eager solicitation of a deepened kiss on horseback. Did she know how much he really wanted? He grasped her hands and stood, pulling her up with him. She was far from naive. Sarah turned her palms to his, squeezing his hands with a tugging motion. Her hands went around his neck, his arms around her waist and they coalesced full length, hard and passionate, for an immeasurable moment before separating just enough to look into each other's eyes.

It was so right, like the thrilling kiss on horseback. She pressed for more. From chest to knees she thrust forward. He felt her urgency and so badly wanted to match it with his own.

"I'm not sure how good I..." Matt waited.

"It's been a long time." Sarah hedged.

"We'll never know unless.."

His hands scurried over her shoulders, her spine, her hips. She felt so good. She felt so right. With tender hands and exploring fingers, he worshiped every curve.

"I like it already."

She breathed raggedly, her fingers combing through his hair, rubbing his neck, undoing the knot in his neckerchief, freeing buttons on his shirt, testing the springiness of his chest hairs, leaning into him nose first, nuzzling at his nipples.

"God, I do too."

He moaned, pulling her tighter against his length, pleased that his manhood made a proud impression against her pelvis. Oh, this felt so good. Now all he had to do was follow through. He took her face in his hands and she raised her eyes to his. Hope and promise traded owners. He took her hand firmly, her palm to his, with great and glorious purpose. She accepted his grip with strength and acquiescence, in equal partnership

He led her to a room she had not seen, to a bed where he had slept alone, to an act each experienced with a different mate, to a joy neither dreamed possible.

First touches were tenuous, full of adoration, yet some trepidation, failure always a possibility. Fingers danced on sensitive areas, hands brushed away fears.

Braver movements in hidden creases built higher expectations and brought sweeter rewards. Bolder caresses established a firm foundation that sought a warmer moister destination.

Two fully mature, fully experienced adults, became as lost in each other as completely as Alice was lost in wonderland. With their separate desires, individual longings, they carried each other to unbelievably fantastic heights of ecstasy.

Each hook undone, opened another area of flesh begging for exploration. The challenge was met with vigor, with heated passionate breathlessness.

Neither had lost their touch, nor their awareness. Each was eager to shed the other's clothes, fondling the skin uncovered with every garment. Their yearning overtook them with fervor.

Precociously they joined. The union was perfect, no residue of a past lingered. They found themselves in sublime heights to which neither had gone before. Their lips fused once more before they stiffened in mutual climax.

Neither body had been too old or too out of practice after all.

Sarah's future took on a different direction, a different purpose, a different meaning. A hope of solid companionship and loving replaced the void she felt before. She was fulfilled and cuddled against him in appreciation. Matt's outlook improved with passion spent and he found courage to face his future head on. The brightness of it drew him forward. Now problems ceased to exist. What a woman she was! He hugged her tighter and grew hard.

And they reveled in a second consummation.

A long time later, they parted, dressed, and faced each other with renewed respect and understanding. Neither spoke of love. All had been said with the most primal act of devotion ever shared by man and woman, an act of love in which articulation had no place.

Matt wrapped his arms around Sarah and held her tight, burying his nose in her hair. Maybe the breath she felt was a heated thank you. Those were the words she breathed against his shoulder.

In silence and mutual sensitivity, they returned to the dude ranch, hands entwined, thoughts racing, intentions clear.

Sarah was beyond thinking. Reciprocal love. What a glorious reality.

Chapter Twelve

Oh, jealous heart

When Sarah crept into her room, her eyes adjusted easily to the shadows in reflected glow of the security light and she made her way to bed. Lou was lying on her back with her knees up, her most favored sleeping position. Sarah laid down quickly, fully clothed, and listened to Lou's measured breathing.

"You can turn on the light, Sarah. You should undress." Lou spoke quietly, her words dripping with sarcasm.

When Sarah held her tongue, Lou asked, "Are you already in a state of undress, or too exhausted from your night of passion?"

Sarah gasped in surprise at the disgust in Lou's voice. She had no idea what time it was. Just very late. All that time she hadn't given Lou a minute's thought.

"I couldn't call you," she apologized. "He has no phone."

Lou's covers flew back and her feet hit the floor. Sarah could see her hands on her hips in the familiar belligerent stance.

"Oh, Melanie told us Matt was taking care of you so I knew where you were."

"Then why are you so angry? I'm free, white and over twenty one - and so is he."

What continued to be so incredible to her was the heights of ecstasy to which she soared under Matt's ministrations. Her age, nor his, it seemed, was no barrier to exciting physical satisfaction. She felt no guilt, only deepest fulfillment.

"Dammit, Sarah, I thought you were injured and scared of horses. I was worried about you. That's how dumb I was. All this time, here you are, secretly horsing around with the big boss."

Sarah jerked upright and stared at Lou.

"You won't have to feign illness to avoid the safari tomorrow," Lou revealed, relaxing her body but continuing the scathing sarcasm, "The safari is postponed because of trail damage in the National Forest. You're free to horse around another day."

Reprieve from riding wasn't an exhilarating thought for Sarah. Lou's accusations stung deeply, not only because Sarah had lost Lou's trust, but because Sarah saw how incriminating her actions looked. What was Lou talking about? She was obsessed with creating a passion between Sarah and Matt. A passion that turned out to be all too true. Incredibly, the impressions Lou formed were caused by Matt's description of her muddy fall, his concern allowing her subsequent absence from the ride, Lou's conclusions about subdued conversations she'd witnessed between Sarah and Matt, and Lou's own fantasy built around Matt's mysterious motive for the sunrise ride.

Sarah avoided rides for her own reasons and her spare time was not spent with her best friend. Was Lou envious of the pleasure Sarah enjoyed elsewhere? Sarah did not set up meetings with Matt. Nevertheless she was glad when they happened. The meetings were serendipitous and too often for Lou to believe they were accidental. What Lou had seen so clearly was obscured to Sarah because she was the focus of the action, not an observer. She did not think to confide in Lou because she was too close to the vortex to expect eminent disaster, which Lou foresaw with unerring intuition, or with overriding jealousy. Lou looked for a release of her friskiness, as well. No telling where her indiscretion would lead. Sarah sat on the edge of the bed, wrapping the bedspread around her shoulders.

"Lou, what is this about the big boss? But you better let me tell you the whole story."

The pinkness of the dawn sky roused the geese, turning on their incessant chattering by the time Sarah completed her description of the episode in the hidden ranch kitchen, her discovery of Eric at the bat cave, and her narrow escape in the rocks. She glossed over the warmest moments that lay like live coals in memory. Memories to be rekindled by Matt alone. She had returned to the scene with him after dinner, explaining that Matt wanted her to describe Eric's raid in the kitchen and the direction he took when running off.

"That must have been some story, to have taken all night to run through." Lou remarked. She squinted an eye and tilted her head in a most skeptical expression.

"Well, there were times when the discussion only referred to Matt's boys indirectly. He's very concerned.."

"And you consoled him? Right?" Lou's innuendo was very clear.

Sarah's cheeks turned a pink brighter than the sunrise. She stifled a stammered denial. He was downhearted. When he finished articulating his hopelessness he expunged his residual despair in her receptive body. The recalled pleasure swept through her like wildfire through dried prairie grasses. How could she explain something like that?

"I do sympathize with him, Lou. What's wrong with that?"

"Nothing at all, my dear, nothing at all. All this time I thought I was fabricating hanky panky to create excitement. You had us all fooled. You know that?"

"I wasn't hiding anything. The boy was on another ranch and Matt asked me not to mention him. He didn't want to pique the curiosity of all these strangers."

"Given your propensity for solitary roaming and determined refusal to ride, you were mysterious," Lou surmised, "and with your infatuation of cowboys I should have known you'd get the hots for him if he gave you a little encouragement."

"I was attracted to him from the beginning," Sarah admitted, "I can't help but be thrilled that he is attracted to me, too."

Lou shook her head in disbelief. She sucked in a breath of contemplation and leaned toward Sarah, "Oh, I don't doubt he's attracted to you."

"Is that so impossible?" Sarah did not doubt it before. Matt sent signs of his attraction unmistakably, several times on that first day. They were too blatant for her to be mistaken. She didn't understand Lou's disbelief when the evidence was so strong.

Lou let out an exasperated gust of air. "Any thing's possible, I suppose, but did you bother to look at it from his side? He saw your goo goo eyes a mile away and decided make the most of it. Think about it."

"Oh, yes, I did think of it. I took your advice and played the part of the cowboy's sweetheart."

She flung Lou's suggestion of the part back at her indignant friend. That remembrance did little to cover the doubt that reared like a cobra's hood to poison her in the aftermath of an exquisite union.

"We're paying guests, Sarah, our registration fees pay his bills. Each one is important in that respect and don't you forget it."

How could she face that if it were true? She added to the farce building in her mind.

"You said so yourself. Have a role in this vacation adventure. I got into the act. I know it will go nowhere."

Sarah's voice was low and surprisingly calm, considering the horrifying way her stomach twisted at the thought. Her heart thundered a denial. Her part had long since ceased to be a contrived role for her, yet the possibility of Matt's perception otherwise was disturbing, horrifyingly so. Had she been so receptive to a movie-like cowboy's advances that she merely read what she wanted in his desires? Lou could be right. She dated more men than Sarah did, and obviously was far less trusting. Men were known to accept what was willingly offered. Society seemed to expect them to be lustful and Matt had years to perfect his seduction. He made a pathetic plea for her capitulation and she insisted on yielding.

How gullible she was! Sarah's aching heart could not concede to such a travesty. He was tremendous in bed but he affected her deepest core many times in more innocent circumstances. But she ruefully admitted she didn't know how to read him.

"If it's an act, he's very good," she conceded, "I still want to believe he's sincere."

"I suppose he could be. The cowboys wondered what was going on when you showed up on Matt's horse."

"He saddled it for me that first day when you told him we wanted to ride."

"That's what made them suspicious. Nobody else ever got to ride that red mare, mostly because it never let anyone get on except the big boss."

"Just what do you mean by 'big boss'?" Sarah's forehead took on the furrows of a harrowed field.

"You know, designer, director, perpetrator, head honcho."

"Do you mean Matt's the owner?" Sarah spread her open hands in a wide circle to indicate everything in sight.

"That's exactly what I mean."

"I thought he was one of the cowboys. He's got a little homestead down by the river. That's where we were tonight."

"From what Tad says, Matt owns half the county. Got a boy's ranch where we're going to a rodeo tomorrow." Lou squinted at the window, reassessing her announcement in the dawn. "I guess it's today."

"I didn't know he was the big boss." Sarah lay back on her bed, stunned to think of the implication Lou brought up about being used. The possibility seemed more plausible than ever given his wealth and manipulative position that gave him.

Matt's motive for attention seemed innocent enough when he asked her to the hidden ranch, although her feelings toward him were ambiguous before she faced his despair and read the passion in his eyes. Everything about him, his concern for the boys, his attention to her, his austere home, everything she saw or felt wrapped around her heart and bound her to him. True, an uneasiness about the developing relationship lurked in the back of her consciousness. But that turned into a innocuous detour sign as she moved forward, a signal her life was taking a new road. She wrapped herself in the knobby bedspread and contemplated Lou's admonition. Since discovering he had a more lofty occupation than cowhand and owner of a modest ranch, her uneasiness resurfaced.

"He told me he had twenty boys at *The Singing Ranch.*"

Sarah wouldn't use the expression 'troubled' for those she hadn't seen, but Matt mentioned two that were headed for trouble. He was trying to control their actions and help them. What he could do to help wasn't clear to her but he had a strength of purpose and a unique insight into young people's minds.

"I don't think they are ordinary paying dudes like us. Kids doing wilderness training, more likely. We'll get a look for ourselves at the rodeo. Steve's taking us over in the van."

"I'm going to get some rest before breakfast. My leg throbs like the dickens. I guess the bruising was worse than I thought."

The bruise on her psyche was too awful to contemplate. The few hours sleep did not bring much relief to Sarah's aching body. Her dreams kept the passion that burned between Matt and her intensely vivid and left her spirit vitally energized. She managed in her fantasy to block out suspicious motives in Matt's display of passion, successfully blotting out Lou's accusation. But as much as she refused to let it niggle at her mind and put a damper on the euphoria she experienced, in full daylight it lay exposed for her examination.

When Sarah thought of Matt as merely a cowhand he held the thrilling appeal of an accomplice in a movie plot. His image as the big boss, rich landowner, important public figure, scared her beyond description. How could a man of that stature come on so strong to a stranger, a widow unexpectedly filling in a guest list, unless he was out for a quick seduction?

Could he have an honest need for her affection? Could he have the same uncontrollable desire for her that she felt for him? She held to the positive gut feeling. She desperately wanted it to be true. Nothing in his loving touches revealed hypocrisy on his part. She was thoroughly submerged in ecstasy, enjoying his tender, fierce loving. Nowhere in her subconsciousness did she detect the slightest hint of falseness in his touches. Could he be such an experienced lover that he could fake all that passion on a body he did not love?

Sarah admitted she had no such experience, neither in identifying feigned stroking or crooned intimacies, nor in employing false ones of her own. She could not believe Matt had duped her. She simply did not want to believe such a travesty. And yet, the man's life was so different from her own. Oddly, she hadn't thought so before. Why did the concept of wealth change his image? Matt did not appear at the breakfast table or at any time during the leisure hours before the buffet luncheon. Sarah was caught up in the excitement of the coming rodeo. Steve advised the guests to wear hats for protection from the midday sun and take light jackets in case the weather cooled before the rodeo ended. They should use sun screen or otherwise protect themselves from the long exposure to the sun.

All twelve guests climbed into the large passenger van, a two-toned gray vehicle, otherwise unmarked and unpretentious. There were seat belts and space for three people in each of three bench seats that did not reach the full width of the van, allowing for easy passage into the full width bench seat at the rear, which could hold four passengers if needed. Steve put Terry in the front seat beside him and channeled Pete into the rear seat near his parents. He was aware of the need to separate the siblings. He let the other guests choose their own seats.

"We'll have snacks and drinks available all afternoon," he announced, "We want you to have a pleasant time."

The trip was a short one, *The Singing Ranch* being only seven miles away by paved roads. They could have ridden a shorter distance across the hills but the trail was a dusty one and *The Singing Ranch* had no accommodations for guest cleanup. They would be better spectators if they didn't endure a horseback ride beforehand. Steve started a canned speech about *The Singing Ranch*. A built in amplifier carried his voice throughout the van.

"The boys are between the ages of sixteen and twenty, all learning about ranching and especially the raising and training of horses."

Sarah almost blurted out a contradiction. Matt said Rusty was fourteen. Maybe she had misunderstood. She held her tongue. Steve drove carefully, his eyes slipping from the road to the rear view mirror to monitor the interest in his description. He opened the way for questions. Pete piped up immediately with the question the adults were too polite to ask.

"Are they prisoners? Is it a reformatory?"

"No." Steve answered unequivocally. He could never answer that the way his heart wanted to, because he was most successfully reformed. It was a reformatory in the sense that it reformed the broken lives of the ones lucky enough to get there. It was a hospital, healing injured minds, curing invisible ailments. Completely opposite of a prison it was a haven, a new beginning for boys on the brink of manhood. He had been encouraged and succeeded in making a respectable life for himself.

"No. It's more like a foster home - like the old concept of the orphanage. State agencies place their wards with adults who will guide them but when they reach age sixteen, foster parents won't accept them as children, sometimes agreeing to the adoption to use the boys for labor. Boys at that age feel too much like adults to take council from strangers and do not easily adjust to a foster home."

Sarah didn't understand the mechanics of it, but she had an insight about the guidance *The Singing Ranch* provided from Matt's description of the work done there. Her appreciation of Matt increased knowing he was somehow responsible for its existence. A void in her knowledge about the actual development of the concept was as wide as the open range. She suspected the founding was rooted in the past of the mysterious man whose emotions were entangled with hers, real or feigned. Once again she looked toward Lou and silently refused to believe Matt would use her for sexual gratification. He had stature and resources to buy that service. Jealousy pierced her breast at the thought. Sarah missed the next question but forced herself to listen to Steve's answer.

"The boys enjoy the thrill of competitions. The timing of each event is serious and meticulously kept. The boys work the hardest to break their own records. To compete in front of a cheering audience is the most fun. That's where you come in." He paused for their reaction before making his suggestion.

"I hope you'll cheer like crazy. It's a public acknowledgment, like a reward. Accolades for the tedious work they do every day. The horses you ride were bred, born and trained right there on *The Singing Ranch*."

Terry heard Matt tell her parents that before. She asked, "Why is it called *The Singing Ranch*? What's to sing? Not the horses?" That was a question burning in Sarah's mind as well. Somehow amid last night's more interesting developments, she forgot to bring it up. A folk guitar stood in Matt's front room. She strained forward to hear if it held any significance.

"The boys work hard and need relaxing activities that direct their interests in a healthy outlet. Music fits that because of its versatility. They learn to play instruments or sing. Because various ensembles played for the public, the music program was expanded and locally it became known as *The Singing Ranch*. That was favored by the boys so it stuck and was eventually registered that way."

The van slowed and the motion pressed Sarah against the seat. A high white board gate blocked the road. A tumbling row of music notes amid silhouettes of romping horses adorned an overhead sign. The playful symbols evoked excitement and promise. Ray grabbed the handle of the sliding side door of the van, volunteering to open the gate before Steve brought the vehicle to a complete stop. White rimmed corrals and barns lay in dips and rolls of the high desert surroundings. The extent of the ranch was not visible from the entrance.

Trees, tall and stately, low and spreading, were everywhere, making a lush oasis. Sarah noted a different layout of the buildings than she found at the Bar X, although construction of the structures themselves bore a similarity. She saw no resemblance to Matt's place except for the profusion of greenery that cooled the area and soothed the mind. The largest structure had an upper story on the center section, two single story wings reached out from either side. Steve quickly told them that was off limits to outsiders, it contained living quarters for the boys and adult supervisors.

"You will find refreshments in the smaller low building toward the corrals. You can take them to drink while watching the action from the bleachers. The heat can be oppressive towards noon. One of the boys will come around with items if you need more."

Steve continued to point out that most of the area was devoted to corrals, barns, both walled and open. He indicated the arena with an exposed tier of wooden benches for spectators. Cars filled a parking area. The rodeo was an event sought by others in the community from other states and even Canada.

Steve drove past the public parking and stopped the van behind one of the adjoining barns, with the suggestion they leave their jackets in the van. "I'll leave it unlocked so you can retrieve them if you want. Go on and be ready to enjoy the action."

He thought it unlikely they would need a jacket unless they all stayed beyond sundown. That had happened in the past. Sarah took Lou's arm and walked toward the building pointed out by Steve on the way in. She wasn't as anxious to get something to drink as she was to explore what buildings she could on *The Singing Ranch*.

Sarah gathered every bit of information to fit together in the puzzle of Matt and his boys. Perhaps she could find some clue as to how he started a project of this proportion. Why had he started it at all? Somewhere, somehow, she hoped to unearth a key to his character, to verify that he was the decent loving man she desired. She pulled Lou into the refreshment building.

"What sounds good to you?" she asked as they looked over the selection of soda pop and sparkling water.

"Where's the beer?"

"That's not allowed here, Lou. The boys are not yet legal drinking age. Besides, we want to enjoy the show."

"I can hoot louder with a beer under my belt. Won't the cheering help the boys put on a better show?"

Sarah couldn't answer that. She had never been to a rodeo but she was here to do more than be a spectator, as much as she looked forward to cheering at the boys' accomplishments. She was looking for reasons to put Matt out of her heart or, perhaps, clasp him closer, as she really wanted to do. The low building looked to be one long room with assorted soft drink dispensers on a wide counter at one end. She chose a large paper cup and filled it with lemonade.

"I have a cup full of caffeine here, my dear, and I'm ready to holler. Are you coming or not?" Lou frowned at the absent look on Sarah's face and followed her gaze around the room.

"Go on, Lou, I'll be along in a few minutes. I want to look at that."

Sarah took in the museum quality of the remainder of the room. Display boards diagonally supported at three foot intervals against the end wall stood like small parking slots. She sipped her drink and went for a closer look. Black and white photographs and text paragraphs in a professional arrangement led her through what appeared to be a visual history of *The Singing Ranch*.

The first panel showed a large corral of horses, with construction equipment tearing into the sage covered land. She studied the date and quickly calculated it was twenty five years back. Matt hadn't said exactly when, but he bought his place a long time ago and she wondered if it had been around the same time as he built *The Singing Ranch*. The men and machines in the pictures were shown working on various stages in the construction process and with the progression of time photos of completed structures appeared. The display told Sarah that *The Singing Ranch* was well planned and patiently developed to its present state.

One panel was devoted to action pictures of bronc and bull riding champions with information about their records. There was no indication of the men's origin or their relationship to *The Singing Ranch*, although names were included. Steve's name was one she found familiar. Matt's was not there, nor was Buck's, although that probably wasn't his real name anyway. The build and dress of the men were so similar she gave up trying to find either man among the winners. Many men were shown repeated winners at rodeos in the western United States and Canada. Sarah had no idea there were so many awarding competitions. The concept did not strike her as a lifelong profession and she wondered what the men did between times, especially if they did not earn the winner's money.

The door of the building continually opened and closed with the passage of the people choosing drinks and snacks. At one time her peripheral vision revealed Rusty putting his arms through straps attached to a tray of drinks. He was one of the boys delivering refreshments to the bleachers. She remained engrossed in her search of the history boards. Sarah did find Matt in pictures on another panel standing with horses labeled with impressive titles. She pulled a ridiculous expression with her set chin when she imitated a haughty straitlaced madam and read:

Periwinkle out of Standby Lightly. Buckle Up out of Charisma Queen.

She remembered Steve mentioning the horses raised on *The Singing Ranch* and chuckled at the outrageous names of studs and dams that those horses boasted for parents. An acquaintance from Boston came to mind who bragged endlessly of his lineage to Miles Standish. At least the ranch horses demonstrated their bloodlines in successful service to people. No verbal bragging for them. That thought reminded Sarah of the rodeo action she was missing. She could hear Lou's voice the moment she stepped out the door. The thumping and yelling from the corral indicated that an exciting event was in progress. She tossed her empty cup into a trash bin and hurried to the bleachers.

"Yah hoo! Do you believe that? He stayed on twenty seconds and that's one mean horse!" Tad yelled to be heard above the cheering when one of Matt's boys was helped off the ground.

Tad slipped through the railing and ran to congratulate the young bronc rider, supporting him as he limped back to the chutes where other boys were waiting their turns in the contest. Sarah felt the excitement of the crowd but couldn't see a whole lot of glamor in being jerked and tormented on the back of a horse or bull just to receive accolades when thrown into the churned dust of the corral.

Matt's boys challenged each other's riding and roping skills in a series of fast moving, dangerous looking events. They must practice for these events by the looks of the success they managed to achieve. Training to cope with the spontaneous actions of the wild looking broncos took stamina and courage. Sarah could imagine the challenge was more exciting when witnessed by a noisy audience. Every guest yelled, groaned, or teased the participating boys in good clean fun. And she was no exception. She cheered until she was hoarse. Her leg began to stiffen and pained her as she sat on the wooden plank of the bleachers at *The Singing Ranch*. She was glad they were driven to the rodeo in the dude ranch van. She overheard the alternative was to ride horseback over the distance and she wouldn't enjoy doing that.

Sarah couldn't have ridden that far anyway. Her leg hurt worse after sitting on the bench than it did when she went to bed. She was not surprised. How could she expect roll in bed with a virile male without ramifications beyond the normal emotional delight? That didn't strike Sarah as a difficulty at the time.

Now she was depressed over her culpability. Despair struck when she confronted the possibility of Matt's deception. That was a different, more devastating pain. His love and attention renewed sexual longings she thought were burned away with age and physical abilities she thought were impossible to revitalize. And the thought that they were not, lifted her spirits. But had she entered into an empty brief affair? When she accepted Matt's invitation it was with no doubts, no misgivings. Then the union itself was reward enough. Now she wanted more. Despair came with the awareness that there was nothing more. Lou made her painfully face the sordid possibility. In her future, the act of lust was no substitute for trusted companionship and devotion.

She got up from the plank seat, a bit wobbly, and made her way to the solid earth at the bottom of the bleachers. Her throat was sore from cheering and she coughed dryly. Rusty was nowhere in sight so she went to get her own cool drink. No one took notice as she went between the barns. All eyes were riveted to a brilliantly colored shirt jerking on a lanky figure who clung one-handedly to a fishtailing black horse that suddenly stiffened its legs and hopped like a pogo stick around the perimeter of the corral. She didn't have to be clairvoyant to know the outcome. She screwed her face in distaste at the imagined impact and hurried away

Only a few hundred feet from the bleachers to the building where a cool drink waited, the distance seemed interminably long, her leg completely stressed. She walked along the tree covered path around the parking lot. Other spectators felt the same discomfort on the hard benches and walked to get refreshments.

She leaned against the wall inside the door and closed her eyes the moment she entered. She knew there was no place to sit in the building but she was thirsty. She could rest again on the bleachers. She stiffened at a sudden voice.

"Sarah. Sarah, honey? Do my eyes deceive me?"

A strangely familiar voice caught her attention. She opened her eyes in surprise at the man who stood before her.

"Bill. What are you doing here?"

Sarah reached for the hand of the top salesman in the company from which she retired. He was well groomed, suave, rotund, and gregarious. He was expensively dressed in a very western looking suit that disguised his overweight in a debonair manner. He looked successful, rich and excessively excited to see her. He touched her extended hand briefly but refused to be satisfied with an impersonal handshake. He enveloped her in his arms and hugged her tightly. He smelled richly of cologne and cigarette smoke. That and the surprise nearly choked Sarah.

She was pleasantly reminded of her past by someone she knew for years from work that she hugged him and laughed. Her head was forced back and she looked beyond Bill into the hardened eyes of last night's lover. In a flash of honesty she saw his disapproval. The reunion with the salesman, a casual acquaintance, angered him. She was stunned.

"Sarah, honey," Bill said, as he grinned and stepped back with an arm remaining loosely around her waist, "I want you to meet Matt Bannister. He's one fine man. Got a dandy spread." When in Rome - an expert salesman reverted to what he thought was the local language.

Sarah's body went cold.

Matt watched with characteristic coolness, all expression masked.

"We've met," he said with a curt nod.

"Well, of course you have," Bill went smoothly on, understanding that a wealthy rancher would not be overwhelmed by an introduction to a retired reprographics worker, no matter how pleased Bill was at seeing a familiar face. He continued his inane gregarious pitch, saying so many words, imparting so little substance.

"I take it you came to the rodeo, did you? Mr Bannister had me on a dandy tour of his operation. We've got some business to discuss. I'll call you later. You'll excuse us won't you, honey?" He removed his arm from Sarah and turned ingratiatingly to Matt, "Can I get you a drink, sir?" His open gesture indicated the counter.

"No, thanks, but please help yourself," Matt nodded, "We'll move on when you're ready."

He invited Bill to get his own drink in such a commanding way the salesman accepted his directive in an act of subservience. He moved obediently to get something for himself.

Matt made no move. He was still facing Sarah and taking in her actions, angered at the greeting he saw, mistaking it for deeper affection than it was, jealous that she could be so happy at seeing another man. His eyes roamed her figure.

Sarah had not recovered from the initial shock of Matt's response to the intimate greeting of the salesman. She was not surprised that Matt was angry. It seemed to be his first reaction every time they met. This was the first she faced him knowing he was the wealthy owner and she stared, wondering why he looked no different. Yet her own arrogance swelled. She felt different. She was no longer a guest at a ranch where he worked. She saw him through Lou's discerning eyes. She was a dollar sign in his register, a paying guest he went all out to please, a willing subject for his lust. Her gaze flitted to Bill and back to him, measuring, judging, choosing.

Matt was not only physically taller, but more appealing and many times more desirable than the man she had just hugged. Matt inwardly recoiled at the disappointment he saw in Sarah's features when she compared Bill's suit to his. He hadn't put on such an expensive suit since he left Nashville and he wouldn't again. Not for any woman. He turned away from her with that thought, dipping his chin and touching his hat brim. He joined Bill at the counter.

Sarah's eyes burned to withhold her tears. She had to get away from him. She stepped outside and closed the door behind her. She had no strength or desire to return to the bleachers. There was no energy left to cheer at the events in the corral. She made her way toward the van. Solitude might restore some sanity to her mind. The van was the logical place to get her weight off her hip and knee. Her joints never gave her any trouble before and a little rest was what they needed now to revitalize. She better make her body comfortable. There would never be relief from the torment in her mind.

The van was in the cool shade. It was unlocked and no one was around. She could lie down and rest. She cleared the jackets off the rear bench seat, tossing them over the back of the next seat. She stretched out almost full length across the width of the van. She laid on her left side, her offending leg resting comfortably on top of the other. What a comfort that was. While she relaxed she threw one of the light jackets over her legs, and before long, another over her shoulders. With the comfort of her position, she could no longer shut out the discomfort in her thoughts.

Memories of the night before assailed her. She fought Lou's view of Matt's willful seduction and deceit. With every recall she was thrilled anew to think of sharing Matt's bed.

When she first saw him, he was the perfect cowboy hero. When they were entwined in bed, he was the perfect lover. He made every cell in her body come alive in a way she had never dreamed could happen after the vigor of youth was gone. She responded with her own hands and body in ways that inspired him to further adventures and he was as pleased with her as she was with him.

Their compatibility went beyond comprehension, their satisfaction pure delight. Those were the sensations she felt then and she stubbornly held to the certainty she were not her imagination.

She drifted in the luxury of sweet recall.

Chapter Thirteen

Ole Chisholm trail

Sarah felt a humming reverberating through the memory of passion. She smiled and kept her eyes closed to hold on to thoughts of Matt, their shared passion. She pressed the memories to her breast. So precious they were and she relived every moment.

She recalled his bed, his ranch – his place he called it when he invited her to come with him. It was the hidden ranch. She happened upon it by accident the day before. The building where she went in and found Eric. A boy that wasn't his boy. A boy he must find for the boy's sake. A boy he thought she could find for him. A boy the sheriff was certain Matt was hiding. She knew better. The humming lulled her and she held fiercely to those passionate moments.

She moved her leg and remembered she was laying in the back bench seat of the van. She tired of the rodeo and went to rest in the van. She laid down on the back seat of the van, parked in the shade. Her body needed rest.

Her thoughts kept her mind restless. She must sort out her feelings toward Matt. No. Sorting was not necessary. Her feelings were well established. She loved his tall muscular body. She adored his angular jaws. She admired his dedication to the boys. She respected his civic determination. Lou was wrong. Lou's accusations that she was being used for sex because she was handy and willing. Matt was a wealthy man. She was shocked to find that he owned the ranch, that he was not a ranch hand. Their loving took place between a dude and a ranch hand. How could that change when she was a paying guest and he was the wealthy owner? They were still the same people.

Matt told her he loved her, told her he needed her. She believed him. Lou insisted she was being duped by the big boss. Sarah would not accept that. She tried to shake the humming from her thoughts. She blinked and opened her eyes. And suddenly she realized what the humming was. The van was moving. The engine was running and the tires were humming and the van was moving along a smooth highway. She rubbed her eyes.

Oh how deeply she had slept. Steve was taking them back to the lodge and she tried to raise her head. The vehicle swayed and forced her back against the bench seat. Looking over the seats for an instant told her that no one filled the other seats. Well someone was driving. New technology was advanced but not to the point that the vehicle was directed by radar like some toy cars she knew about.

"I don't like it," a voice yelled. Sarah thought it sounded like Eric. He couldn't be driving. He was too short to reach the gas peddle. Then who? She could only hear a mumbled reply. She strained to listen. She dared not raise her head too high in fear of being seen. Obviously someone took the van and Eric was along for the ride.

"I don't care. It isn't right." Eric yelled again. Sarah stiffened and held her breath.

"Oh don't be a baby. The old man won't even know we're going for a ride. We'll be back before he misses the van."

Sarah couldn't hear any more but she had a sinking feeling the voice was Rusty's. Matt knew the boy was trouble and was watching him but apparently not close enough. Matt was trusting. Rusty was selling snacks in the bleachers in full sight of an audience and the ranch administrators. Matt was also engrossed in the ranching business, too deeply concentrating on economics to keep an eye on any kid, no matter how important the individual might be. Or the consequences.

Why the ride? Was Eric's only objection that it was not right to drive the van without permission? Or had Rusty given some other reason for their plight? Sarah cringed with a sudden fear. She had a miserable feeling that Rusty had a secret, and had let Eric in on the secret, at least a part of it. Sarah closed her eyes and wrinkled her face in denial. Could the fourteen year old be even a worse character than Matt believed?

She knew the boys did not suspect they had a passenger. What could she do? She had to remain unseen. But for how long? And what would she do when discovered? The boys talked in tones she could not hear. They weren't arguing of that she was certain so Rusty must have convinced Eric of his ability to put things right. Matt said Rusty was a schemer and could talk others into actions or at least thoughts that coincided with his best interests. Sarah wondered what those were. Matt said Rusty obsessed about money. Did he intend to sell the van?

Her thoughts went back to Matt. He had a huge burden in running the ranch – ranches - she amended, now that she knew the full scope of his holdings and the expectations of civic leaders. He trusted Steve and Melanie to handle the dude ranch operation and with Buck and others they did a superb job. He was deeply disappointed that Eric had not been found. Well she found him. Another accidental meeting, not quite like the others.

Had Rusty helped to hide him? How did he find him otherwise? And what were they up to? Sarah knew Rusty was crafty. She saw him shoplifting expertly in the store while Lou was getting antacid remedy in the small town before they arrived at the dude ranch. Sarah remembered Matt sent Rusty away from the veranda when Lou parked by the lodge. Those were the only glimpses she had of the red head until she saw him in the bleachers selling snacks. This minute he was in the driver's seat taking the ranch vehicle away. To where? She would have to wait and see. Momentum drew her forward and she braced against the back of the forward bench seat. The van was slowing down and turning. It stopped. She could smell gasoline.

"You stay here while I fill the tank," Rusty ordered and he was out and slammed the car door.

"But I gotta pee," Eric informed him and Sarah heard a second door slam.

Sarah raised her head slowly. A Chevron station. She looked for another identifying title. No town name that she could see. A flashing sign boasted 'Breakfast Anytime' and she remembered The Coffee Cup. Could this be the same town where Lou had stopped for antacid pills? She leaned back and scanned what sky she could see through the van windows hoping to see the water tower she thought of as a spider hovering over its prey when they first saw the town.

Rusty talked to the station attendant and she dared to raise her head higher. A pain stabbed her thigh like a knife. Her leg was stiff and the slightest movement hurt like nothing she'd ever felt before. Her predicament was worse than ever. She dropped her hand to the floor in despair searching for her bag. Her cell phone was in there somewhere. Would she be able to activate it and get a call off without Rusty's knowledge?

Sarah had better well try. Who to call? She didn't have Matt's number. But she did have the lodge. She talked to someone there a few days before she left home. Now searched for the number and punched it. She heard footsteps alongside the van and pulled a jacket over her head. She breathed slowly and very shallow. The phone rang. Could she whisper a message? She knew if Rusty looked in the window he would see the bench seat. She hoped it looked like a heap of jackets. Babs answered and Sarah had to do something so the phone didn't get hung up. She put her lips against the phone and whispered.

"Call the police. Rusty and Eric stole the van."

Silence. Was Babs thinking this was a crank call? Why didn't she speak up? Sarah heard liquid running into the tank below her. She took a chance that Rusty was too busy working the hose and she whispered louder.

"Babs, call the police. Tell Melanie." Sarah began to panic. What if Babs didn't believe her?

The gas stopped running into the tank. The handle clinked on the pump. Rusty replaced the gas tank cover. She heard him walk away.

"Babs do you hear me? This is Sarah. I'm in the van with Rusty and Eric. He stopped to get gas. He is taking Eric somewhere the kid doesn't want to go. Tell Melanie, call Matt. Do something."

"Sarah you're scaring me. What can I tell them? Where are you?"

"I don't know. I think it's the little town where I bought the CD and Lou got antacid pills. I don't know its name. Hurry."

Rusty yelled at Eric to get back in the van. She snapped the phone closed and held her breath.

Rusty opened the door and she felt the van wobble under his weight when he stepped inside. The van shook and settled down when both doors were shut.

"Here, I got us some candy bars."

"Where'd you get money?"

"Never mind. Just pick the ones you want. We still got a ways to go."

"Where are we going?"

Eric was asking more questions but Rusty wasted no time in starting the engine and Sarah heard nothing more. She didn't think Rusty bothered to answer Eric. Or maybe his mouth was full of candy. She was forced back against the seat as Rusty accelerated and they were once more moving on the highway.

Did Babs understand what was happening? Would she tell Melanie right away? Where was Melanie? Why didn't Melanie answer the phone? Would she call Steve? Or Buck? Somebody? Anybody?

Sarah slowly moved the jacket away from her face. Why didn't she make her presence known? Why didn't she confront Rusty? Was she so dulled from sleep that she never once thought about it? No, she only thought of Eric. He was here. In a way he was safe from the horrors he hid from. Should she let them know she was here? What could she do? Her leg ached and she gritted her teeth.

Think. She must think. If they were going beyond the small town Lou passed through to get to the ranch then they must be heading for the city where Lou met her at the airport. She tried to think how long it would take to get into the city. Would the van be reported stolen in time for state police to apprehend them? Would the van be reported stolen?

Babs called Buck when she couldn't find Melanie right away. Even then minutes passed before Buck was called to the phone at *The Singing Ranch*. He and Steve informed the local sheriff and the state patrol of the theft. They puzzled over the situation while Steve punched Matt's number in his cell phone. He was passed on to voice mail and left the message to come to the ranch office.

"I parked the van among the trees behind the machine shed so it would be in the shade. I left it unlocked like always when parking on the ranch but I have the keys."

"I put Rusty to work in the bleachers. He's careful about handling money. I didn't think anything of it when he didn't come for another tray of snacks. Do you suppose Rusty knows how to hot wire?"

"The counselors haven't plumbed all Rusty's secrets. Matt's working on getting him into the State Center. The paper work isn't completed yet. We all agree Rusty doesn't belong here." Both men had grim faces at the prospect.

The sun lost its intensity as it leaned toward the western horizon but the heat it engendered sunk deep into the desert

hills and living things sweltered from it. Pigeons lined the edges
of the bleacher roof to watch and wonder over the wild romping
going on in the arena. Doves looked like beads strung on the
wires between the buildings. They were startled into flight when
the crowd roared, flurried for a moment, then settled back with
eyes on the people watching the dusty action in the big open
space of the arena.

A ride was rewarded by an appreciative audience as cheering
burst from the arena. A collective groan followed. Not entirely
successful when condolences were expressed like that.

"I guess Tad didn't make it that time," Buck said in
sympathy. The boys were taught how to curl and roll off quickly
when thrown. Consequently few bones were broken. Bruises
were something else. Buck earned his share. He never rode in
competition but he was not immune to a bucking horse. Always
climbed back on. Where else would his nickname come from?

"That's what this rodeo is all about, isn't it? Even in his failure
he won. Matt had that right. Every male has to prove himself."

Matt came across the ranch yard at a slow jog, a very fast
walk. His grim expression indicating something very serious was
up.

"It's Rusty. He took the van," Steve announced immediately.

"Are you sure? When? Where is he now?"

"Somewhere south of Marion from what Babs said."

"Babs? How did she find out? Didn't you know the van was
missing?" The information exchange was rapid but the details
were unclear. Matt scowled with impatience.

"Start from the beginning and tell me what you know," he
demanded.

So Buck filled him in about the call Babs got and what she
relayed to him. The source of the information was Sarah and at
that revelation Matt's long muscular body went cold. He gripped
his craggy chin with a his hand on his mouth in deep despair.
His eyes narrowed. His thoughts churned at some unseen
implication.

"Why was Sarah in the van? Did Rusty kidnap her?" Oh god, he thought, if she's in danger.

"Babs didn't say. Sarah was whispering and was hard to understand. They were at a Chevron station. Sarah saw the Coffee Cup and thought that was the same town where Lou stopped at the variety store. We figured it was Marion. That would be the main highway for a getaway."

Matt puzzled over the lack of details. How could Eric be with Rusty? Frantically he thought of a dozen scenarios. All put Sarah in danger. None answered his real concern.

"Sarah said Rusty was taking Eric some place that he didn't want to go. Sarah's anxiety came through pretty clear so Babs called over here since Melanie wasn't right handy."

"So what did you tell the authorities?" Matt's eyes glared at Steve.

"The van was missing and being driven by a red headed underage kid."

"And Eric was being taken somewhere he didn't want to go." Matt repeated the message Sarah had whispered. How did Rusty get a hold of him? Was he with Sarah and Rusty took them both?

"Well Babs and I talked about it and she was sure the boys didn't know Sarah was in the van. We couldn't figure out how that could be. It was obvious to Babs that Sarah didn't want to be overheard."

An awful thought occurred to Matt. "Do you think Rusty might have a gun?"

"I suppose he could have but Babs thought Sarah was more concerned about remaining undetected. She couldn't figure out why Sarah's voice was so muffled."

"Could Sarah have been in that bench seat in the rear? Resting? I could tell her leg injury was bothering her when I saw her leave the bleachers. Maybe she even fell asleep when the boys got in the van. Everyone left their jackets knowing how warm it would be watching the action."

Matt interrupted them. "When did you call the sheriff?"

Buck pulled his watch from his vest pocket and scratched his temple as he calculated the time. "About forty five minutes, maybe longer." He did not pay attention to the exact time he spoke to Babs and got the first message. Then he conferred with Steve who made the call.

Matt took out his cell phone and moved away from Buck and Steve mumbling about touching base with the sheriff. Buck contemplated Matt's reaction and cast a meaningful look at Steve.

"I don't think the van is his biggest concern, do you?" Buck chewed at his bottom lip and took off his hat to wipe at the sweat gathered under the brim. He glanced at the lowering sun with the hope of relief from the heat.

"Not by a long shot," Steve agreed, "Melanie doesn't like it - what she sees going on with Sarah but Matt keeps getting her involved. You know if the van isn't apprehended before the kid gets into Idaho Falls..." he did not want to imagine what would happen then.

Matt returned to ask, "What's left on the arena schedule?"

"Calf roping and barrel racing after the last bucking horse. Be another hour at least before we get our guests back to the lodge for their supper." Steve's job was to look after the dudes, a job he thoroughly enjoyed. He would tell them about the van and they would be indignant and do what they could to help.

"Most of those folks will be happy to ride the few miles back to the lodge after sitting in the arena all day." Matt had ridden Ruby over earlier and he knew his mare would welcome a hard ride back.

"That's what I figured. We won't need another large van." Steve agreed.

"Buck you handle the buyers. They already made their bids on our stock. Those folks won't leave till sunset." Matt was tying up loose ends. No way was he going to sit around waiting.

"I'll have the papers ready," Buck acknowledged and the big men shook on it.

"Ruby's saddled and waiting. I'll ride back to the lodge. Be gone before you're finished here." Matt raised his cell phone and nodded in a reminder of how to keep in touch. He settled his sweaty Stetson firmly on his head and dashed toward the corral to get his horse.

Sarah rubbed her thigh, flinching at the pressure. Her eyes burned from the flashing lights of the State Patrol cars blocking the van and a big Cadillac. Rusty was pulled from the driver's seat unceremoniously and rather rudely handcuffed. Eric was taken from the passenger seat by a young officer who spoke quietly and lead him to a patrol car. Sarah came out through the sliding door on the right side of the van. The officers appeared to know her and their questions were directed to her.

"I'm Sarah Wilson and this van is the property of the Bar X Dude Ranch." The information she offered was received with nods from the patrol men.

"Yes, Mrs Wilson, we want to verify who you are for the record."

Rusty was shocked that she had been in the rear seat the whole time. He was angry enough to boil when he found out she was responsible for the police. He would kill her if he got the chance.

"Rusty is only fourteen and has no license to drive." she explained to the officer who took charge, a tall, broad shouldered, authoritative man without a hair over half an inch long, Sarah quickly noted as he raised his uniformed cap to her when they met.

"What have you done with Eric? He has nothing to do with the theft." Sarah wanted to be sure Matt would get the boy.

"He is being taken to Mr Bannister. He has special plans for the boy. And don't you worry Mrs Wilson, the boy will be well cared for. We're aware of the man's reputation, don't ya know?"

"I didn't steal anything. We was just out riding," Rusty said, sounding very innocent, struggling with the handcuffs.

"You are being taken into custody for your safety, young man, we have explicit orders." remarked the officer holding Rusty's right arm. He was being hustled into a car marked as a State Patrol.

Whose orders, Sarah wondered? Matt of course. Her message to Babs got through, filtered to Buck, Steve, and ultimately to Matt. Where was he? Sitting behind his desk at the ranch issuing orders? She didn't want to ask for her orders. The officers apparently knew what to do with every one else. What did Matt order for her? Sarah didn't know what to expect. She didn't want to sit still so she forged ahead.

"Shall I drive the van to the ranch?"

"No ma'am, your sheriff will return you to the Bar X Lodge shortly. We have some forms to fill and then you can be on your way."

Sarah recognized the man who mistook her for a kitchen helper days ago, approaching between the cars in the barren parking lot. She looked around and saw nothing familiar to her. Surrounding trees and houses were obscured in the deep onset of dusk. The area looked something like a truck inspection lot but no buildings were in sight. She smiled at 'her sheriff' knowing he would not recognize her but relieved that she would be driven back to the ranch soon. There was nearly a week left of her vacation. Lou was surely going to broadcast her role as a hero for all to hear. And berate her again for consoling the big boss. Sarah still had to argue about her movie role as sweetheart of the head honcho in the crazy mix up she'd made of her life.

When she was led to the sheriff's car she wondered about the tan colored Cadillac that stood off to the side. The interior was dark and she saw silhouettes of two men and knew they spoke to the state patrol beforehand. She put them out of her mind. All she could think of was Matt and what happened between them the night before. Or two nights before? She lost track of time, what with Lou's tirade about worrying where she was. She did not intend to stay out so late but she wanted to know about Matt's boys. Lou implied that Sarah comforted him far more than was called for. Lou would never know how far that comfort went.

Their coming together meant something to her. Was it possible Matt was only using her because she was handy? Was sex part of the service extended to the clients? Her shoulders slumped and she felt desolate. She buckled into the passenger seat beside her sheriff.

"Are you all right, Mrs Wilson? Matt said your injury was more severe than you thought at the time. None of the activities since then helped it I'm sure. Want to lay the seat back and rest? Sorry I don't have a pillow."

Oh if you only knew, Sarah thought. She slept all the way to the lodge wrapped in her light jacket and the warmth of the police car.

Matt waited in the motel suite for the case worker to look through her records. She graciously came at his request to work out a plan for Eric. He had been mistreated, a fact unknown to her until confronted by the boy.

"So what do you have in mind, Mr Bannister? I removed him from the abusive foster parents. Are you accepting him at your ranch?"

"No, *The Singing Ranch* is for boys sixteen and older. They are no longer required to go to school as Eric is. He needs a stable home with a couple who want him for the boy that he is and nothing else."

"I take it you have a couple you would like us to investigate for adoption. Is that correct?" The case worker was hopeful. The boy was a bright child whose psychological profile indicated he would respond to a decent and caring home.

"Must he stay in some strange halfway house during the investigation?"

"Can you offer a better solution?"

"There is room at my ranch in the lodge."

"Is the couple you've recommended nearby?"

"They are my guests as well."

"I left Eric in police custody until I met with you. Here is authorization for his release to your ranch. When I spoke with him it was his dearest wish. I made it clear he would not be able to stay permanently so further explanation is up to you."

Matt took the paper and thanked her. When he closed the door behind her he was guardedly optimistic. The investigation would not take long. And he was reasonably certain of the outcome.

Rusty was something else. There were other obstacles with that young man which would take more time to resolve. He must put that off until tomorrow. Matt called the lodge and left instructions with Steve. He removed his clothes and slid between cool clean sheets. He marveled that Sarah managed to be in the right place at the right time. She was in danger while the van was in motion with Rusty at the wheel. No telling how he would react in an emergency. They could all have been killed. Matt was relieved that Sarah was back in her cabin at the Bar X, although she still may be in danger.

One man from the porno ring had escaped. The other was identified as the kidnapper of a two year old that Rusty scouted for him a few months before being accepted at *The Singing Ranch*. What a bazaar this twenty four hours today had been. Could he put the activities out of his mind? Tonight he wanted peaceful rest. He put his mind to sweeter things.

Chapter Fourteen

Oh, bury me not

Sarah's expectations of Lou's take on her adventure in the van were correct. Sarah was the heroine, whisked away by a bad guy, dared to call the authorities, arrived at the lodge with a police escort.

"C'mon Lou, the sheriff isn't exactly a police escort. He lives around here too so it wasn't anything special."

"Sarah, you're too modest. You did a brave thing to sneak a call to the lodge. What if Rusty had a gun or been a bad driver? You could've been killed." Sarah thought of that herself.

"And your injured leg. Did you ever see a doctor about it? No course not. You went to Dr Bannister and he kissed it all better."

Sarah rolled her eyes.

"Lou will you stop it. I laid down on the back seat of the van to rest. I covered up with a couple of jackets so I wouldn't get chilled. My leg was injured at the bat cave. My muscles were stressed by standing around in the museum before the rodeo. In the bleachers I stamped and yelled a lot for those boys on the broncos. I was all worn out. So I fell asleep. I wish you wouldn't make so much of it."

"Well OK. But it's exciting and you are a celebrity whether you like it or not. Let's go to dinner."

Sarah's thoughts were completely filled with Matt. She was a fool. She was a plain widow thrust into her dream of the old west. Of course she wasn't what a rich rancher would take to his heart. When he took her to his bed she romanticized it for what she wanted. To her it was what she wanted and if that wasn't the way Matt wanted it her dreams were shattered. She couldn't confide in Lou who thoughts were exactly that - a simple retired accountant, a willing widow, would mean nothing but handy sex to a wealthy rancher. Oh how the truth of that hurt.

No doubt the dinner was as delicious as ever the way the food disappeared but she was choked up with memories. Was Matt playing with her? He seemed so sincere. How would she ever know the truth? Imagine asking him. Maybe she would if she ever saw him again. He made himself scarce since the van episode. Well he wasn't here now so she had better put him out of her mind. She sat down to listen to random conversations reiterate the thrills and spills of the youthful rodeo. Her role in the van theft was a short lived topic. Rusty rated castigation for stealing from the generous rancher who was helping other kids get a life.

Criticism eventually degenerated into personal antidotes far removed from the day's events. Sarah enjoyed the snatches of conversation, an after dinner brandy in her hand. Marianne joined her, dropping cross legged at her feet.

"I got a look at Buck's art work," she revealed, surprising Sarah with a bright conspiratorial look on her full features.

"He was going to show me but hasn't had time. How did he manage time for you?"

"He didn't. He doesn't show anyone. Babs showed me. She thinks they're too good to hide."

"What do you think?" Sarah asked. She wasn't going to take Babs glowing critique at face value but Marianne's opinion was something to be reckoned with. Sarah had no clue to Buck's talent, not having seen any of his work herself.

"Superb. Outstanding. And several other superlatives I can't pronounce. He truly has talent and he developed a style that I want to promote in my gallery."

"Then congratulations are in order. That means a new star will shine in Denver." Sarah raised her glass in salute, pleased at Buck's success.

"It's not quite that easy. I have to convince the public to buy. But first I have to convince Buck to show."

"Doesn't he want to?" Sarah thought that was incredible.

"Babs says he won't. But she says the real barrier is Matt."

"I don't understand," Sarah frowned, until recalling Matt's statement about putting foolish ideas into Buck's head.

"On second thought, I do understand," Sarah said. She didn't know what to do about it but Marianne's appraisal would be powerful in convincing Matt to stop discouraging Buck's artistic talent. That was one more reason to understand the relationship between the two. Sarah contemplated on when and how to confront Matt with the new found fact. Her heart tripped a beat at the thought of this evening's trip to the hidden ranch. Later she scanned the room, disheartened because Matt was not there. She went to talk to Melanie, who was in the office on the phone.

Patiently Sarah waited for the boss lady to put down the phone and frowned when Lou was signaled to take the call. Melanie left the office, and Sarah stepped in front of her to speak. Melanie stayed her with an upraised open hand.

"There's been a death in her family." Sarah feared Lou's brother had died and it was sadly so.

She hugged Lou and helped her pack. "Don't you want a night's rest? You could leave in the morning." Sarah urged.

"I couldn't sleep," Lou mourned, "You know it was so unexpected. The doctor said he was recovering. Then he had another attack that struck him. Caroline needs me. The sooner I get there, the better for us both."

"Drive careful. Pull off the highway and rest if you get sleepy," Sarah insisted. "Maybe I should go with you." As close as she was to Lou, it was not Sarah's family, it was not her place. It was only a few hours drive. Lou had driven that much many times.

"It's not that I don't want your company, but I'll be just fine," Lou explained, and Sarah understood.

Lou apologized, "You'll have to find another ride to the airport." Within the hour Lou was on her way to stand by Caroline, the bereaving wife of her brother.

Sarah stood alone in the rustic room, her thoughts of Caroline reflecting another widow, another time, another place. Sarah remembered all too vividly the loneliness of the first days and months of her own widowhood. The freedom later realized: decisions made according to her desires, by her standards, with her resources.

She grew used to being alone, even enjoyed it for awhile. Then it wasn't fun anymore and she found Lou's companionship filled the void. Lately Sarah realized the void wasn't filled at all, just obscured with a thin veil of bustle and conversation. She longed for more. She longed for something different. She longed for a focus to cling to. She longed for Matt. His image filled her mind and she rushed into the lounge. He would be there by now, waiting to take her to his place, the hidden ranch.

But Sarah was wrong. Matt was not there.

Sarah leaned over to speak privately to Melanie. "Have you heard from Matt?" Her voice quivered.

She was concerned about the progress on his case. She pressed her fingers hard against her mouth to steady her nerves. Her interest in Matt or his boys was not entirely philanthropic, she anticipated another evening alone with him, or even the entire night, now that Lou was not there to worry. Matt said he could wait until tonight to hear her further defense against love of Buck. Sarah couldn't imagine where that came from. She thought his jealousy of Buck was exaggerated but if that was the excuse that brought her to Matt's bed again so be it. She anticipated using demonstrative passion in her closing arguments.

Given the mood in which they parted that night Sarah expected him to show up well before dinner or send a message if something came up to prevent his coming. That was more than yesterday. That was before the theft. Matt was gruff and angry when she hugged Bill near the arena. She did hug Bill too tightly. Bill surprised her and she couldn't help returning the enthusiasm. Matt did not enjoy her pleasure. She could explain that too, given the opportunity.

Where was he now? He was on his way to check with the sheriff, his word required to move the case against Rusty. He awaited the summons. She expected him to inform her about a hearing, she being a witness, in a way, to the crime.

There was the child pornography operation, a Mickey Mouse setup that was nipped in the bud and would now go nowhere. Sarah approached Melanie with the question. Melanie was trained to sequester *The Singing Ranch* and Matt's activities from the guests. Sarah's injury and the theft of the van seemed innocent enough. She was apprised of Sarah's accidental excursion with Matt's boys, though not yet convinced that Sarah's involvement went far deeper with Matt himself. Melanie's protective shield was still very much intact, giving Sarah only the general progress.

"He will be scheduled to attend a hearing," Melanie grudgingly volunteered. "He will let you know more."

Sarah smiled thinly, hearing the added implication, *if he wants you to know* and resigned herself to accept the meager information. Would Matt tell her more in his own good time? Maybe. He wasn't all that open with the details of his life. She hoped he would come soon and not just to give her more details. After his remark this afternoon, she expected him to whisk her away to the hidden ranch long before this. And the more she thought about it, the more she worried. Had something terrible gone wrong? Surely not. Her selfish desire for him left no room for his personal neglect. Of course he would   be here if he could. But he was not and the tension in her grew. She wandered through the conversing guests, nodding with a gentle smile at their greetings.

Muted noises of dinner cleanup drifted through the slatted barrier dropped across the pass-through above the barren buffet table. Pots of fresh decaffeinated coffee and hot chocolate were there, the last vestige of service by the kitchen workers.

Steve and Melanie called for attention. "I have the van ready to transport you to the Grange Hall. There is a dance and we have another easy day tomorrow. Matt had to go to Boise for a couple of days. He wants you to enjoy some country dancing for a few hours after your sedentary day. How about it?"

The one thing his guests didn't need was to sit and mope over the death of a man they didn't know. It wasn't healthy for them and it wasn't good for business. Furthermore, they had very little exercise this day and a dance provided more fun and excitement than a ride among the flowers. Steve didn't wait for refusals. If some chose to stay at the lodge that was their concern but he was certain there was no desire for a Puritan wake or a walk to their rooms. He expected this homogeneous group to come as one. And they did.

"Let's go," Marianne tugged at Sally. The young women pulled at Sarah. "You, too." They knew she was the closest to Lou's tragedy and would face it in her own way. From the looks of Sarah when they sent Lou off, she had already come to grips with enough in isolation for one evening. They would do their best to lighten her perspective.

Sarah no longer held back to keep a date with Matt even though her heart was heavy. He was detained with important matters and would not come for her tonight. Separation was his choice. He had a ranch to run, several ranches in fact. If a partnership of love was in their future, Sarah would patiently step back and wait for him to take care of business before keeping promises to her. She straightened her shoulders, smiled at the young women and followed them into the van.

Minutes later, they found the Grange Hall huddled in an isolated corner of an alfalfa field somewhere along the country roads that wound through the treeless hills of range and farmland. Surrounding it were cars and utility vehicles, empty and alert for passengers who whooped it up in a loud hoedown inside the stark building.

"Let's find us a filly and kick up our heels," Ray announced, imitating the western lingo of Gabby Hays, jerking his head toward the double doors that openly invited the latecomers. His companion nodded and grinned, already a step ahead of him.

Sarah felt a lift of her spirits as she walked into the wide expanse of the hall, big enough for several squares of dancers with space along the walls for tables laden with plastic glasses and bowls of punch. Men and women, but mostly men, stood admiring the dancers, waiting for a change in the dance tempo. Sarah smiled as she contemplated the admirers.

Where did all the people come from? Her eyes were drawn to the corner where the square dance caller stood. Behind him was the band, two fiddlers, a drummer and an electric guitar player. Several other young men sat nearby with conventional guitars perched lazily on their knees. They leaned entirely into the music, swaying and tapping toes to the beat. They looked oddly familiar. Maybe from western movies she saw long ago. She scrutinized each gangly knee bobbing against soft denim to the consistent beat, each brushed Stetson individually shaped to fit a personality as well as the head it was meant to protect, each neckerchief boldly outlining young clean jaws. Their young clean faces.

Of course! They were Matt's boys. They were some of the bronc riders and steer wrestlers from *The Singing Ranch*. This was where the musicians came to play. This was a time and place with a purpose, giving incentive for their learning, providing reality for their practice. It was part of Matt and Buck's plan to instill healthy habits by providing activities in the lives of boys - men - that would benefit them all their lives.

A shaft of pleasure struck her then, a bolt of love for the man with drive and foresight to start *The Singing Ranch*. Would he be dancing if he were here? Her leg wasn't ready for a dance, with him or anyone, and she was glad she didn't have the need to refuse. She thought of the guitar in Matt's place and saw him strumming with the band instead of dancing and wondered if that was where he would be. Where was he now? What sudden occurrence took him to the state capitol? Ranch business? Sheriff business? Ordinarily, ranching itself was a complex mixture of wise predictions, hard work, and dogged patience, but this rancher, with paying guests and orphaned boys, had a range of interests that required broader management skills.

Yes indeed, quite a range. She couldn't help but smile at the concept. A pun worthy of any sly linguist. Either range suggested that she was completely out of bounds to think of sharing Matt's life. The breadth of his range, literally, was overwhelming in itself. The extent of his interests was breathtaking. The impact of his efforts was mind boggling. She could think of nothing she could do that would enhance his life. She could see now that she would more likely be in the way, be demanding time from a man already spread thin over his chosen responsibilities. The effect of those thoughts was not as uplifting as Steve intended this evening of dancing to induce.

"Come here, Sarah, and sit down," Steve urged, pulling a chair over to her side. "Matt told me you injured your leg near the bat cave. The way you favor it, I suspect it's worse than you let on."

Sarah worried just how much Matt revealed about that episode. Although Steve gave her the opportunity to deny or confirm his suspicion, she did not feel uncomfortable about his noticing her hesitation to dance. She had no intention to make any statement that might bring up more questions than it explained. She sat down and watched him expectantly as he pulled another chair over and sat down beside her. He apparently did not intend to dance either. Melanie was not here and the crowd already consisted of more men than women. He was not going to add to the disparity.

"Too bad you don't feel like dancing," he added, "there is a noticeable shortage of women for partners. The aggressive fellows will start leading the willing men any minute." He let his eyes roam over the crowd, amused at the tapping feet that would precipitate the spectacle of two men dancing together.

"I don't think I ever saw that," Sarah admitted, a perplexed look on her face.

"That's the only way we could dance while we learned at *The Singing Ranch*."

Sarah turned a more surprised countenance to Steve as his words made a strange impression. She blurted the obvious, "You're one of Matt's boys?" She didn't realize how easily she came to think of all the young men on *The Singing Ranch* as Matt's boys after Matt questioned her about seeing Eric and asking her help to find him. Steve's name was on *The Singing Ranch* history boards as a rodeo winner so it was natural to consider him in the same way.

"Matt's boys?" Steve's eyebrow shot up curiously then he shrugged with pleasure as he recognized the significance of her reference and nodded in agreement. "One of his first."

Sarah bit her tongue to keep from plying him with questions. She sensed his willingness to say more and tried furiously to think of something quickly that would draw more information without appearing nosy. She could not. She simply leaned forward with an approving nod and said, "Oh."

"I was very lucky. Matt is a very remarkable man." Sarah agreed wholeheartedly but she was careful not to show too much enthusiasm.

"I'm beginning to see that." she replied simply. She would listen to him talk about Matt if he must, but she would rather hear more about *The Singing Ranch*. Silly, she thought, how could the two be separated?

"I don't remember any boy that had Rusty's determination to make his own trouble. Most of us were foolishly independent but everything Matt had us do illustrated what a boy really had to learn before he could be independent, be a man. We were dropouts."

"He made you go to school?" That question just popped out. She always believed education was a major key to success.

"None of us liked school. If we thought he was going to teach us, we probably would have run away from him, too. He didn't make us do anything, except make us like the work and grow up in spite of ourselves." He rubbed the back of his neck in a slow pensive way.

"He hired the right people and they conspired to give us self pride, made us want to go to school. Made us see what we could really accomplish." He dragged his hand down to his lap where he clasped them both and shrugged. Sarah didn't see the surge of pride that she expected would follow. Something else was on his mind, she could sense it. Steve was looking at the fiddlers but Sarah thought he was looking into a past he was proud of. She waited to see if he had more to say and her patience seemed to pay off.

"Rusty lost that chance when he took Eric in the van." Steve turned slowly to Sarah and held her gaze.

"Matt thinks he failed Rusty. He's been unnecessarily distracted lately. He doesn't take failure very well." Steve looked at Sarah, curiously.

She bit back a remark about Matt's curious attitude fluctuations because she didn't understand what caused them. At each occurrence, she blamed them on her response, or at least on the circumstance she found herself, which was not always favorable. He was either rescuing her or getting her out of his way. She would call herself a distraction all right but she loathed to think she was unnecessarily so.

"When the Boise trip came up, he insisted I take everyone to this dance and especially announce his absence. He doesn't usually make the final decisions on guest activities. And he never informed them of his movements before." Steve took a moment to critically observe Sarah's reaction before asking.

"Have you any idea why he did that, Sarah?"

"No. Why?" She answered in less time than it took for her eyes to flick to her clasped hands. Then she drew back and looked at him slightly wide eyed, not so sure she wanted him to have the answer. She voiced the one she thought of when the announcement was first made.

"We were all depressed over the death of Lou's brother. I saw no point in mourning for someone none of us knew, except for me, and I didn't really know him either."

"I agreed with Matt on that, but I didn't see why he should make a general announcement of his personal plans. And you know what he said?" Of course she didn't.

"He said it was too impersonal to give you a private second hand message. A general announcement would suffice until he could personally explain to you." Sarah blushed. Not a bright colored blush but a darkening flush beneath her tan. She did not squirm or otherwise appear nervous.

"He's a genuine anomaly," she admitted, with a tender smile.

Steve suddenly noticed the crowd around him as eavesdroppers. "Let's go outside."

"Last winter Matt began turning over *The Singing Ranch* operation to the professionals. They don't think he should quit *The Singing Ranch*. His trip today is most unusual from their point of view, also."

Steve paused until they settled in the van. He had left it unlocked but the keys were secured in his pocket. Sarah thought earlier that Steve would enlighten her about Matt's multifaceted operation. Now she understood less than she thought she did before in regard to Matt's boys or any other part of his operation. She wanted some answers, deserving or not.

"What professionals?"

"How much has he told you about his project?" Steve asked, speculatively.

"About that much," Sarah answered, leaning toward him with a raised thumb and forefinger spread less than an inch apart.

"I thought so," he sighed. "It's not my place to tell his side, but I want to say this much: Matt built a very important place for boys. I consider him a special friend. I think he needs fulfillment in his life. Some of us, well, Buck and I anyway, think you just might be what he needs." Steve caught his breath.

That needed an explanation and his thoughts scrambled for some way to do that. A few couples already left the Grange Hall in their own cars. It was after midnight and he expected the finale of the night would soon follow. And *The William Tell Overture* came over the loud speakers as it was adapted for the theme song of Bonanza, a popular long running TV program. That signaled the end of the dance.

Sarah's expression was blank. She stared at Steve with her mouth open. What was she to think? Matt needed her? For what? Sex? He already had that. How could she bring fulfillment to his life? She had nothing to offer. Couldn't everyone see that? Lou certainly had - and bluntly informed Sarah in no uncertain terms that the big boss had everything a man could want.

Sarah stammered, "P-p-please explain that. What can Matt possibly need?"

"Some real stability in his own place - the little ranch where he lives. More than just a house he needs someone there to love." Steve was adamant about that. His lips folded together and his head, his whole body, nodded with approval.

"So how do you get Matt to love someone, let alone me?" Sarah shook her head in an expression of disbelief.

"He already does, Sarah. Matt is in love with you so much he has difficulty keeping his mind on every aspect of the business."

Steve watched strange expressions flash and disappear across Sarah's features. He could tell her more but stretched his hands out and held up his spreading fingers. The music stopped. No more could be said tonight.

Matt loved her? What was to be done? Could Melanie put a stop to the distraction Sarah so innocently precipitated?

Chapter Fifteen

Right or wrong

Sarah didn't try to figure any of Melanie's accusations. From the parting remark Melanie's protectiveness toward Matt seemed to have softened. At least Melanie was willing to wait for Matt's return to straighten it out, not that Sarah understood what *it* was to straighten. As far as she was concerned, her life would never be straight again. No matter how she denied it, her emotions were so knotted around Matt that she felt like a ball of yarn left impossibly entangled by a batch of silly kittens.

Unlike Melanie, Sarah was not patiently waiting for Matt's return. He couldn't conclude his trip too soon to suit her. It was her impression when they parted that he was as anxious as she was to resume a private interlude. Although that was several days ago she remembered his words clearly. If Melanie had overheard and wanted to stop such a meeting, could she have arranged for Matt's departure? Sarah doubted that Melanie had power or influence to such a degree. If Matt was so easily controlled he was not the kind of man Sarah could respect. And she respected him in a big way.

The shade no longer protected Sarah's lawn chair from the direct sun. During the last hour she became increasingly exposed and rotated her shoulders for some relief from the heat. She had no intention of swimming when she left her room this morning. The bruises on her leg turned a sickly yellow streaked with deep purple and she wasn't going to parade those in public. Matt's advice was to keep them covered and not even mention her injury. She wasn't going to until it became clear that the muscle of her thigh was damaged so severely she had to favor it. The accident was explained, although Matt only admitted to finding her after she pulled herself free.

"Sorry you didn't bring your suit?" Babs asked.

"Do I look that forlorn?" Sarah retorted. Her loose cotton slacks stuck to her legs and she had all she could do to keep her mind off the water. The delicious smell of barbecuing beef was overwhelming and produced a different desire. Vic had continually spread the Bar X brand seasoning sauce on the meat and its browning filled the air with the magic that caused human salivary glands to run like artesian wells.

Steve's riders came in and Sally and Jane readily joined the romping in the shallow river waters. Babs dived in with the rest of the swimmers.

"You shudda seen Steve plunge that hypo into that bleeding cow," Terry shouted, "Then Buck and him lifted the critter on the flatbed." Steve prevented the injured animal from thrashing around and used a sedative he carried in anticipation of such problems. Steve was no novice when it came to animal injuries or how to handle them on the range. Buck wasn't either.

Norm and Arlys rode on to the lodge to clean up. They would return with either Steve or Buck in time to eat with the gang. Jane stripped down to her suit and joined Terry and Ray in the cool refreshing water. Dirk walked over to watch Vic put the sauce on the roasting meat.

"I see a spot right here you missed," Dirk tormented as he leaned over and grinned. Teasing came easy with this group

Melanie was happy to observe. They experienced hunger pangs at the delicious smell of roasting meat.

"Hey, boss lady, When do we eat?" Dirk called to Melanie. His overhanging midsection indicated he hadn't skimped on any previous meals and his tone suggested he was not about to start now.

Sarah was amused at the success of the barbecue. What was there about eating outdoors that's so appealing? Whatever it was Melanie's barbecue more than filled everyone's expectation. The beef, baked potatoes, and tossed salad were enjoyed, plate after plate, before the guests settled down to a mellow Mitch Miller "*Sing Along*" between beers under the mauve sky. It was well past dark when they were taken to their rooms. The night was long and star filled.

Matt returned the next day, at least, Melanie said he would. Sarah did not see him.

"I want to join the ride this morning, Steve," Sarah said as she rose from the breakfast table.

She decided to take her own advice and participate in the planned activities which that day included a morning ride. Her motive was to impress Matt, she knew, but that was that. If she had courage to ride without him, he would be surprised but pleased, and the thought warmed her. Some perverse reasoning led her to believe her leg would become stronger and more fit because of it. Buck saddled Ruby for her and helped her mount. When he stepped away, the horse danced against Sarah's lack of control. She held fast to the saddle horn with her strong right hand, her left holding the reins firmly. She planted her feet rigidly against the stirrups with her heels down. She didn't think of how strong her leg felt in lifting her weight slightly as she strained to relax. Trying intensely not to panic, she spoke softly, in a reprimanding tone to the big red mare.

For several heart stopping moments, Sarah thought her tactic was successful. She released her death grip on the horn and reached out to pat the horse's neck. Ruby felt her hesitancy and stepped sideways, tossing her head high then briskly down. The movement was swift and naturally fluid and Sarah was smoothly ejected over Ruby's head.

Stunned, Sarah hung on to the reins and carried them forward over Ruby's head. Sarah's weight stopped the horse, none too delicately. She was pulled to her feet by the reins with the momentum of her rolling body. Buck ran to save her. A meaner horse would have stomped the thrown rider, but Ruby did not. Buck was relieved but didn't stop to consider that was unusual. Ruby didn't have a reputation for being the most docile horse on the ranch. That Matt would let Sarah ride the mare never ceased to amaze Buck. He regretted his impulse to allow it this morning as he took the reins and put a steadying arm around Sarah.

"Are you all right?" Buck asked inanely.

She was trembling, angry at her presumptuousness, relieved she was not hurt. Hell no, she was not all right! What ever made her think she could ride the big red horse?

"I'm sorry, Sarah," he moaned at her angry face, "I should have known Ruby wouldn't behave without Matt around. I'm sorry." He leaned down to ask, "Want to give up this ride? Or should I get a gentle horse?" He looked doubtfully at her but still held Ruby's reins while the horse arched its proud neck and eyed Sarah with the haughty look of a smart aleck.

Sarah's chin came up in chagrin but when she caught the look in Ruby's eye her expression changed to indignation. She reviewed with mounting anger how the agile horse choreographed a debonair dance with the smooth sassy toss of the regal head and the cocky bowing retreat that tumbled her delicately to the ground in a royal ritual. Sarah dusted herself with determined slapping hands, noting how Ruby shied away with doubtful eyes. She slowly reached toward Ruby's head, held within in her grasp by tight reins in Buck's hand. She took the bony jaws in her hands and held fast, forcing Ruby's head down without benefit of the bridle or bit. Her hands firmly pressed, she spoke in an authoritative tone.

"Don't you do that again. Hear me?" Sarah looked resolutely into the animal's deep liquid eyes while jerking her hands in a forceful shake that conveyed her determination without moving the huge animal in the least. Moving beyond the head she stroked the glistening neck as far as she could reach. She moved to the side, caressing Ruby's neck as she went.

"Buck, will you help me mount this majestic steed?"

"You're not going to get on this damn horse again, are you? She's been idle too long."

"I'm in training for the circus tumbling act, Buck," Sarah's tone calm and even, her words alone conveyed the ludicrous idea that left onlookers with open mouths, struggling with mounts impatient to be underway. She approved of her own stability. There was no residue of pain. Sarah confidently stroked Ruby's quivering withers, murmuring encouragement as she remembered Matt doing when she first met the horse in the stable.

Buck carefully pulled the reins over Ruby's head and measured the horse's reaction against Sarah's courageous stance.

"You're the nervy one!" Buck breathed, and lifted Sarah by the waist. She settled confidently in the saddle, setting her boots firmly in the stirrups, watching Ruby's ears swivel with her head slightly turned in complete approval. If the lanky cowboy she loved trusted her with his horse, by golly, she was going to trust the horse!

"Lead on!" she waved to Buck. The ride proceeded as intended, Ruby alert but not mischievous. Sarah's ride was by no means smooth, but the horse made no move to dislodge her during her awkward moments. She ached from top to bottom long before they returned to the corral. Without Lou to tease, Sarah felt lost. Matt was not there either. Sarah felt bereft.

After a soothing shower Sarah enjoyed the broiled salmon, delightfully smothered in Melanie's special caper sauce. Matt was not at the table. Sarah was uneasy but at a loss as to what she could do about it. She hesitated to ask Melanie, to even hint that she was concerned and Steve was too close by to question privately. Buck would be more helpful. Sarah hoped he would be waiting until Babs finished for the night. She glanced at Melanie, spotting her attentively in conversation with Arlys. Assuring herself that Melanie was properly occupied, Sarah slipped unnoticed into the kitchen to find Buck. He wasn't in the kitchen, he was too discreet to blatantly wait for Babs there. Sarah made a conspiratorial face at Babs and proceeded directly through the back door. Buck immediately materialized among the shadows.

"Have you seen Matt?" she asked.

"Isn't he inside?" At that negative thought Buck shrunk into the shadows fearing disclosure to the incomprehensible man.

"No. Has he returned from Boise? I thought he might be still talking to the authorities." Sarah's anxiety heightened. She didn't believe his business could take this long.

"No way. He settled that stuff hours ago. He said he had to run a couple of errands. He seemed very anxious to wind up things and return here."

"I thought he was, too," she murmured, "But he gets uptight and unpredictable."

"Matt don't mean that. He's pretty sensible," Buck said, a strange look in his eye. Sarah wondered about the relationship of these men. They worked well together, yet she saw a friction between them, something personal and far beyond her understanding. Her real feelings for Matt was her more immediate interest.

"He was really angry when he saw us together here before. He thinks I was too intimate with you. He didn't like the interest you were showing," Sarah said, knowing she could be honest with Buck about her feelings because of what was going on with him and Babs. She was unprepared for the dawning look stealing its way across the young man's handsome features.

"So that's what's eating the old fart," he snorted, throwing his head back, his wide shoulders shaking in quiet laughter."

"Now you wait just a minute." Sarah insisted. She wouldn't stand for this impudent young man, no matter how handsome or talented, laughing at Matt for any reason.

" Don't you jump on me for criticizing him. I get that from all the regular folks around here. He's been doing some strange things lately and you've just verified my suspicions."

"What do you mean?" Sarah demanded. Her eyes narrowed angrily.

"He was ready to kick me out when you left me in the storeroom but he wouldn't tell me why," explained Buck, "just gave me a bunch of nonsense about finding a place in my own generation. He hasn't spoken a civil word to me since." Buck pressed his lips together in a hard line to suppress a laugh and his shoulders jerked harder in silent mirth the more he thought of it.

"And why do you find that so amusing?" Sarah's brows knitted together in total consternation, her hands on her hips as she confronted him.

"Because now I know what put the itch in his jeans," Buck said, with a sympathetic look as he thought it over.

Sarah was so perplexed she could only frown and stare. The intimacies she shared with Matt flashed through her mind and her eyes got rounder. What else could Buck be referring to, when he had agreed that Matt needed something more than female adoration?

"He hasn't thought about anything but his ranch for so long he hasn't had a personal life. Before Babs made me sit up and take notice I figured he never needed one." Sarah glimpsed a concern in Buck that was not there before.

"You sound like you know his personal life pretty well."

"Well enough, I guess."

"His dedication to the boys is very obvious. I saw the pictographic history at *The Singing Ranch*. Steve said you and Matt set up the program there."

"Yes, we did. And he's meticulous about the implementation. But he always managed the problems there with stubborn patience. That's not what's bothering him." Buck stood like a man who knew what was.

"Well?" Sarah strained forward looking like she had dentist's tools for pulling out the information if he didn't reveal it on his own.

"You came along and he was challenged with feelings he never had for a long time. Now I don't suppose he knows exactly what to do about it."

Sarah reared back with a glare of disbelief. She stared at him a moment until her posture relaxed and her face softened. She sensed a puzzling ambivalence in Matt but, without audacity to place her charms at fault, she attributed his changing moods to disrespect and coldness. Could a man flounder with the same misgivings she had at the thought of loving so deeply? Especially at this age. The thought was a heady one. She wanted to believe it so much she couldn't deal with it at the moment.

"What have you got to do with the Boy's ranch, anyway?"

"Matt established that when he finally realized what a mess I was making of my life," Buck reflected, sadly.

"What did your life have to do with his?"

"He thinks I would've done better if he hadn't made a mess of his life first."

It took one reflective second before a dawning light came over Sarah's features. She knew the answer to that now, the melding of the strange relationship between the two strong men. Except for the build of their bodies, there was no surface similarity. The strength of wills, the set of chins, the relentless determination marked the mold that shaped them both.

She smiled faintly, wonderingly,

"He's your father."

"It's no secret," Buck shrugged. Only the ranch workers knew how many relationships among the staff were stronger than blood.

"He treats you like hired help," said Sarah, "with little regard for your feelings."

"Makes me work as hard as he does, filling in with stuff he has no education for."

"But you're a grown man.."

"Yeah...I know...one who ought to be on his own. But you know what I did when I was on my own? Humiliated him... that's what. Ruined his life."

"Is that what he thinks?" That was difficult for Sarah to accept.

"It's true. At age fourteen I was implicated in a crime serious enough to put me in a prison work gang."

"And you are still paying for that?"

"Matt got hit with real guilt over neglecting me then, ended up punishing himself...but that turned out pretty good in spite of everything. This land became a lasting monument for needy boys." Sarah didn't see the ruined part of Matt's life. What she did see was a crisis caused by Rusty's selling himself and Eric to an evil man.

"Where is he?" Sarah insisted on an accounting of Matt's whereabouts, as if she was entitled. Buck gave her a blank look that filled with curiosity. He listened as he noticed how Sarah's attitude affected her tone.

"I'm worried. He gets moody, closes up on himself. I'd like to be with him." Sarah's tone of voice and urgent hand on Buck's arm was a revelation.

"I saw his interest in you but didn't hold much hope you would take a liking to him. That's why Steve talked to you like he did at the grange dance. Now there's hope if you're sweet on him, too."

To Sarah '*being sweet on him*' was an old fashioned statement, a term old timers often used for love. She was more than starstruck, but not totally convinced she was really in love. Being sweet on Matt was decidedly possible. That would explain why her body chemistry went berserk at the thought of him. She didn't have enough insulin to counteract the sweetness. Her thoughts were getting silly.

"We were going to his place after dinner. He should have been here hours ago. Do you know where I can find him?"

"So." Buck eyed Sarah with a strange knowing expression. "Maybe we should find out what's keeping him." He explained Sarah's concern when Babs joined them and led her by the hand. Sarah followed to Buck's jeep.

"We'll see if he's home," and they headed for the hidden ranch. Buck's vehicle had no trouble manipulating the rough trail past the corral and over the grazed terrain taken by the guests on their daily rides. Buck turned and headed on the trail Sarah took to the hidden ranch. She felt the trail more than she could see it until she spied the rock outcroppings that pierced the star-studded sky like stalwart sentinels standing guard. Buck shifted into a lower gear as the vehicle began the descent into the valley, the engine ground noisily in the stillness of the night. Lights shone through the windows of Matt's place, beacons of welcome that should have gladdened Sarah's heart.

Instead, apprehension flooded her senses and she touched Buck's shoulder, "Hurry. I'm afraid something's wrong."

He accelerated, tearing up the dust that followed to envelop them as he came to a sudden stop, headlights revealing a dust settling in the yard as if recently disturbed. Buck turned his jeep using his headlights as a beacon up the road toward a departing car. Matt's pickup stood silent near the broken lattice. The departing car gathered speed, disregarding the dog blindly setting in its way. The driver twisted the steering wheel, squealing the wheels, sending the car in a crazy careening pattern, scraping across the massive trunk of an ancient cottonwood tree.

"Follow him," Sarah urged, "I'm going inside." She dropped out of the back seat, grimacing as she landed on her injured leg. She ignored the dull pain, her chest racked by her fearful heartbeat as she stared at the silent lighted windows.

Had Matt been kidnapped, too?

The screen door slapped against the wall when Sarah threw it aside and entered the living room. Her heart stopped at the sight of Matt's body heaped upon the coyote skin in the middle of the floor.

"Oh No! No. No. No." Sarah rushed to his side and took his rugged jaws in her hands. Matt was limp and unconscious.

She straightened his legs on the soft rug and laid his head back, horrified to see his arm grotesquely twisted. She gritted her teeth as she straightened it, relieved to find it was not broken. She squeezed her eyelids tight until her sanity returned to make sense out of the chaos. Her hands explored his bones, his features, desperately fearful about the extent of his injury. His face was bruised, his nose bloody, his body limply unconscious. There was no other sign of blood.

Western heroes got shot and she blindly searched for evidence of a bullet wound before realizing she wouldn't know what one looked like if it was there. The blood and gore in movies was only catsup anyway. She pulled the edges of the coyote skin around him for protection from body shock. She felt helpless and frustrated and angry. None of those reactions was reviving her lover.

Her lover.

Admit it.

Her desire was to embrace him into vibrant health. That was not possible, but she didn't want to take her arms off him. Sarah's basic reflex was to wipe his face. Matt was bleeding slightly from his temple and his cheekbone. She finally reacted sanely. She retrieved a clean tea towel from the kitchen, soaked it under the cold tap, and tenderly wiped the blood from Matt's battered cheekbone and swollen lip. She pressed the cool towel to his temple while crooning encouragement and assurances that Buck was after the attacker. Sarah turned as the peripheral noises took an extra moment to register in her anxious mind. Sarah had cleaned the blood from Matt's face and held his head in her hands. Babs and Buck burst in the door.

"Call a doctor," she ordered Babs, who held a cellular car phone, then to Buck she asked, "Will a doctor come out here?" At his skeptical grimace she suspected one would not. She crooned encouragement into Matt's unconscious countenance but he did not respond.

"Let me have a look," Buck insisted. He pulled aside the rug and bent over Matt. He searched every inch of his body with the same expertise Sarah had seen Matt use when he saved the calf.

"There's probably a broken rib," he decided, not sounding overly worried. That happened before during the years of horse training Matt had undertaken. His body may bruise more easily than when he was younger and more vital, but Buck suspected Sarah's ministrations would ease his present discomfort in more ways than one. He examined Matt's head even more carefully, frowning at the ugly bruise so close to his left eye. He gave a grunt of relief.

"Here's why he's out cold," he jerked his head, showing Sarah the lump behind his left ear.

"Is he going to be all right?" Sarah asked, eyeing Buck curiously as if she had watched a physician's complete examination. He sat back on bent knees and braced curled fingers on his thighs. His studied gaze traveled up and down Matt's length and came to rest on his bruised face. He reached for the wet towel Sarah clutched in her hands. He turned the cool side against Matt's temple. Babs leaned down with the phone loosely held in her hand, punching the off button.

"Doc Whitney's on his way to Jacobs. He'll call us when he gets there. Martha is having her fourth baby." That meant a long wait. They would have to do what they could. Sarah couldn't take her eyes off Matt's face.

"What do you think happened? Is he going to be all right? He's badly beaten. Why doesn't he wake up?" She was kneeling opposite Buck at Matt's side and crouched over him. She touched his shoulders tenderly, her hands pausing on his jaws, knowing that was not enough.

"Help me move him to the bed," Sarah ordered. They had to make him comfortable and warm. Babs pulled back the coverlet so Buck and Sarah could lay him on the sheet. She removed one boot and Buck removed the other. He reached over to pull the blanket up and found Sarah unbuckling Matt's belt.

At Buck's raised eyebrows, she nettled, "He will be more comfortable without his jeans." And she proceeded to ease them down around his hips.

"But.." Buck stammered. Then he made a defenseless gesture and acquiesced. He took the bottom of one pant-leg and pulled it over Matt's foot and then the other. By that time Sarah had Matt's jeans down to his knees and Buck was able to slip them off all the way. Matt lay naked from the hips down, with only the long front ends of his shirt tail tucked modestly around his male parts. Buck watched Sarah tuck the covers around Matt's full length without a glitch as if she seen it all before. She bent to kiss him and moan encouragement.

Buck nudged Babs with his elbow and gave her an astute glance with raised eyebrows as if to say I told you so.

Relieved that Matt was as comfortable as she could make him Sarah thought of what had reduced him to his battered condition.

"Did you catch that car?" His attacker must be caught and punished.

"It had too much of a start. I don't think we'll be able to identify the car because I couldn't get the license. I came back to make sure Matt wasn't in it with him."

"That never occurred to me." Sarah admitted. But for one instant it had, except her premonition brought her directly, unerringly, to his side.

"Who do you suppose that was?" Buck shook his head, at a total loss of an explanation.

"I don't know. It could be some partner to the guy who took the kids. Seems odd that Matt should be a target but I suppose there are others who would get rich with boys like Rusty and

Eric and when they are thwarted would retaliate with violence just for the pleasure they get from revenge."

"Is there any chance of finding them?"

"I told the sheriff which way he's headed. The car won't be easy to find since we couldn't give a decent description. If he's stopped before he cleans the blood off his bumper, the sheriff will have him cold."

"Blood? What blood?" Sarah couldn't figure how Matt's blood could have gotten on the car.

"Fella's." Buck barely choked the name.

"The dog was run down in the yard," Babs explained, understanding Buck's inability to speak.

Fella was as much Buck's friend as it had been Matt's companion. Loss of the old animal was inevitable and both had concluded it would be put to sleep if it began to suffer, but for Fella's life to be wiped out with such sudden violence was more than Buck could discuss at the moment. He stood with slumped shoulders pouring his unspoken regrets of it upon his battered father. Babs hugged his waist and Buck slipped his arms around her shoulders. He looked from Sarah to Matt and knew the injured man would appreciate her comfort more than anyone else's. Buck hoped Matt would come around soon. Seeking his own consolation, Buck hugged Babs more tightly still.

"Let's find a blanket to wrap Fella's body," Babs whispered quietly. They might have to wait until morning to find out if Matt had a particular place to bury the dog, but her man needed to be doing something, not silently wallowing in worry and regrets.

"I'll leave the phone with you, Sarah," Babs said, putting it on the dresser as they left. Sarah wasted no more thoughts on the attacker. She ran loving hands over Matt's hair, her fingers lingering on his stone shaped jaws with touches more delicate than a feather. Without taking her devoted eyes off his face, she checked the contours of his thin body to be sure the blanket snuggled against him. She longed to lie beside his body to warm

him with her own but this was no time for such measures. The
extent of his injuries had to be decided. All she could do was
wait, until he regained consciousness or the doctor came to assess
the damage. A wave of profound love swept through her and she
leaned lightly upon him.

"Wake up, you big galoot," she whispered sternly, her lips
brushing his bruises. She held them there, soft warm healing lips.
She would restore him with her love if that were possible. She
thought a stillness settled on his body and she drew back to view
the consequences. There was a moment when she thought he
would awaken and she quickened with a sucking of her breath,
hoping against hope he was reviving.

To her alarm his body wilted almost immediately as a puppet
slackens when the strings release it. Sarah freed her breath in dry
sobbing bursts and her face went down against his in hopeless
submission. She was too dazed to believe words were coming
from his mouth.

"If I didn't hurt so damn much, I'd swear I was in heaven."

"At least you're not hurt so much you can't wake up," she
responded, her lips on his before he wasted energy on another
word. He held still for her kiss unable to bring his head toward
her without getting clubbed with tremendous pain. His arms
struggled to be free of the covers, and even that brought a grimace
of pain. Sarah leaned away and pulled the covers back, her eyes
radiating a joyous relief at seeing him awaken, concerned that he
was hurting but thrilled at his response to her presence.

"How did you get here?" He had many other questions but
in his grogginess, it was the fact that she was here that touched
him most.

"I had Buck help me find you. I worried that you were
detained, gone longer than you intended." Her expression told
him that she had an intuition where he was concerned. Matt let
his eyelids close on the thought of what a treasure she would be
if she would always be by his side. His aching head brought him
out of his dream.

"Where's the scum that caught me unawares?" Matt's hands held Sarah's and she sat on the edge of the bed.

"Who was he?"

"Didn't you see him?" Matt's eyes blinked to restore his reason. He couldn't imagine what had transpired since he blacked out.

"We had no idea someone was here until a car left in a big hurry. Buck couldn't get close enough to identify it."

Sarah leaned to put a hand on each side of his shoulders, bracing her weight above him, but closing the distance, her intent one of checking the extent of his injury, not ready to reveal the terrible thing that might ultimately identify the offender in Matt's beating and another tragedy as well.

"Something may come up," he offered, always patiently expecting solutions. In his own solid way, he demanded them. He saw in Sarah a 'something' that came up but he was encased in an awkwardness that made him unsure of his approach. She was a willing lover, respecting him in bed. He reveled in the admiration that poured from her eyes now. He saw evidence of it at other times, but it came and went like the light of a clandestine firefly. It would be bright for a time, then disappear, her expression replaced with wariness and anger. It had puzzled him and he hesitated to speak his mind.

He needed her so much he ached from it. That put him in a quandary. His physical aches surfaced as his most immediate problem. She was here and this was now. He ought to appreciate what he could get. She was sheltering him and it was a good feeling. It soothed him, brought a small relief from his throbbing pain.

Matt's hands slipped up her arms in a caressing welcome. "I'm lucky you came along. That man wasn't willing to give up." Matt didn't describe what he thought might have happened.

"Buck thinks you've got a broken rib." She tipped her head to indicate the lump behind his ear. "The depth of that will show up later." Matt blinked slowly, his inner eye assessing his injuries.

He couldn't keep from being silly, so satisfied he was with Sarah's attention. The corners of his mouth turned up and he insisted, "I bet I'll live after all."

"You'll have to answer to me if you don't." She closed her eyes and her mind to the troubles ahead. She lowered her lips to his and knew he was going to be all right.

Ominous details reared as insurmountable obstacles in his life, and hers, that had yet to be resolved.

Chapter Sixteen

I'm tired of livin' alone

Sarah took the call from Dr Whitney shortly after midnight. In whispers she described Matt's condition, sorry the ringing phone disturbed him. He became alert at her guarded tones and raised his hand toward her. Sarah was relieved that he showed that much desire to regain control. At Matt's beckoning fingers, she sat on the bed beside him and handed over the phone.

"Hello, Elwood. Yes, I'm fine," Matt insisted, his eyes lingered wonderingly over Sarah's silhouette, her features dimly visible in the reflected light from the living room. He paused and listened with eyes dimly glazed as if searching his memory.

"Yes, thanks to you I got that straightened out yesterday. Sorry Buck bothered you tonight." Buck and Babs left after Matt regained consciousness. The sheriff was phoned the description Matt recalled of his attacker: height maybe five seven, weight maybe hundred sixty, build wiry, hair light, features soft, knuckles overlain with hard metal. Matt's recollection was drawn more from action than from observation, the attacker had been swift, his intent murderous. If not for Buck's arriving jeep lights,

Matt would not have described his attacker at all or anything else again. Matt smiled insolently and regarded Sarah with loving eyes. He chuckled and shut his eyes in bliss.

"I'll have you know I've been thoroughly examined by a well schooled horse doctor and nursed by an old woman who can't keep her hands off me." Matt grinned like the Cheshire cat until Sarah playfully swatted the air at him. His cringing reflex brought on an implied grimace of pain. Her response was a smug downward nod that plainly told him the pain was fitting reward for his outrageous statement.

"Just go on home, Elwood, I'll come see you tomorrow, or this afternoon, whatever the case may be." Matt didn't know what time it was, or even what day, and he didn't care. He got satisfaction out of authorities in Boise regarding Eric. What could be done for Rusty was yet to be determined, but it was out of his hands. He put those thoughts aside. He wanted no distractions. His every cell was attuned to the way Sarah touched him, kissed him, glowed at him. She was that attentive from the moment he regained consciousness and made his heart throb with strong joyful beats.

"Yes, I will. I'll be fine. Bye." Matt surrendered the phone to Sarah, his hand falling across her lap in sweet possession. She turned the phone off and laid it in its charging cradle, her other hand holding Matt's in place with her own decisiveness. She gazed at him in the dim light, and leaned toward him.

"I should have left the phone in the living room. I'm sorry you were wakened. Just go back to sleep. OK?" Sarah braced her hands above his shoulders and decided against planting a kiss on his bruised cheekbone. Before she could get up to leave, she was captured in Matt's arms and pulled down against his chest.

"Oh, no you don't. You stay right here. Dr Whitney said I had to take my medicine and you were prescribed."

"Are you sure you can handle a pure unregulated dose?" Sarah cuddled her cheek in the hollow between his jaw and shoulder, warming him with her suggestive breath. She laid hard against his chest, then raised and twisted so she could swing her legs up on the bed to lay against, almost atop, his full length.

"Treat me gently. I can handle everything you'll give. I'll have to go kinda slow at first" Matt nuzzled her temple, his hands adoring her shoulders, upper arms and back. He caressed her waist and slowly slid his hands tenderly around her curves. He pressed her hips to his, her buns firmly held in his large calloused hands.

"Take all the time you need, big boy, but take it easy," Sarah urged, her breasts flattened against his hard broad chest, the pearl buttons impressed in her soft flesh. The blanket swathed him below his shirt, protecting his naked body from her sight, but not her thoughts.

"I like your concern, woman. Settle down here." Matt turned slowly, his head none too clear, his eyes closed against the throbbing that exploded behind his ear at every sudden move. He rolled Sarah to his side pressing her closely to him. His head ached and he wanted to sleep but he couldn't let her go.

"Are you all right?" It hurt her to know he was still hurting.

"It's easier this way, Sarah. Stay by me." His tone was imploring, his breath ragged.

"Buck's block and tackle couldn't drag me away."

"Does that mean you forgive me for owning property?" She knew he referred to her reaction when she learned he was the owner and not simply a ranch hand. She had no quarrel with his property. Not then or now. Sarah was concerned about her place in his life but his recovery took precedence so she did not want to bring up that distressing item.

"Will you go back to sleep? I'll be close by." Her arm was pressed to the pillow under his neck and she tried to disentangle herself from him, leaning her head back, her free hand pushing against his shoulder. He would have none of her departure. His arms were tough and hard and held her fast against her token resistance. Her concerned gaze searched his face but his eyes were closed, his mouth grim.

"I want your answer first," he demanded, his dark eyes suddenly open and intent, his whole being alert with anticipation.

Sarah felt the apprehension stiffen his full length through the bed coverings. They had many things to discuss regarding their relationship and she suspected he was not going to be put off. She couldn't think of the right words, soothing words, yet decisive, to explain how she felt.

No matter how much she loved him, she was not going to become another piece of acquired property, a body for his comfort. Her eyes refused to be held by his. Instead they roamed his high cheekbones, his sharp jaw-lines, his dark hair. She lovingly fingered the wild strands curling around his ears. His white sideburns curled in presidential abandon.

"You're here. Is that your answer, Sarah?" His embrace loosened and he raised his head with great effort to get a serious view of her face.

"It's your business what you own." she said, but she held the statement like the loose end of a rope that had to be fastened with the securing hook yet to be found.

"I know my business, Sarah." He pushed his head wearily against his pillow, his entire length wilted in fatigue. "I knew my business very well until you came along."

Sarah had disrupted his life, of that she was well aware. So far he did not place any blame on her and it was now coming out in the open. Like Melanie said, she was an unsettling factor in his life. Did he consider her a nuisance to be brushed away? Would things settle down if she left? His earlier question hung heavily in the air between them. Still it was up to him to do the talking. It was he who really held the answers.

"And now? You don't know?" She suspected from Buck's description of the itch in Matt's jeans that he was suffering from too much hormone activity just as she was. How he related that disturbance to the future was critical to her.

"I know all right," he breathed as he crushed her to him and rocked her with tiny jerks that gently swayed the bed, "I can't concentrate on business anymore. I don't want to think of business. You're totally distracting."

Sarah's arms tightened around him. Tell me more, she urged silently, tell me what I want to hear.

"I can see that. I could leave but I promised Buck I'd stay with you," she said quietly.

"I don't want to hear about your promises to Buck." His arms fell loosely and he laid back to look into her face. The move brought the painful throb pounding at his ear. He hid a grimace and realized her eyes were closed, tightly, obstinately.

"What about promising me?" he insisted, putting his palm under her chin and turning her face to his. He silently willed her eyes to open and pinned them with that deep penetrating yearning that left her helpless.

"Promise you what?"

"That you'll stay with me - for me. That you'll be my wife."

Sarah held her breath. That was what she wanted to hear, wasn't it?

Matt didn't understand her hesitation. "Is that so bad? I love you. Don't you know that?"

Until now, she hadn't known. Only hoped. She took a long mellow moment to absorb the fresh knowledge, like the outburst of a developing seedling. Her body swelled and she retreated to make room for the crashing eruption of her fulfillment.

He misread her action as withdrawal and he agonized. How could he make her understand how much he needed her, how much he wanted her? In his helplessness, he panicked. The room slowly spun around him and he dreaded his loss. The adrenaline kicked in to allow him to cope with the refusal to accept his love. He heard only the throbbing behind his ear and faded away, his body wilting back against the mattress like a stringy piece of kelp released from a receding tide.

If Sarah said 'yes' to help him recover, she could change her decision later, it was obvious to her she had so little to add to his life. He would realize that when he healed and his system returned to normal. She didn't realize how stressed he was over her failure to answer. Nor did she understand that he viewed her hesitation as rejection. The stress had put him in suspended condition not unlike loss of consciousness. She withdrew her arms, cupped his jaw in one hand lifting his eyelid with her thumb, and was stricken with fear. Was his injury worse than Buck surmised? Or had he given up to despair?

What was she to do? Buck earlier used a wad of cotton saturated with some vial smelling stuff under Matt's nose to revive him. She went in search of it, instantly remembering Buck returned it to the bathroom. Ice would help subdue Matt's pain and she hurried to prepare a cold compress as well. Furiously Sarah rushed to do those simple things, confident she could revive him, resolute with purpose. The odor of the remedy Buck used led her unerringly to the cotton in the bathroom, she didn't need the light to get it. She went for ice from the kitchen, moving like one possessed, knowing she could revive him, needing to restore his well being, wanting to answer his question.

Her eyes were accustomed to the dark, the pale reflection from the light in the living room illuminating her way, making passage quicker by not stopping to search for unfamiliar light switches. She dumped ice cubes in a plastic bag, pausing to wind it in a towel before returning to Matt, her goal, with reviving remedies in her hands.

She stopped.

What was that?

An unfamiliar movement in the living room. In horror she watched a figure stealthily approaching the bedroom. It was a man, no one she recognized, and his ominously raised hand was threatening. Sarah flew into action, without thought, without reason. She leaped at his back, knowing she must prevent him from harming Matt, making no correlation with the next move that would jeopardize her own life.

Her man was endangered, her drive instinctive, her target sinister. The man went down under her weight, his lungs bereft of air, his surprise complete. The ice pack in Sarah's hand was braced against the attacker's neck, in a position of protection for herself against the fall. The vile cotton wad further stunned him. It fell under the man's nose, his face turned sideways as he hit the floor.

The ensuing scramble blurred in Sarah's consciousness. Overpowered by the burning along her forearm she fell against the bedroom wall. Buck was suddenly there, with a strangle hold on a slighter man. Babs kicked an object under Matt's bed.

"There's rope in Matt's truck, honey, go get it. Quick!" Buck insisted to Babs and she reacted without question.

The scene came together for Sarah almost as quickly as it had been lost in the scuffle. She squeezed her eyes shut and knew Matt was saved but he was still to be revived. She went to him then to shield him, if necessary, with her body. Babs asked what happened.

"He was awake and fainted," Sarah explained, examining Matt again, finding him stirring weakly, hearing grunts and wheezes behind her, seeing in her peripheral vision Buck throw the attacker to the floor, an arm twisted behind his back. She raised Matt's head gently in her cupped hands, willing his eyes to open, his mind to return to consciousness.

He responded as if on cue, his thoughts on the same track as they were when he last spoke. "Are you going to say yes?"

"Yes, yes, yes," she murmured into his cheek, her eyes closed in relief at his revival, her heart opened to the wisdom of her promised word. She caressed his face with feather-like kisses, not missing a crevice or a ridge of his rugged jaw. She was rewarded with his encircling arm, unaware of Babs return to assist Buck in securing the man he had subdued.

"Shut your filthy mouth, before I clobber you," Buck was saying loudly over vile obscenities pouring between gasping breaths of the stranger. Babs switched on the bedside lamp and peered at Sarah in the sudden light.

"Are you all right?" she asked.

"Yes, yes," Sarah murmured, at first simply repeating her assurance to Matt then aware that she should answer Babs.

"I'm fine." She raised up and looked from Matt to Babs. "He blacked out and I went for ice."

Babs' horror stricken focus was on the bloody blanket and she gasped, "He's been stabbed."

She pulled Sarah away and ripped open Matt's shirt to attend to his injury, drawing back, puzzled at seeing his chest clean and unbloodied. Babs saw the real source of the bleeding.

Sarah had been stabbed. Her arm bled profusely. Babs was unaware of the damage done by the knife when she kicked it away from the attacker. She pressed the hand towel against the Sarah's wound.

"Buck, you've got another patient," Babs called, anxiously, her attention returned to her dazed boss as soon as Buck came to take over the care of Sarah.

"What happened?" Matt asked weakly, wanting the walls of the room to stop turning like a merry go round.

"Where's Sarah?" Oh god, had she walked out on him? He was ready to jump off the bed and go after her.

"Keep your shirt on, old man, Sarah isn't going anywhere." Matt recognized Buck's voice and hated that Sarah preferred the younger man. Sarah came into view on Buck's arm. Among the austere furnishings there was no place for her to rest but the bed.

"You might as well lay down beside him," Buck insisted.

"By the looks of things, you lost a lot of blood in saving this old man," he said, affectionately gazing at Matt, who was glaring back at him. He explained what happened with a smug look on his face, sharing with Sarah his knowledge of Matt's jealousy.

"You're the one that did it," Sarah asserted, obediently stretching herself alongside of Matt, accepting the gesture as a reward, settling her head on his outstretched arm, smiling into his eyes before turning her attention back to Buck.

"Where did you come from?" she asked of Buck, as he covered her with a blanket retrieved from the chest of drawers.

He and Babs had left hours ago, after Buck established that his father was not seriously injured when he regained consciousness. She assumed they would continue with whatever plans she interrupted when she asked them to help her find Matt. That was precisely what had happened.

"Buck and I left here, intending to go on to the movie," Babs offered from the protection of Buck's encircling arm as they stood beside the reclining couple. She looked up at Buck to let him add to the explanation, which Sarah knew must eventually include a report of Fella's death. Buck chose not to bring up that painful fact right away.

"There's a nice hideaway just a few yards downriver, where we went instead," he revealed, squeezing Babs a little tighter.

"We decided to find a better place to, ah, do what we were doing and saw a car approach without lights. That was suspicious and when we came to investigate that guy was sneaking into the house."

Matt frowned and glanced at Sarah's bandaged arm and back to Buck.

"I didn't get here in time to stop him but, as it turned out, I didn't have to. Sarah already did that. She surprised him and I had little to do but tie him up."

Sarah knew it wasn't that simple. "I didn't see the knife. I was afraid he wanted to hurt you and I couldn't have that." She stiffened and huffed. "Well could I?" She couldn't remember the details but the knife was directed to her and she would have accomplished nothing, if not for Buck's intervention. She hugged Matt's arm tightly across her stomach, ultimately relieved at their good fortune.

"The sheriff's on his way out here to pick up the guy and get your statement. He'll want the whole story." Babs laid a fresh ice pack for the throbbing lump on Matt's head. She had given him another dose of aspirin.

Some time later the intruder was charged with attempted murder and taken away. The sheriff radioed and discovered he was the accomplice in the pornography ring. He had deputies search the grounds and was satisfied no one else was around to cause more harm. One patrol man stayed on the porch just to keep things safe.

Matt's head was clearing without the searing pain. He felt rested. He sighed with such relief Sarah suggested he tell them what was on his mind. He nodded and was gratified to share his latest accomplishment.

"I got the authorities to override the bureaucracy and allow Norm and Arlys temporary custody of Eric which all expect to become a permanent arrangement. The time I spent in Boise was not very productive. Rusty..." His voice faltered and his eyes closed sadly. Rusty appeared to be a budding psychopath and the staff and facilities at *The Singing Ranch* were not set up to handle that disorder. Matt thought Rusty's future looked dim, but the boy was too young to be given up so easily. Maybe later.

Matt's arm tightened on Sarah and a wonderful assurance passed between them. Their bond was beautiful to see.

Appreciating it, Babs put the obvious to words.

"You reached an understanding?" It was a positive statement. She knew what she had witnessed earlier between the two.

"Sarah promised to marry me," Matt stated with great pride, his eyes gazing on her face in wonder. Then he frowned.

"I think she did," he drew back to look more carefully into Sarah's face.

"I didn't dream that, did I?" Matt suddenly became wary, worried that perhaps he just imagined she said yes. Sarah's upturned face beamed at him as she reiterated her answer and two smug mouths fused briefly.

"Well, that's settled then," Buck said, as if the whole world had been set to rights.

"I still don't understand half of what's going on," Sarah said, "I've agreed to marry a man whose past is a mystery, whose future I'm not totally convinced I can enhance."

"If that man can't explain everything right away, he will in time, I'm sure." Buck countered, with a confident grin at Sarah and a nod toward Matt. Buck's voice reminded Sarah of his talent and refusal to show his work in Denver.

"I'd appreciate if you would explain why talent should lay dormant around here. Tell me exactly why you won't let Marianne show some very promising work." She felt Matt's breathing resume.

"I insisted he pursue more practical endeavors." Matt explained.

"But why? He's very talented," she insisted. She hadn't told Matt that before. Perhaps he needed a real expert's opinion.

"We made a pact a long time ago." Buck said, his focus moving from Sarah's face. "Matt will have to explain that."

A sheriff's car had taken the intruder away. Matt and Sarah had given statements and their intention to press charges. The attacker made no statement but from his vociferous outbursts during his capture, Buck accurately surmised him to be some sort of beneficiary of the kidnapper. His record was found and he had been taken away.

Buck and Babs left. They would be at work in very few hours.

"What must I do to convince you how much you will enhance my future?" Matt asked, when they were alone. He would give up everything he had if that's what it took to prove it, he knew that as surely as he knew she risked her life to save his.

Sarah slowly shook her head. Somewhere in the past few hours she lost her concern for the unknown future and for the unknown past, of this wonderful man. She couldn't account for it but she knew it as surely as she knew she could not think of spending the rest of her life without him.

"I know so little about you," she ventured.

"Then why did you bother with me?" His amazement at her saving action was the *bother* he referred to.

"I love you." It was a bold statement and blatantly true. Her eyes shone with the brightness only an inner adoration could inspire.

Matt hugged her tightly and kissed the top of her head. "Then let me tell you - " he broke into song huskily with the words from 'The Prisoner's Song,' " - a story that's never been told -" His voice was unmistakably the one from the recording on her CD.

"Your talent?" He told her once he tried to develop his talent and it only got him into trouble. She was told the full story then, of Matt's prior success, his failed marriage, his wife's suicide, his son's search for attention.

"We made a pact - Buck and me - to give up public display of our talents. I expected then he would take up singing. Both wanted, yes, needed, to devote our lives to boys disrupted in similar circumstances. Buck went to college and got a degree in psychology and counseling." The years since had been difficult, his final goal achieved in the establishment of a place where his own son found a decent future and helped other boys do the same.

They spent the dawning hours over coffee and a breakfast they prepared together, Sarah needing assistance from Matt, his arms unencumbered by a sling.

"I see even less I have to offer," Sarah revealed when Matt concentrated on his coffee, his gaze upon her so completely adoring, "You do all the giving. I reap all the benefits."

In exasperation he threw aside his cup. In apprehension her eyes went wide when coffee spilled on the Formica table top.

"You're the feistiest woman I've ever met. Won over my horse. Passed her tests. Oh, I heard about that the minute I got back. How you got thrown off and buffaloed her into behaving." Sarah smiled dimly in retrospect. Horseback riding wasn't her favorite activity and it wasn't relevant. She continued her skeptical gaze. He wasn't going to let up one minute.

"You're the brightest woman I know, sensible in so many ways." His eyes roamed her unpainted face and short hair, its waywardness combed into submission with her sturdy fingers. He spread his hands and leaned closer to her.

"Sarah, look at me. Don't be blinded by a rosy picture of a man's success. Just look at me for once and you'll see a man lonely, a man who found a wonderful woman he wants to spend his life with, a man who can hardly believe his good fortune at having a beautiful woman love him, a man whose looks are more of a turnoff than an incentive for admiration - let alone love."

She was appalled at his self appraisal. She slipped off the sling and rushed to open her arms, hoping she could make him believe how she cherished the thought of remaining forever with him. He lifted her bandaged arm, resting her hand against his shoulder. Then he crushed her to his full length, hoping in his lifetime he could make her understand how much she meant to him. Sarah had no difficulty in putting Matt in her future, to be by his side, talk things out, encourage him, care for him.

Oh, how she cared for him!

In their ensuing coalescence they both realized their hopes would be fulfilled. Their hands roamed and roused. Kisses fell softly on reachable surfaces, until Matt held Sarah back with his lower body tightly against hers.

"I've got a terrific yen to look at that bright blue underwear of yours," he teased, his arousal more physically apparent, hers no less real.

And a long time later he actually looked at the bright blue puddle of satin on his bedroom floor.

About the author

Naomi Sherer is a widow who travels extensively, having been to twenty four countries in six continents. She grew up in Minnesota just as rural electrification brought labor saving devices to farmer's lives. Educated at the College of St. Catherine in St. Paul, the University of Minnesota, Duluth Branch, and Washington State University, Pullman. She edited scientific papers for a contract research firm for twenty years. Since retiring she teaches natural science at the Environment Education Center on the McNary National Wildlife Refuge in sagebrush grassland of central Washington state. Naomi Sherer

Naomi began writing at age ten and keeps a journal. She is a widow who travels extensively, having been to twenty four countries in six continents. She participates in the International Interdisciplinary Congress On Women with posters and presentations.

She grew up in Minnesota just as rural electrification brought labor saving devices to farmer's lives. Educated at the College of St. Catherine in St. Paul, the University of Minnesota, Duluth Branch, and Washington State University, Pullman. She edited scientific papers for a contract research firm for twenty years.

She teaches natural science at a National Wildlife Refuge. Naomi is especially interested in the native plants of the desert in which she lives and works in the native plant area within the education center of the McNary National Wildlife Refuge. She maintains a wide variety of evergreen and deciduous trees on her residence, reaping nuts and fruits for her efforts.

Naomi operates a hand-and-rod puppet in performances to illustrate disabilities to elementary schools that help children to better understand those people who cannot do simple tasks that are usually easy for others to do. She supports the work of the state-wide association for people with disabilities called the ARC.

She serves the city of Richland, Washington, as a trustee on the Public Library Board and Committee for Library Expansion. She maintains a large library of books ranging from scientific research to biographies, taxonomy, romance, nature, travel, and history.

She hiked South Sister in Bend, Oregon, and takes nature excursions with Mark Smith of Portland, Oregon, to study birds, plants, and habitats in Jamaica, Belize, Peru, Patagonia, and Brazil.

Naomi has five grown children who live close to the Pacific coast, requiring hours of driving in her two-door Hyundai over Snoqualmie Pass for frequent visits.